# The Amazing and Somewhat Sarcastic Tad

by Tim Toterhi

Published by Plotline Leadership

Book Design by Stephannie Beman of RuisPublishing.com
Cover Design by David Amaya

Print ISBN: 978-0-9968485-1-0
Digital ISBN: 978-0-9860646-3-0

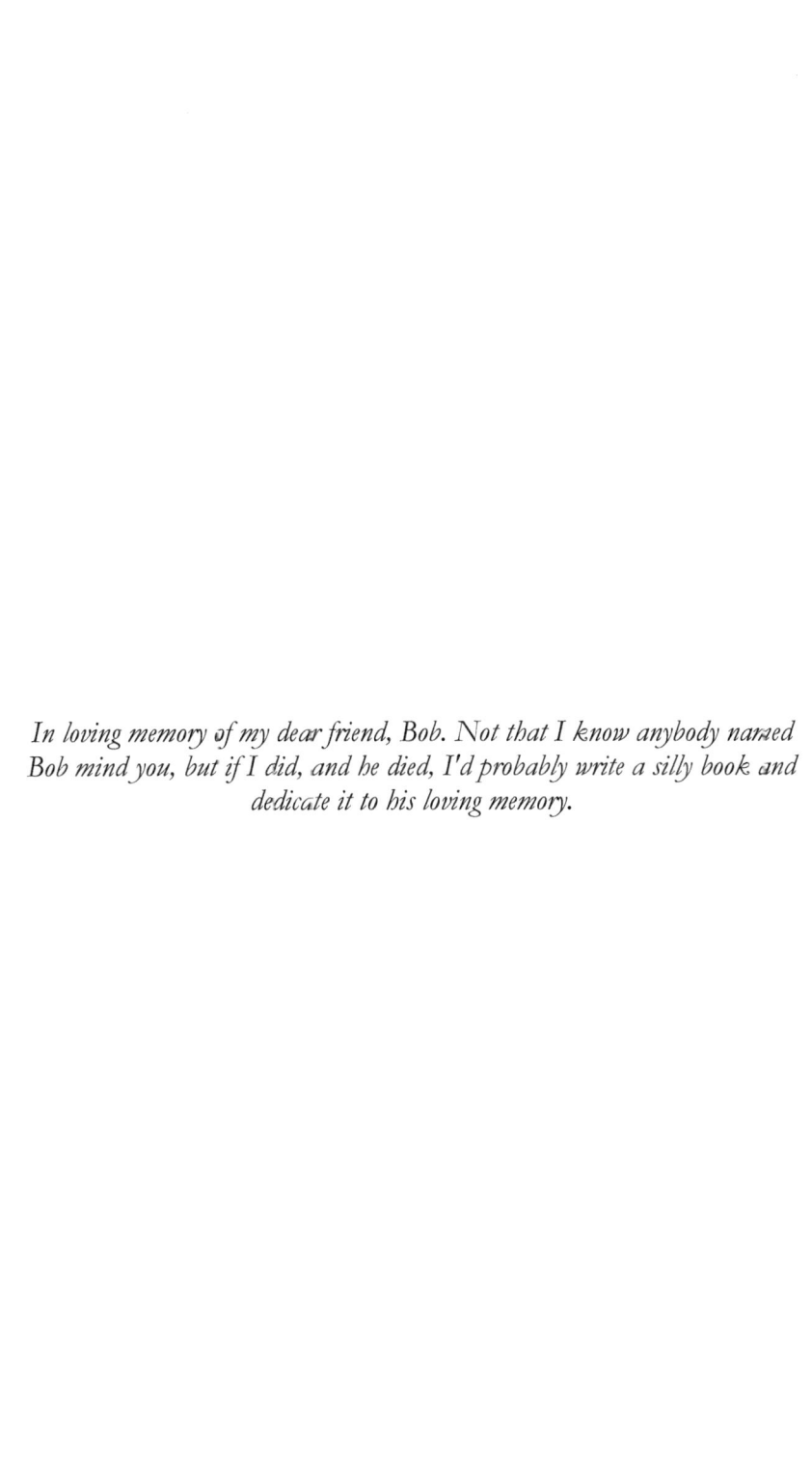

*In loving memory of my dear friend, Bob. Not that I know anybody named Bob mind you, but if I did, and he died, I'd probably write a silly book and dedicate it to his loving memory.*

## Fiction by Tim Toterhi

# The Amazing and Somewhat Sarcastic Tad

# PROLOGUE – May 1988

Okay, here's the deal. My name is Tad, but you can call me The Amazing and Somewhat Sarcastic Tad. I initially planned to abuse the power of authorship by spouting a mindless string of controversial obscenities like: religion is a social evil. Politicians suck the sweat off a dead gorilla's balls. And, some of the more stringent mandatory qualifications of a lunchroom monitor are that they be hairy, homely, and highly hefty.

Such statements would indubitably piss off the part of the population that likes to be soundly sleeping by 9:30. Now I love controversy as much as the next guy on the talk show stage. Unfortunately, controversy leads to hate mail. And though I enjoy receiving creative literature from the straight and narrow folk, I can't stand the guilt arising from leaving such correspondence unanswered. So, in the spirit of the Do Nothing

1

Generation, I'll play nice and spare myself some poetic obscenities from the mostly miserable masses.

Just so you know, this book is so incredibly cool that once you finish you're gonna want to buy me lunch and ask me over to meet your mother. I realize this is a bold thing to say considering this is only the two hundred and tenth word. But hey, it's a fact-wrapped truth with an accurate, nougat-like center of verifiable authenticity.

Anyway, because this book is so monumentally cool, I don't want just any "Rent-a-Nerd" reading it. Therefore, I have prepared the following, *"Yo, you can't read this because you are a loser and I don't like you"* list.

If you're a Yuppie, you can't read this book. If you wear a suit every day or don't own a pair of sneakers, you can't read this book. If you sell anything door to door or pass out religious literature, you can't read this book. If you're mentally over thirty, go grab a copy of *War and Peace*. If you're illiterate, you can't read this book.

Wait a minute. That was cold. I take it back. Let's continue.

If you're one of those girls who pretends to be the easiest lay since the Material Girl and then makes a guy wait four months before he gets any, you can't read this book. If you're the kind of guy who waited for that girl, then ah...beat it. If you're into politics, religion, Save-the-Whales nonsense, or any other system-oriented affair, scram. If you constantly bitch about racism, sexism, ageism, or any other "ism," calm down and go have a cream soda. If you're one of those immoral individuals on late-night TV who tell the moronic masses they can buy the world for no money down, you're a dildo with wings. If you're a sex-craved preacher, a crooked cop, or a crime figure of any sort, you should have your Charmin toilet tissue secretly replaced with a nice box of Brillo pads and no, you can't read this book. Finally, if you're a stupid person, you know, the kind who drives forty-five miles per hour in the left lane of a highway with his right turn signal on, you should merge slowly into the abyss of despair and no, you cannot read my amazing book.

Ah! I feel better. Don't you? I realize it's going to be an intimate audience now that I've asked all the posers to go shit in their hats. But I could do with a little intimacy in this cold, calculating, corporate-obsessed existence. So I invite you remaining idealistically inclined individuals to join me as we embark on this wonderful, mostly true, somewhat sarcastic, slightly sad, but all in all fantastic story.

Our destination will allow you to once again view the world through the optimistic eyes of a child. It's the place you loved, laughed, played, pondered, and slept through the night without waking up in a cold sweat wondering if your parents lied when they said everything was going to be all right. This is the place I want to show you. This is the place I hope we find as we travel through this mental monstrosity I've created. I say *hope* because I'm directionally impaired and will likely get lost.

Our guides will be six recent high school graduates. We'll track them through a week's worth of happiness, hardships, and wonder. We'll help them overcome conflicts with themselves, each other, a few spirit-like substances, and a bunch of double-crossing mobsters.

You're probably asking yourself what mobsters have to do with a story about growing up and the development of your personal philosophy? Well, the truth is, nothing at all. But damn it, this is my book and I happen to dig mobsters. So if I want to bullshit about a guy named Vito Devito for a while, I'm gonna do it. As long as I reach my point I don't see the big deal so just relax and get ready for the world's greatest, almost-true story.

Oh, by the way, the reason I know so much about the whole thing is because I am one of the six teenagers. It's just lucky for you that with drugs out of style and sex hard to come by, I've got nothing better to do than sit here, munch on some pathetically processed fast-food beef, and type. So buckle up, folks. It's time to get rolling.

# CHAPTER 1

As the cool water chased the humidity from my bones, I casually reflected on my complete and unyielding hatred of warmer climates. Yes, summer sucks. I was never too fond of winter either, but summer definitely slobbers the one-eyed sea serpent.

What could God(?) be thinking? Does He like watching people with Jerri-Curls burst into flames while walking down the street? Or is it the joy of seeing me take my sunglasses off the dash of my wickedly cool 1980 Monte Carlo and have them shear to the top of my skull while I scream a variety of imaginative obscenities? I don't get it. And how can a stream of wonderfully tanned Floridians whiz by happily on their *radical* skateboards while this displaced New Yorker cringes at the thought of leaving his air-conditioned bedroom?

5

I know, you probably think I'm being a wimp and that I'll eventually get used to the weather. Well sorry, buddy, you're way off. I've been living here for two years and I still believe that Tampa summers are one of Mother Nature's more elaborate bad jokes.

So before we go on, let's get something straight. I'm the one telling the story and I don't need you second guessing everything I say, rating my jokes, or analyzing the deep statements I'm going to make in upcoming chapters. If you desperately need to do so, please close the book so I don't hear you because it really pisses me off. Oh, and another thing, don't read the last page because it has an exceptionally cool ending and I don't want you to spoil it. Got me? Cool beans, baby.

Life should be air-conditioned. The environment is going to hell anyway, so why not throw a dome around the planet and live out our lasting years in comfort? Okay, I'll admit it's not the greatest idea, but heat makes me crazy. Just be thankful I'm not analyzing Earth's mysteries. Like why do they pronounce "Rolodex" "roll-a-desk" if it doesn't roll? If you think about it, when you're looking for a number in a Rolodex you spin it, so shouldn't they say "spin-a-desk"?

I turned off the shower and questioned my sanity. I always knew I was weird, but lately I was talking to myself for no apparent reason and I had begun to question everything that was once an apparent truth.

Is there a God(?)? Will I become a productive member of society? And why do croutons have an expiration date? Let's face it; we are talking about stale bread. And if that's not bad enough, they come in a stay-fresh pouch. I mean seriously.

I think I need professional help. People say that an eighteenth birthday is a stressful time, but they never say when the stress will end. Suddenly I find myself finished with over twelve years of totally worthless education and faced with the monstrous dilemma of which totally worthlesser college to spend all my beloved cash on.

(I am completely aware of course that "worthlesser" is not a word. However, I, The Amazing and Somewhat Sarcastic Tad, believe that it should be. Therefore, as a direct insult to every English teacher who ever ripped on, snapped upon, dissed in the highest, or otherwise cast a royal aspersion at my handwriting; I declare, in a rather arrogant tone of voice, that from this moment forward the word "worthlesser," as well as any other grammatically incorrect, but otherwise incredibly useful adjective I choose to grace with my presence, will be perfectly acceptable in this book, any of your high school term papers, or those incredibly boring "What I Did on My Summer Vacation" essays.

Please note the last sentence *ran on* like a man with his balls aflame solely to add insult to injury. And what the hell, as long as you're noting things, all non-homeboys please be advised that the above-mentioned "snapped," "dissed," "jousted," etc. are congruent in denotative form to the phrase, "a few slang words for severely screwing up someone's personal schemata via various derogatory comments.")

Anyway, if you think my educational predicament is pathetic, realize that most of America's graduates haven't got the slightest idea as to what is going on in the world, and are probably no more prepared to deal with life than when they left grammar school. Come to think of it, I didn't want to leave. I liked it there. I didn't have to worry about being cool, impressing girls, or the latest income tax laws. Life was simple and dreams were possible. I could become famous and little Tyrone could become President. Yup, the world was roses and it would remain so as long as I kept watching Bugs Bunny instead of the six o'clock news.

I grabbed a towel, dotted the water from my eyes, and stepped to the bathmat. I tried in earnest to turn off my brain, but failed. It was morning and I always get verbally and mentally irregular in the morning. And so I rambled on, words dropping from my mouth like candy from a piñata.

Sometimes I think I'm a psychomaniac. Then I think I'd like to be a psychomaniac so I'd have an excuse to go to a psychiatrist. It's not that I'm for real crazy or anything. It's just that I'd like to be able to lay on one of those comfy couches and bullshit like a madman about anything I want without having to worry about what the listener thinks of me. I'm sure the shrink wouldn't know much more about the cause of my concerns than anyone else, but at least he'd be okay with listening. There has to be tons of people nuttier than me out there.

Actually, I secretly hope that if I ever got the courage to go to a psychiatrist he'd think my life was kind of boring and fall asleep while I was yakking away. That would be great. You know you're sane if your shrink starts snoring in the middle of your bitch session. It's when the guy's on the edge of his seat that you're really screwed. It's like when you get in a car wreck and the ER doctor barfs after looking at your mangled body. Call me crazy, but I'd welcome the reassurance. Maybe one of my friends could get me a gift certificate for a free counseling session. Kinda like a back rub for the subconscious. Only now that I think about it, I bet the doctor would make up tons of weird shit just to keep me coming back. Money-grubbing bastards, they're worse than lawyers.

Sufficiently dry, I tossed the towel to the hamper and heard an imaginary swish as if I made the winning three-pointer in an

NBA final. The sound lingered and brought a moment of clarity. I suddenly understood the cause of my confusion. I was growing up fast, faster than I wanted to, and I was scared. I wouldn't mind becoming an adult as long as I could hold on to myself in the process. Something told me the answers weren't far off, but I wasn't prepared to deal with the questions at the moment. In life there's always a to do list, always an excuse. Today's was a trip. We'd planned it for months and I had to be at my friend Pete's house in an hour.

He rented the place a couple of months ago after going a few rounds with his old man. Pete was kinda prudish with the details, but the gist is, he told his pop he'd prefer a rusty rectal probe to a career as an army officer. The move settled things for the short term, but the two would have to have a serious sit-down or the old guy would try to run his life forever. I felt sorry for the Luke Skywalker-type hardship he would eventually encounter, but couldn't afford to dwell on it, so I cleared my head and began my bathroom ritual.

I combed my hair and brushed my teeth with this nasty brand of toothpaste that tasted more like battery acid than winter-fresh gel. I'm all for good oral hygiene, but do they have to make mouthwash that brings tears to your eyes?

In any event, I spat the stuff out and…. Wait a minute, there's no way I'm going to have the word "spat" in my book. I mean that has to be the wimpiest word in the universe. Can't you just picture some bearded old Jewish lady saying, "Murray, Murray, you just spat all over the whitefish." In light of this, I'll say, "I spit" or rather, I had, "hocked an incredibly green and somewhat slimy loogie into the sink."

Anyway, I wiped the foam off the corner of my mouth, did a few muscle man poses in front of the mirror, and decided that I looked more like Pee-Wee Herman on steroids than Conan the Barbarian. I knew I could stand to gain a few pounds, but it was harder than it seemed.

You see, fat people don't understand. They think losing weight is harder than gaining it, which is completely false and utterly moronic. Look at it this way: Did you ever lose your keys? Now what was harder, losing them or finding them? Why, finding them of course, and this proves my philosophy that in general it is much easier to lose something than to gain it. What? You're not convinced. Then look at it in the context of money. What is more difficult, working to gain a five spot, or spending that same fin at the nearest fast food joint? I rest my case!

"But wait," you say, "I've found a hole in that theory, Mr. Amazing One. I'm sure it's more difficult to get rid of a cold than to catch one."

Well, you're absolutely wrong. You see, before you contract the illness, your body is fighting incredibly hard not to get it. However, these diseases are generally more physically able than the beer-guzzling masses and thus, following a not-so-gallant struggle, the body loses and Mr. Disease enters our domain.

Unfortunately for him and increasingly more fortunate for us, once he's inside he has to confront Mother Nature, who by the way is getting quite annoyed with her lack of press. She is often pissed off at the overabundance of corrupt blood-sucking doctors in the world and slowly (without any help from the above-mentioned beer guzzlers) heals the body before the medical community can extract the poor slob's financial fluid. But I digress.

Where was I? Oh yes, I was talking about the abstract possibility of me one day looking like I actually went through puberty. It's just not in the cards I guess. I mean, last year I worked out for over nine months, ate all kinds of overpriced health food, and only managed to gain two pounds, which by the way were lost after the flu season.

A friend suggested steroids, but I felt that I looked good enough at five feet nine inches tall, and one hundred and forty-five pounds. Besides, steroids are for stupid Guidolopiouses (Guido-lo-pi-ouses) that have the intellectual capacity of Cheez Whiz. I don't understand it. They go on steroids to get huge and attract the girls, but by the time they do, Mr. Penis wants to hibernate. It kind of defeats the purpose. Don't you think?

Oh wait a minute, how utterly rude and otherwise uncool of me. I forgot that the greater portion of the reading audience has probably never seen a Guidolopious. Let me explain. Guidolopiouses are Italian, New York-based, child-like barbarians. Typically named Vito or Tony, these gold-garnished Goliaths have huge attitudes and no hair whatsoever on the sides of their Cro-Magnon-like craniums. They generally travel by Mustang convertible or IROC Z-28 that they purchased by either working construction or beating up on guys like me and taking their lunch money. I hate these muscle-bound manifestations of some genetic experiment gone astray. However, I must admit that I am often overcome with the desire to mount their shapely, mindless Guidette girlfriends and sing old game show tunes while celebrating the moments of my life. Unfortunately, the overall humongousness of the males prevents me from acting out this fantasy.

Morning Philosophication complete, I left the bathroom and walked toward my bedroom. This was my castle, my cabin. As a shelter for my creative thoughts and dreams, it was a positive oasis in a mostly miserable world.

It was filled to the breaking point—no rather quite past the breaking point—with posters of awesome individuals. I had everyone from music stars like Billy Joel to great leaders like… like…. Okay, so I can't think of any great leaders considering that the world has about as much sex appeal as a four hundred-pound farm girl dressed in Rollerblades and a Spandex leotard.

Anyway, it was your basic eighteen-year-old guy's room, overflowing with dirty laundry and fast food containers. The only differences were my bookshelves were armed with self-help novels, and a poster featuring the word "can't" crossed out and a caption that read, "Don't use four letter words," hung over my bed. The poster was cool, but I later discovered the books were crap. You have to admit though that self-help and 900 lines are a couple of the greatest scams ever invented. You see, I don't mind getting ripped off if it's done with some creativity. I figure that if you have the balls and brains to do it, I ought to be impressed not pissed.

I grabbed some socks and a pair of underwear with a huge red dragon on the front. They were a gift from an ex-girlfriend and I actually thought about wearing them, until I spotted ones with the cartoons. Maybe it's me, but I'd rather have little Wilmas and Betties hanging out with Mr. Penis than something that could eat spear-wielding cavemen like hors d'oeuvres.

I threw on a pair of dark gray pants, some cheap deodorant, a white tank top, and a charcoal-gray button-down shirt. I fastened the bottom two buttons, leaving the rest undone in order to expose the white "Giny-T-shirt" and three elegant and extremely unlike-the-Guidolopious' gold rope chains. I left the shirt out of my pants, flipped the top off my shoulders, and popped the collar. No wait. There's more! I laced up my, *"Gee, I used to be white,"* high top Converse, and splashed on some freshly stolen cologne from my father's unsuspecting dresser. Looking cool, I

12

headed back to the bathroom.

I brushed back my hair and decided that I was somewhat of a stud. I'm not saying I'm a complete stud, mind you. My nose is a little too big for my face. And, although I was officially eighteen, I still only shaved on the second Tuesday of every other month if there was a full moon and a man named Obe singing a wonderful rendition of "The Night Before Christmas" in the middle of my street. But despite these minor flaws, I still rated myself a semi-stud.

Hey, that's right, my fellow humanoids, I am a man now! I'm eighteen damn it and the world's at my feet. I can drive a car, ride a girl, die pitifully in a jungle somewhere for no apparent political reason, and travel to exotic lands to meet strange and exciting college professors. Granted, I still can't legally purchase certain complex sugars at all-night convenient stores, but other than that and some things like a mortgage, three screaming kids, lower-back pain, a nagging wife, and an ulcer in the works, I'm an adult. Happy birthday, Amazing Tad!

I checked my watch and realized I was philosophizing at the ungodly(?) hour of 5:00 a.m. I never understood why people get up so early to go camping? It's not like the wilderness is going anywhere. Let's face it. You dump on the environment all year and then the one time you decide to go see what you're destroying, you act as if you're Paul Bunyan. If it were up to me I'd leave about two in the afternoon, get there before dark, set up, and then relax and appreciate the one thing God(?) didn't screw up—the view of the stars from a campground at night. It's simple, it's pure, and it doesn't piss me off.

Because I, The Amazing Tad, am always early, even when I'd much rather be very late, I had some time to kill. Therefore, I headed back to my castle and turned on the radio. Feeling satisfied with the slow song currently caressing the speakers, I sat at my desk by the window, grabbed some paper, and opened the blinds. I had sunrise on the brain, but a series of storm clouds denied the image. They lined up neatly like English redcoats and chased the sunrays to safer sky. I admired the ominous scene for a moment and then got down to business.

I worked for a small pizza place and I had to finish my inventory list before I went on vacation. I was supposed to do it last night, but the guys came by and asked me if I could hang out. Things were slow for a Thursday so Buck Johnson, my boss, let me go early. He was a pretty cool guy so I didn't want to let him down.

Yes, that's right, folks, I have a real job. I don't know about you but I hate reading novels where everyone is fake. The people in those books never work, and if they do, it is always some wonderful job that allows them to fly off to exotic places to track down a vicious killer or meet with an incredible, Gumby-like lover. Get real! Why don't you ever read a book about Ordvil, the eight hundred-pound welder who has to work in a factory fourteen hours a day and then go home to beat his eight starving kids and make love to a woman who looks like Jabba-the-Slut?

Also, people in books have way too much money. And even if they're not exceptionally wealthy, that trip to Paris is always within their budget. This is all sad, but what drives me crazy is that sex comes too easily for them.

Modesty aside, I'm an intelligent, good-looking, humorous guy. Yet more often than not I find myself embarking on a quest for sex, while Biff and Troy get laid every other chapter. You know the deal. Chad meets a chick at a party on page twelve and by page fourteen you're reading things like: "Well, I pulled open his zipper and his immense manhood rolled onto the carpet and down the hall, where it was used as a jump rope by my little sister." Give me a break!

This is why women need to study my philosophy of The Mighty, Manly, and Mostly Imaginary, Magical, Mystical, and Mainly Impossible, Major Shlong. This is the impossible concept of the thing most people think they understand, but then again, don't.

In this world, some men were given more than others in the way of... well, ah... to be blunt, dicks. Some of the more unfortunate dweebs of society were given penises to make up for the fact that they drive BMWs, live in million-dollar homes, and generally shit all over the less financially fortunate. The penis is a rather small, stumpy-looking ligament that serves no purpose other then to excrete certain hazardous bodily fluids and keep its owner's left hand occupied.

Next up is of course the dick. The dick is the average-sized sexual tool of the average-minded, average Joe. Unfortunately, this particular model comes with a dark-sided counterpart known as the prick. Lawyers, please note the *Star Wars* reference.

The prick is an evil entity solely concerned with self-satisfaction and maybe bragging to pathetically depressed penises. Ladies, if you feel yourself being approached by a prick, just stay calm, tease it into a false sense of security, and then squash its two favorite meatballs into hamburger hash.

Next on the list is the capable cock. This is a truly enormous individual. In fact, if not for the Mighty and Mostly Imaginary Major Shlong, it would be the largest sexual tool. It is nice, stupid, and ready to be abused by any willing female in the area. Women adore this one.

Unfortunately, because we are all greedy and miserable

creatures, women seek The Mighty, Manly, and Mostly Imaginary, Magical, Mystical, and Mainly Impossible, Major Shlong, which by the way died, or rather ceased to live long ago. I think. What I mean is, if in fact it ever did exist I'm sure it must be gone by now. Still women will long for it, just as most of these same women still long for that hippie in a handbag, Elvis, who, by the way, may have been the proud owner of this fictional fabrication of human flesh.

I honestly believe that if women knew this philosophy the world would be a better place and guys like me would get laid more often. In any event, the point is I'm nothing like these fictional buttheads. Rather, I'm simply a pissed-off idealist who is sick of dealing with the corrupt corporate crap and the idiotic masses that follow it to their detriment.

With this in mind, I finished my list, my Morning Philosophication, and headed to the kitchen for some Black Blood of the Earth.

# CHAPTER 2

Coffee sucks. I don't see how anyone, armed with an intellect greater than a mass of molted refrigerator fungus could purposely pump such poisonous potions into their system. What's the attraction? It has no nutritional value. It tastes like burnt dirt. And it was indubitably picked, fondled, and otherwise entertained by a cast of hygiene challenged Columbians who are wage raped by their imperialistic overlords.

And yet, at that rare and rather unique moment I was struck with the unyielding desire to cautiously consume a charismatic cup of the liquid I, The Amazing and Altogether Incredible Tad, have dubbed Black Blood of the Earth.

Perhaps it was my birthday, yes, the inevitable passage of time that led me to this change of heart. Or was it the lack of sleep, the early hour, or the awaiting wilderness adventure? Oh, let's face it, I wanted a cup of that crud because I was stressed out, pissed off, and hadn't been laid in many, many moons.

With this pathetic problem in mind, I grabbed my previously packed suitcase and headed for the kitchen. As I sleepily strode down the freshly painted hallway, I noticed the kitchen light was in the utterly on position. This could only mean one thing: The highly insomniacousable (yes, it is a Tad word) Dad creature was astir.

The man never slept. He would get up at four in the morning, drink silos of the infamous liquid, and then go off to sell Nissans until midnight. When he finally returned home, he'd scarf down some microwaved food, a couple of beers, and watch TV until the cycle resumed. Don't get me wrong. On weekends he was a normal person, but within that corporate structure the man was an animal. Still, I had to give the guy some credit. It took a lot of balls to quit his job and move to another state just to fulfill that mid-life crisis void. Hell, it would have been hard enough alone, but he had a bunch of kids and a troll of a wife (your standard issue wicked stepmother) to bring along for the ride. I just wish the happy little workaholic could have found his calling sooner. Sales: it's a no-brainer. The illustrious gift of bullshit runs strong in our family.

But wait! Before I tell you about my father face-off I'd like to pose a question. I was wondering if you like reading novels that explain every God(?) damn thing and spoon feed you stupidly useless adjectives as if you were some kind of feeble-minded idiot. I hope not because I tend to stay away from that sort of thing. I realize some might take this lack of description as a sign of a no-talent loser who is just trying to con the population out of some cashola, but to be perfectly honest, not to mention forward and frank, I really don't give a shit.

You see, if I'm riding in a car, for example, I feel that it's enough to say the car is red, or, if I want to get fancy, "very, very red". But some high-priced, egotistical, megalomaniac-type authors go on and on jerking you off with big words and no booty. This style of writing is nothing more than intellectual masturbation. Given the fact that I hate intellectuals and am quite sick of masturbation, I go the road less traveled.

When I entered the very, very blue kitchen with the not-so-blue tile, I saw the Dad-like creature sitting at the head of the table armed with a steaming cup of java, a wrinkled newspaper, and a slightly filtered cancer utensil.

"How's it going, sport?" said the man who looked like a chubby Michael McDonald.

He never used my name. It was always something like "slick," or "champ." I think the truth is that he never really liked the name Tad. This really didn't disturb me because I agreed. Looking back, I bet he would have let me change it. But then again, how would you bring that up? Should I have said something like, "Yo, Dad, my name sucks. I get the hippie thing, but you must have been on some serious drugs to come up with something so stupid." Frankly, I don't see it happening.

Now where was I? Oh yes, my dad asked how I was doing. It's lucky for me in the world of books the narrator can go off on wild tangents, leaving the rest of the characters hanging. It's as if they are suspended in time with the Amazing Me controlling their destiny. Sure it sounds good, but knowing my dad, if I don't answer him in the next few seconds he'll break that unbreakable rule and kick the crap out of me. Therefore, without further ado, I return to the story line.

"Okay, Pop," I replied in the nick of time.

"So, how does it feel to be eighteen?"

"Actually, I'm not feeling anything, unless of course you count tired, hungry, and frustrated beyond belief."

"You're a pisser. Why don't you grab some coffee and relax a while before you go."

"I'll just have some tea," I said out of a completely habitual anti-coffee defense mechanism.

"Jesus, sport, humor me for once. Tea is for old ladies and Brits."

"All right," I said, pouring cup of swamp-type fluid.

"Aren't you going to take any milk or sugar?" he asked with surprise.

"No."

"You're gonna drink it black? You?"

"Yes."

"That makes no sense."

My Dad never understood my philosophies. This worked out fairly well because I rarely saw him, and when I did, I generally made him so confused that he later tried to have the entire family, including the dog, avoid me for fear of a brain melt down. Unfortunately for him, this approach never worked and we generally wound up in a heated discussion due to his whole Curious George, *"What's wrong with my eldest child?"* mentality.

"Actually, Dad, it makes perfect sense," I said. "You see, I despise coffee, but since I have already agreed to drink it, I might as well enjoy hating the thing which I do not like. If I were to cover it up with milk and sugar, I would miss out on all that fun and in turn, I wouldn't necessarily be drinking real coffee, now would I?"

I thought the statement made perfect sense, but judging by the looks of confusion, frustration, anger, and complete disillusionment, which by the way, does not look very nice when performed together on one face, I decided to drop the subject. I mean there was no point in risking any newly awarded birthday presents.

As I sipped the beastly beverage, I noticed he had the old, *"It's time for one of those serious man-to-man talks that really doesn't get much accomplished, but makes me feel better about the whole father/son relationship thing,"* looks on his face. As I braced myself for the upcoming bombardment of fatherly advice, I noticed a strange sincerity in his eyes. I had seen this look before and although it was a rare occurrence, it was a welcome one. I found it funny that a man who could turn Medusa to stone with the slightest faux Mafioso glance could invoke the warmest of feelings with the same wondrous eyes. Yes, that look was like walking into a hug after being pounced on by the neighborhood bully.

"Son," spoke the great one, who still refused to call me by name, "You're a man now. The world is at your feet. Shit, you can do almost anything now that you're legal. (Notice the, *"Gee, I think I'll throw in a curse right away to show the nameless boy that I'm on his side and am trying to relate to his world even though I honestly don't have the slightest clue as to what it feels like to be a teenager at the ass end of the 80s,"* expression.) Why, I remember when I turned eighteen. I thought I knew it all. I was a wild-eyed, stargazing playboy. Yup, those where the best years of my life. But you can't forget your responsibilities. Get me?"

Of course I didn't. Being a teenager contained the same amount of joy as did a triple bypass without any pharmaceutical magic. Things had to get better. They couldn't possibly get worse. I felt dizzy. Part of me wanted to organize a strike of all humans until the so-called God(?) entity provided better working conditions, and yet before I was able to organize my thoughts and begin to hand out some anti-creationist literature, my mind was summoned by some unknown force (probably the God(?) like entity) back to the subject at hand. I found myself agreeing in a rather confused manner to the question previously posed.

"Uh huh," came my eloquent reply.

"Good, I'm glad to see you still have some sense in that dissident young mind of yours."

"I'm not that dissenting. I just don't agree with society's expectations."

"Yeah.... Look, the point I'm trying to make is that you have to watch your back. You may find this hard to believe, but I was once an, 'angry young man,' but I learned to get through life without getting taken in the process."

I liked that he occasionally quoted our favorite singer in his fatherly talks. These personable, poetic, musical preachings were one of the few things we had in common and they generally helped his points get across the desolate caverns of my mind. I often wondered who taught me more, the father I loved and longed to know better, or the music star whose words I knew and whose personality I didn't. Perhaps it was the combination of teachers who helped create the mixed-up mess you see, or rather read, before you.

"What do you mean, 'without getting taken?' I'm not a dope, you know."

My father was always overly concerned about me getting screwed. You see, being a dissident and work avoidance tend to go hand in hand. Therefore, I often tried various get-rich-quick schemes with the undying effect of becoming quite poor quick instead. His concern was well founded, but I had to protest. That's what I do.

"I realize you're not a dope," he said, "but your track record isn't that hot, you know?"

22

That's the thing about parents; they always bring up the past. Doesn't that piss you off? It's like they keep records of everything you've ever done wrong and then pull the appropriate file when they need to win an argument. Perhaps kids should have secretaries.

"Look, Dad, I've made some mistakes, but I think I can handle the whole life thing as well as can be expected in these pitifully pathetic times."

"I wonder about you, champ," he said while trying not to laugh at my general disregard for universal systems.

"Don't worry. I promise to grow up nice and normal."

"I doubt it, but let me give you a word of advice, something to contemplate while you're trying to get to first base with what's-her-name."

Now if there was one thing my Dad knew almost nothing about, it was my love life or rather lack thereof. Just so you know, "what's-her-name" is a hot little number named Jackie. Don't worry, you'll meet her later, but I'll tell you this much, she's got a great ass. I've tried to con her into bed a few times, but I never managed to pull it off. I know you're shocked. Well, smart-ass, when was the last time you got laid? Thought so. I figured you were…

My thoughts were severed when my father began his dissertation on the meaning of life.

Hey, wait a minute. I'm the author and no one, not even the Dad-like creature, has the power to interrupt me. Therefore I, The Amazing and Somewhat Sarcastic Tad, order time to reverse itself to the moment when this most heinous act of treachery occurred. Hold on! Bang! Zap! Poof! and other travelling-type words.

"*…got laid? Thought so. I figured you were* just a bored penis

Erector Set with nothing to do but read the incredible philosophies of a stressed-out, birthdayed, high school survivor. Not that these philosophies are anything but amazing, mind you."

I just broke your time travel virginity. Was it good for you? Ha! Anyway, now the mighty but recently out-willed Dad may speak. You've got to love that power.

"You see, son, most people are bastards and will do anything to screw you over. This may seem harsh, but you're old enough to know the truth. Trust my opinions, boy. I'm a car salesman."

"So what do you want me to do, Dad? I'm already equipped with the legal amount of cynicism, sarcasm, and eccentricity for a guy my age."

"Look, I'm gonna give it to you nice and simple."

"Refreshing," I said, testing the limits of our buddy-buddy relationship.

"D.T.A."

"What's that?" I asked.

"That should be your philosophy of life, kid. Don't trust anybody. The moment you trust somebody is the moment you get screwed."

"You got your credo from a Sylvester Stallone movie?"

"Yeah. The man's a genius incognito."

"Yeah, ah... sure, he's pretty smart," I said, while trying to adjust my mental alignment.

"Oh don't bullshit me, boy. I know you think he's a moron. Most people do. But the fact is, he's got a hell of a theory."

"So you're saying the only person you can truly count on is yourself?" I asked.

"That's the only person you can trust with your life. Everything else, no matter how sure it may seem, brother to brother or father to son, is a question mark. I know it sounds shitty, but it's true. The only trust that cannot be broken, altered, or amended is the one you have between yourself and your conscience, principles, and morals."

"Wait a minute, there's a hole in that theory, papa-san. People disregard their morals all the time and as far as principles go most people don't even have them."

"Listen, everybody has principles. They may not be of the same design, but they're there. And as far as your conscience is concerned, I'm not talking about little white lies. I'm talking about self-betrayal."

"Okay," I said in a, *"Yeah right, Dad. That almost makes sense,"* kind of way as I came to the realization that I would have to cut this convo short if I wanted to drop off Buck's inventory list and still meet the guys on time. "But people have been known to betray themselves. What about that?"

"That's extremely rare. You can betray your wife, your country, even your kids, but once you have betrayed yourself Life is no longer an option. Do a little research if you don't believe me."

But I did believe him. All at once it made sense and my soul was overcome with a dark sensation. I stood and tried in vain to shake the feeling. It was true and I knew it somehow had a direct effect on me. I vowed that no matter how deeply I buried my feelings, and no matter how much bullshit I spewed to stop others from finding the real me, I would never forget where I put the key to those emotions. Even if I never choose to reveal them, and even if my contempt for the basic lack of moral fiber in this deteriorating miserable world fails to bring about a noticeable change, I will remember. I had to remember. For, the moment I forget who I really was and put in place of that being a society-safe stranger, I'll have betrayed myself and will surely die.

It was all so clear. I don't know if my father was trying to tell me this, or if his message was simply, "Don't get conned when you go back to New York," but whatever the reasoning, I was enlightened and I thanked him for the wisdom I always knew he had. He may have only been there ten percent of the time, but he was there when I needed him.

With the incredibly touching and somewhat-meaningful Dad talk out of the way, I grabbed my suitcase, a couple of Billy Joel tapes, and the keys to my dream car. As I reached the door, I felt my father's hand on my shoulder. He slipped me a twenty and wished me well.

I guess he knew the trip was about us coming to terms with the not-so-distant future. I admired his alleged intuition and when I closed the door I said a silent thank you to no God(?) in particular for giving me a cool dad.

# CHAPTER 3

I was loaded. I had over one hundred birthday bucks plus my life savings, forty-three dollars and sixty-two cents. Coupled with the newly arrived twenty, we are talking some serious cash for an otherwise pathetically poor, and partially pissed, personable person.

In any event, which is probably this one, I walked to the driveway and silently cursed the pitiful patches of, *"Gee I really wish I could call myself grass, but I'm afraid the truth is that I look much more like a rather sick and somewhat sad piece of wilting desert vegetation,"* weed-like substances. I grieved as I passed the wanton wasteland of weary wilderness, for I knew that when the *"I do nothing because it's my birthday and I am King of this land for the entire day"* rite was over, I'd have to embark on a shit-load of mostly miserable gardening.

As I approached my miraculous Monte Carlo I admittedly admired the monumentally monstrous manly machine. It was the official Guido car of the 1980 Winter Olympics and the only thing related to these psychopathic creatures that I could stand for more than eighteen seconds without projectile vomiting through my nose in a most unfriendly and not to mention anti-social manner. In its prime the car had been magnificent.

Of course now, eight years and approximately two hundred billion miles later, it was a piece of shit. Still my beloved baby guided me on the road to freedom, adventure, and of course, cheap and otherwise meaningless sex. We had been through some exceptional times together and although it ran like a two-legged turtle and desperately needed a paint job I loved it unconditionally. Okay, so I'd curse and kick it in the gas tank (which is the equivalent of testicles to a car) when it didn't start, but other than that, we are talking unconditional love. I vowed to have it rebuilt and repainted one day, but those kind of dreams don't come easy at three dollars and seventy-five cents an hour, which by the way, is a pitifully stupid amount to pay someone like The Amazing and Somewhat Sarcastic Tad.

Anyway, after boarding the vehicle, I turned the key and the engine belched a noise resembling the sound a cat makes when you step on him with cranium-crushing construction boots.

"Ah shit!" I grumbled.

I tried again and produced the same effect. The third time charmed as advertised. As I backed out of the oil-stained driveway my baby purred as if to spite the groggy-eyed individuals, who were now standing in their doorways with looks of confusion, shock, and pain.

Yes, I had that old *"I'm up so you're up"* attitude again. I think it's safe to say that my neighbors, even those who thought I was a Special Ed kid who not only rode the short bus to school but also wore hockey equipment and wasn't even on a team, hated my guts with a deep and penetrating passion. I met their imagined ill will with a maniacal giggle.

As I approached the town center, which looked more like a scene from Andy Griffin than a growing metropolitan development, I began to feel most ravenously hungry, so I stopped at Burger King for some speedy nutrition. A light rain started, so I elected to use the drive-thru. I probably would have used it anyway, considering that I'm really a rather lazy bastard whose only form of exercise is an occasional karate class.

I pulled up to the speaker and purposely ignored the menu board. I never understood why they have menus at fast food joints. I mean they've been serving the same stuff for a billion years. And yet, the moronic masses of this brain-dead society continue to strain their necks while endlessly glancing upwards toward the entrancing and altogether insignificant neon menu.

"Ah, prices," you say. "That is the reason for such an annoying and useless piece of equipment."

Wrong! I used to work in one of these hell holes that could make any early industrial factory look like a weekend in Disneyland, and from this horrendously horrid experience I learned an invaluable lesson that will shock and amaze you. Any meal you could possibly order containing one of the three main food groups, (those of course being a meat-like substance, fries, and a Pepsi) will without failure cost either four dollars and eighty-seven cents or five dollars and thirty-six cents, depending on the area in which you reside. That is the meal button, and anything else can be figured out mentally without the use of those horrid contraptions.

After a few moments of rather annoying static the speaker

sprang to life. All at once I heard a kid with a strong Southern accent sing—not say mind you, *sing*—the following rhythmic stupidity.

> *Well, I'm the King of Burgers.*
> *There is none higher.*
> *Sucker McDonald's should call us sire.*
> *To cook our burgers we use a lot of fire,*
> *And I won't stop cooking till I retire.*

> *Now, I rock those orders. They come out correct.*
> *All my drinks are on time and my burgers perfect.*
> *I got the right to eat, and that's what I elect.*
> *Other food joints can't stand us, but give us respect.*

After busting a rather interesting "beat box" for a moment or two, he adjusted the volume on his RUN DMC tape to a bearable level. As the music faded, I reflected on whether I was as bored while working under those conditions. By the time he finished his ungodly(?) musical assault upon my senses, I came to the conclusion that it was probably the graveyard shift that added his extra level of moronical idiodicy, which by the way are in fact new Amazing Tad words.

In any event, he finally asked for my order.

"Yeah, give me ah...shit, ah…a thing of pancakes, a potato-like substance, and a Coke," I replied ever so eloquently.

"You want a Coke at 6:30 in the morning?" he asked.

"No, I wanted a bucket of piss and the secret code for that on Friday is the word Coke."

The strange Southern creature laughed sarcastically and proceeded to piss me off further.

"We don't got no Coke. Would Pepsi be okay?" he asked.

"You got Diet Pepsi?"

"Naw, the darn thing broke the other day. We got 7 UP, Dr Pepper, and orange."

"I'll take a shake," I said. "Chocolate."

"Sorry, buddy. You see, me and my girl, Shirley broke up yesterday. And because she subsequently (which was a rather large word for this over-talkative moron) decided not to come to work, we're short-handed and are still fixing to get ready to start planning on setting up that there shake machine up...eventually."

"Huh?"

What kind of loser discusses his romantical intimacies life over a Burger King loud speaker? I could never understand Southerners. It seemed they spent half of their lives planning their actions and the other half trying to figure out what they just came up with. Yes, this was the great American stupid person. He was the kind of guy that believed the word "wash" is pronounced "warsh." I realized he was just a product of his pathetic "Yee haw" environment and was about to take pity on him, when he assaulted me with another stupid question.

"How about a nice, hot apple pie?"

"No, God(?) damn it!" What a pain in the ass. "Just give me the pancakes, the potato-thing, and a Dr Pepper."

"You sure you don't want the pie?"

"Nooooooo!"

"All righty," said the pushiest son-of-a-bitch I ever met, "that will be four dollars and eighty-seven cents. Please drive thru."

"I'd like to drive through your skull with a rusty harpoon, Druid boy," I grumbled in a stage whisper, as I wondered whether killing this miserable rodent in a loud, grotesque,

Mafioso manner would be worth twenty years in federal prison.

When I pulled up to the window I was not at all surprised at the sorry state of the southerner's physical features. A truly sad specimen of humanity, the chromosome-deficient monstrosity appeared to be a few hundred years behind on the evolutionary ladder.

As I waited for my order, I pondered the purpose of pies. The damn things look more like egg rolls than an American tradition. And why is it that their inventory never dwindles? Sure run out of burgers on game day, but don't neglect to push the pies. Feeling utterly annoyed with life in general, I grabbed my food and screeched out of the parking lot.

As I whizzed down the street with absolutely no respect for traffic regulations, I reflected quite thoughtfully on the fact that eating while driving required great concentration. Over the years—okay, well, year and a half—I had become a master of this art. I could make a left-hand turn while reaching for some fries in the passenger seat or salt my burger while tuning the radio on a nice straightaway.

After about five incredibly dangerous, rather manly minutes of dogging decrepit old ladies and equally sad and somewhat flea-bitten dogs, I came upon my place of employment.

When I pulled into the lot I gave thanks, for I had managed to arrive without mortally wounding one of the mostly miserable masses. Then I cursed the misfortune of having just missed my thirty-forth viciously disgusting road kill. The fact that I chose to run down only pathetically stupid and otherwise useless raccoons instead of my fellow humans was not out of love and respect, mind you. Rather it resulted from a deep and utterly horrible fear of a lawsuit and a confrontation with, perhaps, the most parasitic people on the planet.

I hate lawyers. The rotten scumbags aren't fit to lick the anal drip from a diseased and seriously decapitated, sorry-looking sperm whale's oversized and altogether ugly butt. They are just a bunch of filthy, bloodsucking leaches who hide behind a, *"Gee, all this uselessly dead Latin probably makes us seem highly intelligent, but we realize that if we spoke everyday English society would discover that we are just as brain dead as they are,"* facade in order to extract the financial fluid from the basic population's "wallet-oric" artery.

Now, I realize there still might be a few pro-planet, feminist, liberal losers reading this thing. Therefore, in an incredibly sarcastic attempt to reconcile my last statement, I will say, in the most appropriate free-spirit, "new-woman" sort of way, that not all lawyers are psychotically certified criminals because that would be highly stereotypical of me. But, on the other hand, 99.999999% of them are, so just shut up and go whip up a bean curd yogurt-flavored taco or something.

Once I came to terms with my feelings on these matters, I locked the car, even though no one in their left mind would steal it, and walked toward the creatively titled Italian eatery. Before buying the place, Buck Johnson was a New York City cop. Therefore the establishment was, after much crossing out of other less style-ridden titles, called The New York Pizza Department. Pretty cool, huh?

# CHAPTER 4

When I walked through the Gothic doors of the magnificent and wondrously stupendous restaurant, I found myself transported from the world of disgusting and altogether repulsive indigestion–inducing fast food into the heavenly ambiance of the amazing palace-like establishment.

Oh wait, I can't go on. I don't care how much the owner offered for this pitiful rent-a-commercial, which by the way wasn't a lot. I can't lie. You see the truth is the NYPD is, was, and will always be just the average shit-hole of a pizza shop. The only thing special, unique, or otherwise strange about it was its owner, Buck Johnson.

He's a weird guy. All he did besides make pizza and read spy novels was dick around with dolls. During the two years I had worked for him, I constantly questioned his sanity. I mean let's face it, what kind of rough and tumble New York cop can read for one thing (snare drum), and for another, just as important thing, studies, crafts, and otherwise imports dolls. It just doesn't fit the personality profile of an otherwise-heartless, ticket-giving, power-lusting, no-respect-for-anything-remotely-related-to-justice-thinking, conceited-feeling, *"Gee, I really want to be a cop because you can carry a gun, drive a fast car, and get a kick-ass pension after only twenty years,"* saying loser. As you may have noticed, I'm not too fond of police either, but I'll go into my, *"Why I think the whole justice system really sucks,"* theory a little later.

For now, I'll say the whole best, brave, boys-in-blue ideal the PBA keeps pushing down our throats while the maniacally obsessed, ball-breaking media tries equally hard to do the opposite, is in fact a large and seriously smelly crock of your favorite feces. And just to show you there's no hard feelings, I hate the media too.

Now even though Buck was one of these unfortunate slime balls, he was bearable. In fact, a little better than bearable. He was righteous. (I bet that's a word you never thought an anti-Floridian would say.) A reasonably intelligent individual, he possessed a rudimentary understanding of basic Amazing Tad philosophies along with an admirable passion for recreating those wonderfully rare and altogether exotic Italian dolls. I took his artistic side into account as I entered his office.

If you could imagine the worst old-fashioned, coffee-stained, memo-ridden, *"Gee, I really can't find a God(?) damn thing,"* detective's office you ever saw in one of those black and white movies and multiply the disgusting factor by six point eight nine times ten to the sixth power, you would have in your possession a unique piece of sloppiness that wasn't even remotely close to the chaos and general disorder found in this man's cave. I was positive that if he didn't bribe the board of health, (another agency I loathe with a feverish passion) the NYPD would have been closed in seconds. Don't get me wrong, the eating area was fine, but sometimes when you walked in to get a quick slice, you could somehow sense the satanic horror and complete lack of organization that was hidden behind door number one.

When I entered the domain of disorderliness I found the Oscar Madison-like monstrosity perched in an armchair as he came to the conclusion of what I guessed to be his seven billionth spy novel. I noticed the familiar crinkle of longing and wonder in his eyes as he turned the final page in his incredibly plain-covered and much-too-immensely-huge for its own good, so-called literary work.

I despise any book that doesn't have a cool cover or is over three hundred pages long. I realize this statement may seem completely superficial and otherwise judgmental, but as I'm sure you know by now, I really couldn't give a flying fart. If you can't say something in under three hundred pages, you're probably just making it up as you go along, and jerking off the general population as they follow you blindly down the road of bewilderment, blasphemy (if you believe in that sort of thing), and mental fornication. This, as you know, is exactly the kind of behavior that, when done in the presence of morally decent human beings, or if those same goodie-goodies should hear about such sinful actions while gossiping in a local church, temple, synagogue, or shrine, will be highly frowned upon by the local God(?), deity, high priest (or priestess if you're so inclined), all-knowing wise one, great spirit, or any of the other supreme beings that dot the imaginative and altogether over-dependent religious landscape of humanity. Therefore, because I don't want to offend one of these super creatures, I've designed a pretty cool cover, and kept it to about two hundred or so Amazing Tad-like pages.

In any event, I digress. That's what I do and I'm damn proud of it. But as I returned my senses to the book world I noticed that Buck had finished reading and had been staring at me with those enormous Rodney Dangerfield-like eyes for quite some time.

He was huge, with a sixteen-gallon beer belly that had most likely moved into his incredibly lanky neighborhood during his college years and, in spite of countless weight loss programs, still managed to hold on to its lease. His hands and feet were oversized and his right knee didn't seem to cooperate too well with the rest of his walking apparatus causing him to limp in a rather unusual manner. And yet, I must say, that even though his body was an utter disaster, he had the most charismatic face. The only thing equal to this above-mentioned handsome head was his personality. He was quite charming. It was to this bit of social mastery that I attributed the success of the restaurant. Let's face it; it wasn't the food.

"Hey, Buck. I didn't expect to see you here this early," I said, pulling the crumpled inventory list from my pocket. "I just thought I'd drop off this bad boy before I left this sweaty, hellhole."

Usually one of my negative, *"I hate Florida and the world at large,"* comments would arouse a response from the unbalanced monstrosity, but there was something different about his usual happy-go-lucky attitude.

"How long have we known each other, kid?"

He knew damn well how long we had known each other, and I sarcastically sensed that the question was being used as a tone-setter for the day's second, *"Tad, we need to talk,"* project. What's with everyone? Did the world decide to put on serious hats in the middle of the night without telling The Amazing and Destructively Distraught Tad? Well, since it was becoming apparent that I was going to be late anyway, I decided to play along without bitching about the total disregard for honesty and truthfulness in the world.

"About two years, Buck. Why?" I asked in a seemingly pleasant fashion that secretly harbored a bucket of pissed-off agitation.

"It's just…. I think you're a good kid, and that's not the kinda thing I'm used to saying."

"Thanks," I said, slightly taken aback.

Don't get me wrong, I was flattered, but I always got the heebie-geebies when anyone talked about feelings. I know you're shocked. Well blow me, wise-ass. I just don't have my bearings straight yet, okay? Friendship, never mind love or marriage, freak me out. To be honest, I don't think I even want to get married. For one thing, I seriously doubt if anyone can stand me. I'm miserable in the morning, moody in the afternoon, and an utter shit-head at night. Even if I found the perfect girl, I'd always worry that somehow things would go sideways, and we'd wind up like my own parents—divorced, depressed, and spending the rest of our pathetic lives and money on custody battles over severely messed-up children. I experienced this from one perspective already and I vowed to never see it from the other side.

Whoa, that was deep. After a sensitive personal disclosure of that magnitude, I think the only way to rightfully regain my manhood would be to finish this Quarter Pounder and lay an incredibly disgusting, yet somewhat admirable, unbelievably nasty, wet, greasy fart.

"Piiiiiiitttttttsssss...pcof," said the rather arrogant slice of cheese as it suddenly turned into a green cloud of cosmic dust and floated off into the sunset.

After leaving Buck on hold I felt a tad guilty. (Even though I'm the all-powerful author and he doesn't have a clue that I stopped time to embark on a pitiful "poor little me" story.) In any event, the guilt was there, so when I jump-started the book universe, I reentered our conversation with a little more empathy.

"Is there something on your mind?" I asked, while secretly hoping there wasn't.

I think Buck knew the next few minutes would alter our lives forever. Therefore, in the proper fashion for such a momentous and altogether non-boring occasion, he let out a great sigh and shook his head back and forth a few times before leaking the info.

"Can I ask you something," he asked (A paradoxical question which of course annoys the hell out of me.)

"Anything. You know that."

"Anything?" he asked, angling for assurance.

I hate it when people beat around the bush. I mean, why can't they just say what they have to say and get the damn thing over with? Consumed with a, *"Gee, if this guy doesn't cut to the chase pretty soon I'm gonna tie him to a stake, set his balls on fire, and hire a half-dozen official American Indians NOT to do a much-needed rain dance,"* feeling, I pushed the issue.

"Look Buck, what's the deal?" I asked, growing exceptionally weary of the infinite bombardment of sunshine currently seeking shelter in my anal cavity.

"I need a favor."

Great, he probably wants me to break his cousin Lou out of a

Turkish prison or join the New Zealand shit-shoveling team with his brother Johnny. Buck had a pretty screwed-up family. One time he asked me to take out his niece Conana to celebrate her fourteenth consecutive Weight Watchers day.

"What do you need?" I asked.

"Well," he said, "it's a bit hard to explain."

"Try me!" I said, noting the similarity between this conversation and a recent dental appointment.

"I need you to pick up something for me."

Generally speaking, the first thing that should enter one's mind when an olive-skinned New Yorker asks you to retrieve an undisclosed package would be that you have suddenly been promoted to ass-puppet for some irrational and otherwise psychotic mobster. And yet, in this rare and unusual instance, I knew there was no cause for alarm. You see, I've made deliveries for him in the past and, although he never told me what I was shuttling about, I always assumed that they were the dolls he imported, copied, and subsequently sold. The air of mystery he ordered to surround his side business was mostly for effect. I didn't mind all the cloak and dagger crap because he paid me a shit-load of money to deliver the stuff (about fifty or seventy-five bucks a pop, depending on the location and value, or rather alleged value, seeing as how I wasn't supposed to know what was going on).

I must admit though, at one point I found myself wondering if he didn't have himself a little counterfeit scam going. Let's face it, he could have imported and copied the dolls and then sold the fakes to the highest bidder, while keeping the real gems for his already impressive collection. However, after further consideration I came to the conclusion that this theory was a complete crock of shit and it would be a cold and rather joyful day in hell before I read another one of his stupid-ass spy novels. With this in mind, I reentered the conversation.

"So what are the details?" I asked, glancing rather obviously at my watch for the thirty-second time.

He let out another one of those stupid sighs and then paid me a curious regard.

"Fine. I'll cut to the chase. I'm screwed, Tad, and I really need your help. Is that simple enough?"

"Yeah," I said, noting the platter of seriousness and side order of fear that accompanied his words.

"Good. Here's the situation. I need you to go to the old neighborhood after you finish jerking around with your friends and pick up a package at the old beach and tennis club on Davenport Road. You know where that is, right?"

"Yeah."

"Great. The manager is Bobby Mancini – not too sharp, but tip him if he gets inquisitive. Anyway, you'll be looking for locker number 37. Inside you'll find a suitcase, a package, and the second part of your payment. I want you to mail the package to me at this P.O. box." He looked around as if someone were watching and handed me a slip of paper with the details. "The suitcase will have to be delivered to an associate, and of course, the thousand is yours."

"A thousand dollars?" I said, as my bullshit sensors rang wildly.

"It's two thousand," he said, holding out the first half of my payment. "But believe me, kid, you're going to earn it. The guy you'll be meeting isn't exactly a Boy Scout."

"Are you shitting me?" I asked, admiring the ten crisp C-notes in an orgasmic fashion.

"I wish I were."

"Why can't you go up there yourself? Or better yet, just mail the friggin' key."

"I can't mail it. The package contains one of my dolls. The guy doesn't know about it, and frankly, after all this is over I'm gonna need the money. Besides if I go myself, I'm dead."

"What the hell are you talking about?"

"It's a long story."

"I'm already late."

Buck realized that the situation was too weird to act upon in the blind. Thus, he let fly with the whole heartbreaking, pathetic, *"God(?) really took a shit on me this time,"* story. I listened, understood, and truly felt for him.

Now I don't know if I mentioned it, but Buck has a way of gabbing it up pretty good. Of course, we here in Book Land don't have the time, or to be extremely frank, the mental capacity to listen to a load of crap of that magnitude. Therefore, I, The Amazing and Altogether Insightful Tad, have decided to order up a condensed version of the whole affair. I hope this will provide you with enough info to follow the plot, while at the same time spare you from a couple of horribly boring Uncle Mondo stories. If you are honestly pissed that I have excluded these stories, along with many other annoying antidotes, please feel free to file an official complaint with the Executive Board of Uncle Mondo Story Likers. They, upon receiving your letter, will call you up and snap on your mother in a rather nasty tone of voice. In any event, here's how it went down.

"You remember me telling you about my partner, Thomas Torri, right?" asked Buck.

"Yeah."

"Well, the prick's been blackmailing me for years."

"You? For what? Even if you did something wrong, what

could he possibly take? Ah... no offense."

"I'm not that poor, wiseass, ...or at least I wasn't."

"He started small enough, but greed gets to people. Two years later I lost my house, my savings, everything. All I had left were the dolls. He didn't know about them. Nobody did for obvious reasons.

"I had to get out, so I convinced him I had cancer, sold half my collection, and bought the house and shop down here. For a few years things were quiet. I thought it was over, but about two months ago I started getting his letters again. The shit-head is retiring this year and he wants me to pad his golden years. That's where you come in. I need you to deliver one last payoff. Then it will all be over."

"What do you mean, over? You know every time he needs money he'll come knocking."

"No. This will be the last time. He still thinks I'm dying. So I will, sorta. I'm going to disappear. Look, kid, I'm selling the shop and taking off."

"He could find out, track you down?"

"No. I've got friends who can arrange it the right way. I should have done that in the first place, but then Margie would have learned my secret. Now that she's gone, it doesn't matter what comes to light. She was the only reason I paid him. I just couldn't let her know what I did. But it doesn't matter now. Nothing will until I see her again."

"Oh Jesus(?), don't get melodramatic on me, Buck. First it's the melodrama, then it's the .38 under the chin. The whole suicide thing doesn't sit well with a potential English major like myself, you know?"

He laughed. I was surprised to see him laugh.

"That's why I like you, kid. You don't play by the rules. Shit, you don't even know what they are yet. You have your own system. Jesus, think of that gift! You're only eighteen and you already figured out that the world is just a screwed-up accident."

"Thanks, Buck."

"So, are you going to show some balls and make a little cash? I'm not pulling your chain when I say it will be tough."

"Okay," I said, feeling the pressure of the cash, the friendship, and the need to support my philosophies. "But if I'm going to risk my neck for something, I want to hear the whole story."

He leaned back, took a swig of coffee, and ran a sweaty hand through his hair.

"When I first joined the force I was a bit of a rock star. Don't give me that smirk. I'm serious. I worked my ass off to make a difference and bounced up the food chain pretty fast."

"So, what's the problem?"

"I wanted to work, work. There comes a point where a promotion means riding a desk, but pushing a pencil was not my idea of public service."

"Got ya."

"I had six great years. I made big arrests and got lots of press. The mayor was a prick, and the city was in search of a hero. I guess I fit the role."

"That's cool, man," I said.

"Yeah but at the same time I was making headlines this young hotshot, Scott Adrian, was breezing through the academy. He was good all right, but a big ball breaker. The academy almost tossed him for insubordination, but by the time they were ready to move the media picked up his story. Before long they were billing us as some sort of dynamic duo. Cops knew we hated each other, but the PR was good for the department. A

*Daily News* story later, the arrogant little pissant was my partner.

"I tried to control the megalomaniac for two years, but he was totally reckless. Then it happened."

"What, did he screw up?"

"No.... I did."

I felt two inches tall and even smaller when I noticed his eyes redden. Men don't cry where we come from, but considering the circumstances and my general disregard for cultural norms, I didn't take offense.

He continued.

"We were working a high profile drug-murder case for about eight months and much to the public discontent, weren't making a lot of progress. We knew it was a professional crew, but that's about all.

"Anyway, I was pissed off most of the time because my baby-face partner was getting all the attention. I know that's a shitty way to feel. Cops aren't supposed to want the limelight. The thing is when you grow up in a job constantly being praised for your actions and the attention is stolen from you by a person you see every day it works on your insides. It's kind of like having your wife fall in love and sleep with your brother."

I eased back in my chair and let him work through the scene in his mind. He took a deep breath, closed his eyes for a moment, and continued.

"Eventually we closed in on them. An informant gave me a tip on their location. We entered the building and immediately called for backup. We were supposed to wait, but Adrian couldn't. So we split up and began the search.

"I found them just as our backup team was assembling outside. I heard their footsteps in the next room. I shoulda waited, but I wanted the bust so bad. I kicked open the door, saw what I thought was an armed assailant, and fired. When I cleared my head I realized I killed my partner. He was beaten, blindfolded, and tied to a chair facing the door. The perps were gone."

"Holy shit!" I said.

"The department ruled it an accident and I was back on the street in six months. The truth, however, was that I shot the poor son-of-a-bitch before I even looked at him. I was so gung-ho about being a hero again that I forgot what the word really means.

"For months I tried to convince myself that he would have died from the beatings. I even went so far as to thank myself for ending his suffering. But no matter what I ran through my head, I couldn't rationalize the act. Fifteen years on the job and I killed my partner and covered it up."

"What?"

"Yeah, that's the sin. I taped a gun to his shoulder. Said I fired because I saw the reflection and thought it was one of the perps."

"How could you?"

"I don't know. I couldn't think."

"So you covered your ass?"

"What was I supposed to do? We weren't even supposed to be in there. He was just trying to show me up. Besides, I was scared. I was exhausted. Christ, I was just human. Is it okay to be human every once in a while?"

"Yeah, Buck."

"So how does Torri fit in?" I asked. "It sounds like you two were alone."

Buck flinched as if someone shot his puppy.

"You're never alone, kid. Backup, remember? Torri got there

first. I knew he would. We were friends at the time and when he heard my call he came running. I thought I could trust him. Was I wrong. As soon as money got tight he threatened to turn me in. That's when the blackmailing began. Bastard, it was his idea to plant the gun. He just set me up for the fall."

"Well, why didn't you just waste him too? No witnesses! Oh God(?)Buck, I'm sorry."

"It's okay. You have a right to be ashamed of me."

"I just thought you were bigger than that."

"I was kid. I really was. But Jesus, you can't stay in Never-Never Land forever. One day you wake up and discover you live in the real world. Everybody becomes a realist. You can't avoid it. You can't stop it. It's human nature."

"Bullshit!"

"Believe what you want, but I swear that one day you'll be faced with a decision so clear, so tempting, that you'll just have to give in. And once you make the transition, you'll lose that 'everything can be wonderful' attitude and become one of us."

"I'm stronger than that."

"Time will tell."

"Time has nothing to do with it. But I do and I'll be damned if I sell out."

"You got balls. You know that, kid? So what's the deal, are we going to end this friendship now, or will you help me when I need you most?"

"I'll help you, Buck. Everyone deserves the benefit of the doubt."

"Gee thanks, guy," he said, as the tension began to dissipate. "That's nice of ya. So I guess you'd better be going now, huh?"

"That's a startling observation, Sherlock, but aren't you forgetting something?"

"What do you mean?"

"I have the locker number, but what about the details?"

"That's a good point, wise-ass, and precisely why I wrote it down and placed it in this junior spy traveling envelope. But do me another favor and don't open it until you're two days gone. It's more poetic that way," he said, as he handed me a plain brown envelope with the words "Sarcastic Spy Guy" scribbled on the front.

Buck always had things perfectly planned. Maybe he had been a spy in a previous life.

"I don't suppose I should ask you where you're going."

"You're not as stupid as you look."

"Ah well, it's the thought that counts."

"And I am glad you thought of me."

"Then I guess this is good-bye, huh?" I asked. "I'll miss your sarcasm even if you couldn't hold on to the ideal."

"You'll grow up one day, kid, but for now enjoy your mental freedom. I'll see you in the next life. Let's hope it can be a little more honest than this one."

"Here here!" I said, toasting dreams with an imaginary glass.

"Here here!" he replied.

I shook his hand and left.

"Here here!" That was the last thing I ever heard him say. It's funny how you remember the little things. Two tired words most often uttered by inebriated individuals in dusty, forgotten taverns. And yet, when we toasted, those words seemed alive. Yes, our toast to honesty was honest and that's how I wish to remember it.

# CHAPTER 5

As I left the land of the poetic pizza, a plethora of conflicting emotions ransacked my brain. I was scared for Buck, though he probably enjoyed the situation. It was like one of his novels coming to life. I was also excited about the upcoming adventure and thrilled that for the first time I was going to have more money on me than Jackie. Finally, I was worried that I might get my balls blown off before I really got to break them in.

That's what I hate about feelings. You usually have too many at once. Why can't you ever just be pissed off? It seems that to experience this emotion you also have to feel guilt, shame, confusion, and about forty other stupid and altogether useless sensations. Just once I would like to feel a single emotion without a host of others getting in the way. I know this is strange, but it's consistent. Just look at the way I drink my coffee.

Now that I think of it, these two philosophies (that of the desire to experience a singular emotion and the importance for one to drink his coffee black) are connected. If one were to consume a brewing cup of the demonic beverage without the aid of the cloaking ingredients like milk and sugar, it may be unpleasant, but you would definitely get more out of the coffee experience. This idea also holds true with emotions. If one could conjure just the needed emotion, the person would be able to handle any situation with the clearest thought and the greatest accuracy. This is why I firmly believe that people who drink their coffee black are inherently more cool than those who don't. Of course, if you drink plain tea with a slice of lemon on the side (note the lemon never actually enters the tea, but rather is present solely for the decorative purposes), you will probably have a shitty childhood, write some stupid but altogether interesting books, and subsequently rule the world. This, however, is a completely different philosophy, and I will refrain from going into this amazing and somewhat interesting discussion so I can accurately complete this left-hand turn.

With this task behind me, I found myself driving up Pete Dempsey's block. I checked my watch as I pulled into his driveway. It was 7:30, a half an hour past our meeting time. Knowing I would surely be bitched at by a bunch of tired, stressed-out, pathetic excuses for Grizzly Adamses, I donned a forgivable, puppy-dog face and walked up the lawn. As I approached the door, my buddy Eric came running past me.

"Hey, Tad," said the maniac, as he hurried toward his car.

"What's up?" I asked, while trying to guess what sent him scurrying to his stupid automobile. Personally, I never scurry.

I deplored his car, which looked as if it was owned by a

decaying old man named Gus. He had bought the rectangular, incredibly gray shit box after selling his 1976 Triumph Spitfire convertible. How could he go from a classic creation to an automobile so large that it made that beeping sound when it backed up? What irked me the most about the whole affair was that he did it the exact weekend I planned to con him into letting me borrow the booty-machine.

Ah, but that was Eric, Mr. Eccentric. Once we went to the mall and, while I was looking at the latest trends in women's underwear, he walked into a tobacco shop and spent one hundred and thirty bucks he didn't have on a pipe, a case, and a half-dozen tobaccos. Okay, it seems normal enough if you can get past the inconvenient monetary outlay, but the dude didn't even smoke at the time. He walked up to me as I fondled this amazing pair of leather panties with a four-digit combination lock and said, "Tad, I read that pipe smoke won't give you cancer as long as you don't inhale it."

He then proceeded to lead me into a hat shop where he purchased one of those stupid French racing caps. For two months he drove around in his little white sports car, smoking that horrific cancer utensil and wearing that, *"Gee, I look like a dweeb,"* hat. None of us had the heart to tell him that he looked like a penis Erector Set, and if he didn't start to dress like a normal person, he would end up marrying his right hand. So one night, when he was most intoxicated, we decided to guide him back to sanity.

As he lay on the couch in a most compromising and helpless manner, my homeboy Pete and Darien, his partner in crime, lifted him up and dropped him, ever so harshly, onto the adjoining love seat where Mr. Pipe had taken shelter from Eric's unyielding breath.

In the days that followed the device's destruction, Eric realized the hat was incomplete without the rings of pipe smoke billowing around it. So, in a disgusting attempt to save money, he acquired a gift bag and passed it off to his grandfather as a birthday present.

When I regained my view of reality I noticed Eric was still rummaging through his car, so I took the opportunity to admire his psychoses.

"What are you looking for Eric, my boy?"

"My earmuffs. I can't find my God damned earmuffs."

"Earmuffs?"

"Yes, earmuffs, earmuffs."

"Eric, it's the middle of summer. What do you need earmuffs for?"

"We are going camping, right?"

"Yeah."

"Then we are going to need earmuffs to keep the bears away," he said, as he pulled out six black pairs.

"What the hell are you talking about? You want us to put those things on a bear?"

"Don't be stupid, Tad. The earmuffs are not for the bears. They are for us. I read that if a bear comes across your camp ground you should put on black earmuffs so he will think you are one of the family and leave you be."

"That's ridiculous. Are you telling me that a bear is not going to notice that I'm wearing Converse, a pair of Cavariccis, and have a little less hair on my face than your baby sister?"

Eric smirked and folded his arms.

"It's obvious that you don't know much about bears. If you did you would realize they are almost completely blind and, because they rely on their ears for survival, they generally look at other creature's ears to determine if they're a friend or foe."

My bullshit sensors went wild as I pictured him wearing one of those, *"I'm a hopelessly stupid loser and I like it,"* pins they sell at all-night convenience stores.

"Oh really," I said. "Well, what happens if the bear decides that you're not family, but rather an attractive member of the opposite sex?"

"That's okay, Tad. If you find yourself in that position just put on a hat and run in a circle while waving your arms. The bear will most definitely leave you alone."

I didn't even ask. I just kicked the garage door really hard and walked toward the house.

Dawn answered before I finished the seventh beat in that rhythmically annoying knock everyone uses. She was fairly cute in a tomboy kind of way and had the personality to match. She was dressed in faded blue jeans, powder blue T-shirt, and a pair of old Candies. Her soft auburn hair was up, but even in hiding, it had the ability to amplify her warm brown eyes.

She was naturally gorgeous and the countless hours spent working on cars and hanging with a bunch of barbarians did nothing to tarnish this reality. I wished she would start dressing and acting like a girl, but I wanted this for selfish reasons.

We had a brief fling a while back, but nothing came of it. I know she likes me as I do her, but I don't think either one of us is ready for anything real. Ah well, it's probably for the best. There's too much pressure in a relationship. When you're my age all you should have to worry about is getting decent grades, laid quite frequently, and of course, your daily dose of Pringles. I considerably love Pringles.

"Hey, what's up, bud?" She liked to call everyone "bud."

"Nada."

"Did you bring your earmuffs?" she asked with a smile.

"The kid is mentally irregular. I mean no brain power whatsoever."

She smiled softly and brushed back a curl that somehow escaped her scrunchie.

"Where the hell is Pete?" I asked of Darien as he came in from the kitchen.

"He's in the shower," he replied.

"What? It's almost eight o'clock."

"Lighten up, Tad," said Dawn. "He had to work late last night. Besides, me and Darien just got here a few minutes ago."

"We were supposed to meet at 7:00? I rush to get here on time, with every available maniac trying to deter me from this goal, and when I finally arrive, I realize I'm not late at all. Is this what you're telling me?"

"Correct-a-mundo," they announced in unison. Fonzi would have been pleased.

"And where's Jackie? Or will this upset me too."

"She's ah..." stalled Darien.

"Jackie's here!" screamed Eric, as he rushed through the door armed with a nylon duffel bag and a shit-load of earmuffs. "She needs help with her stuff."

"I got it, ya nut ball," I said.

Yes, Eric had always been different. He was like that quasi-haunted house in your neighborhood. You know, the one all the kids would dare each other to approach. That's Eric. From a distance he looks mysteriously strange dressed in starched, white buttoned-down shirts, never-changing Earth-tone slacks, and dirty high-top Nikes. But when you get past the superficial oddities, you see an entity like every other. It may have different paint and shutters, but it has the same structural problems as the rest.

I often longed to enter that home and witness its settling, but it appeared to have a new lock and the owner was not allowing any righteous handymen within its atmosphere to check its walls for cracks. This was hard to handle. I knew Eric was hurting. The recent amplification of his strangeness was just a warning sign. Perhaps someday I would know him enough to help.

With this in mind, it was almost full. Nevertheless, I ventured onward to help Miss Stuffy, but incredibly sexy, Jackie with her luggage. When I got to her car she was bent over retrieving one of her many suitcases. She looked gorgeous in her skin-tight pink sweatpants. The fact that her white sweater seemed two sizes too small only added to the arousal of every male creature in the galaxy. It was at this point I took a serious, *"what the hell, I might as well go for it,"* chance, and smacked her firmly on the ass.

"Ahhhhh!" she screamed, as she turned around in one of those vicious Italian, *"I'm going to beat the living crap out of you twice,"* moods.

"Just wanted to get your attention, honey. Here, let me help."

"You rat. Do you realize what time it is? Eight o'clock! I never get up this early."

"Early? You must mean incredibly late, because that's what you are. But don't worry, nobody will notice, considering that the master of all tardiness is probably still trying to find his pants."

"Early again?"

"I wasn't early! I was late. It's just that everyone else was much later."

"You're so funny sometimes, you know?"

She kissed me on the cheek (a first), and left me to carry the endless stream of suitcases that inhabited the far reaches of her

Mustang GT. As I labored forth, I couldn't help but wonder if maybe, just maybe, I would get in her pants before I died. I realize this is a crude thing to say, but I'm a guy with Montana sized hormones. Besides, if you spent the greater portion of your life thinking about stupid shit, and the little time you had left writing it down, you would realize that there is only a minimal amount of time for booty conquering. Therefore, when the sarcastic one (that's me) is presented with even the slightest chance for cheap and altogether lustful sex, he must pounce upon the moment with unslow-like quickness. Now, armed with my mental boner for Jackie and my previous (but probably never to be repeated) lustfestations (it's a Tad word) for Dawn, I grabbed the rest of her crap and headed into the house.

When I put the luggage on the couch, I came to the ever-so-obvious conclusion that I had to take a mind-bogglingly voluminous leak. As usual, my timing was perfect because Pete had recently finished his once-a-month bathing ritual. However, as I made my way to the bathroom mentally preparing myself for the appeasement of the porcelain sanctuary, I noticed that the door was locked. After further inspection, which included a great deal of banging and cursing, I discovered it was Darien who was keeping me from my natural duties.

Darien was a fairly cool individual, but our philosophies were polar opposites. I am, of course, an antisocial, sarcastic maniac who has absolutely no respect for society. Darien, on the other hand, is society. He is the youthful precursor to the stable, *"Gee, I wish I could afford a Volvo instead of this beat-up Chevy, but I had to get married really young, have the wife push out a couple of hopelessly stupid but incredibly lovely children, and subsequently save all my money to make them less hopelessly stupid,"* guy next door who probably should have been named Bob. I hated his Wally Cleaver-like attitude towards life, but hey, I can't complain.

Well actually, I can. You see there is one thing (besides his personality) that pisses me off. He can't dress. He would wear the same ripped John Deere shirt for weeks and I don't think he owned any jeans that weren't completely stained with oil. Yes, a fashion mogul he was not, but then again, none of my friends, with the exception of Jackie, could dress.

When Darien finally came out of the bathroom my teeth were doing the backstroke, so I rushed in and pulled out the monster. It took a while for the yellow stream of poisonous piss to begin its descent into the vast reaches of the porcelain pool, but when it finally started, I realized something was vastly wrong with my auto-aiming mechanism. You see, as I began to pee, the tarnished fluid shot out in a "V" formation, missing the bowl completely. As I watched the watering of a certain unhappy looking fern and the inevitable drenching of an equally disillusioned piece of tile, I became horrified. I quickly smacked Mr. Penis on the neck to rectify the situation, but it was too late. The peeing had ceased and the damage was done. The only thing left to do was leave in a hurried manner and blame the whole thing on Darien.

I'm kidding. I'm not that much of a scumbag. Anyway, when I finished the most unpleasant cleaning-like activity, I figured Pete, The Almighty God(?) of Lateness, would be ready, so I did a quick hair check and headed back to the living room.

I returned to find Jackie and Dawn sitting on the horribly stained but *"what the hell, it was cheap,"* couch talking in that whispering tone that always made guys like me nervous. Darien and Eric were in the adjoining kitchen and, by the look on Darien's face, it was obvious that Eric was annoying the crap out of him.

It is at this point where I would like to give myself a quick pat on the back. You see, I may be a heartless, cynical piece of crud, but for some reason people generally feel they can talk to me. Eric and Darien are a case in point. Although they are best friends and have been hanging out since grade school, they have incredible difficulty understanding one another. This is where I come in.

Eric is basically a moron, but being a moron as such, he generally comes up with some pretty cool ideas that I like to capture in my, *"I can't believe you said something so stupid,"* notebook for future enjoyment. Darien, on the other hand, is fairly intelligent, but has that, *"I guess I'll do the exact same thing my father does because I'm way too lazy to look for something I really like and even if I wasn't so damn lazy, I'd probably still not try it because I'm also very scared,"* attitude which will most likely cheat him out of the ever-familiar slice of stupid-burbia that he thinks is his birthright.

What one must understand is when stupidness meets stability, a conflict of the highest proportions is assured. This is of course fairly evident by the, *"Darien looks really pissed,"* scene currently on hold in the kitchen. (Please note the Amazing Tad time stoppage jammy once again.)

The point is that neither one of them could relate to each other's personality quirks. I, on the other hand, have nearly ninety percent of available personality quirks blended within my being. The remaining ten percent, which I have yet to incorporate, have been ordered from that inter-galactic store of mostly stupid and altogether annoying personality traits. Once they arrive, I will be able to effectively bitch about every idiotic stupidism that people are scared to discuss among friends.

Therefore, when anyone has a problem or just something to complain about, they usually come to me for answers and that all-important tear-proof shoulder. I guess this kind of makes me the unofficial leader of the group, but please don't say it too loud for fear that some psychotic Yuppie recruiter will tap me on the shoulder and say, "Hey, son, you've got leadership potential. Now come with me so I can work you into the ground for the best forty years of your life, give you a gold-plated watch, and then leave you to die in a leased BMW."

Anyway, feeling confident that I could effectively rescue Darien from Eric's bullshit tractor beam, I pulled out my verbal light saber and headed for the kitchen. Unfortunately, as I approached the two, the Pete-like creature emerged from his den. I stood in awe of his monstrous outfit. He was the only person I knew that could find a shirt that didn't match itself and would think nothing of wearing it with a pair of plaid slacks.

Still, Pete was my best friend; that is to say we could listen to each other's philosophy of life without squinting a doubtful eye or bowling over from laughter. I don't want to get started on the Jesus(?) thing, but it pisses me off when well-educated people believe to the death (or war) about a skinny little white man who hadn't enough people skills to avoid getting nailed to a block of wood. It's not their believing that gets me, but their total lack of tolerance for those of us who believe (without much vigor) in no real god, just the human spirit and multiple lifetimes. Who do they think they are, treating us (me, Pete, and a few quasi-cool others) as outcasts or children who have yet to see the light. Fuck them. I really hate saying that word in print, but fuck them some more.

Besides the tolerance thing, Pete was an incredibly intelligent individual, who could not only match wits with any Wall Street banker, but could also handle my artistically stupid thought process. I often imagined we were mental twins with each controlling half of our mutual brain. I would operate the creative functions with sarcastic proficiency, while he handled our more scientific ordeals. Yes, we were brothers in thought, but as I continued to gaze at his pathetic ensemble, I began to reconsider my previous statement.

He was wearing gray shoes, tan slacks, and a tent-green shirt with brown and blue stripes running across the back. If this doesn't make you think the child is seriously fashion-impaired, allow me to point out that he accented the outfit with a black belt and a loosely made electric blue tie. Add this to an animated personality and a physical make-up that resembled Popeye the Sailor Man, and you'd have the intense individual known throughout the land as homeboy Pete.

"What the hell is that supposed to be?" I asked.

"What is what supposed to be?" asked Pete.

"Does anyone else see something wrong with this?" I asked, trying to solicit support. The group sat silent, looking vaguely interested, but much more bored.

"Pete, what's with the clothes?"

"What do you mean?"

I was now convinced he was just trying to piss me off. I mean the kid was going to be an electrical engineer for Christ(?) sake. He couldn't possibly be this brain dead.

"Bud, I think he means, why are you wearing those dress clothes?" said Dawn.

"Oh these? These aren't that dressy."

That's it, the pissed-off factor had been reached. I was either going to have to yell really loud or stab him fiendishly in the skull with a large, rusty, bacteria-infested butcher knife.

"You can't be this dense," I said. "First you managed to be over an hour late to a meeting in your own house. But this get up is ridiculous. Do you know where we are going?"

"Yeah, sure."

"And you think it's normal to wear that pathetic excuse for a suit in the middle of the woods."

"Why not?"

"Why not? I'll tell you why not: because I have never seen you in anything dressier than a tuxedo T-shirt. You didn't even wear a suit to Eric's sister's wedding.

"Remember that, Eric? Dude showed up in a polo shirt and a pair of sandals."

"Yeah," said Eric, with a chuckle.

"And another thing," I said, "what's with this new-found love of water? Two weeks ago you formally declared bathing a total waste of time and now here we are, about to embark on a historic camping extravaganza, and you're inside clipping your nose hair."

"That's disgusting!" said Jackie.

"Dude," said the formerly Hawaii-based animal, coming to his own defense, "you cannot hold my past sloppiness against me. It just so happens that I've seen the light and subsequently decided to turn over a new leaf and become a normal bed-making, wipe-off-the-table-when-you-spill-a-beer, prompt individual."

"What the hell...?"

"That's right, bud," said Dawn, cutting off the Amazing One. (I was going to do another one of those Sarcastic inter-bookular time travels to produce a diss-avoidance, but decided against it due to the hornyness factor.) "We didn't want to tell you right away because we figured it would drive you crazy."

"Tell me what? That Pete's a lunatic? I knew that."

"Dude, chill," said Darien in a rare but interesting moment of hipness. "While you were relieving yourself, Pete and Eric made a vacation bet."

"Yeah," said Eric, "Pete bet me fifty bucks that he could stay neat longer then I could go without a cigarette."

"Eric, that's stupid," said Jackie. "You're forever smoking. And just think of all that beer we're gonna have. Tell me you're going to be able to drink without puffing away."

"I know I've got my hands full, but think about it. Pete is an animal at a fancy dinner party. Just imagine his natural instincts come alive when he's in the wilderness. Trust me. This is an easy fifty."

I quickly reminded myself that I had a shit-load of money on me. (One thousand two hundred and sixty three dollars and sixty-two cents to be exact) But, like any naturally scumy human, my inbred propensity toward greed got the better of me.

"I got twenty on Eric," I said. "Any takers?"

"I'm in for fifty, if you can cover it," said Jackie in a playful tone.

She expected me to fold. Everybody folded to Jackie, even her parents. But this time, with the help of my future delivery job, I pushed back.

"Why not make it a hundred?" I bragged, and then immediately wished I hadn't.

I didn't want anyone to find out what I had to do once we got to New York, and this stupid mind game for a possible side order of booty would surely attract attention; especially since I'm generally a cheap schmuck.

"You got it, honey," said Jackie in a voice that was surprised, excited, and aroused.

Darien predictably chickened out and Dawn, who otherwise would have joined in the fun, gave me an undeserved dirty look and sided with Darien.

I had no idea what her problem was. We had only fooled around once, and afterwards we had both gone on and on about how much of a mistake it was and how we were so different and all that phony horseshit. Actually, I wanted to see her again and she did most of the rationalizing. But hey, if that's the way she wants it, it's her problem. Now, just because I'm flirting with Jackie, she goes and gets all pissed-off. Whatever!

Hey, that reminds me to remind you to remind me to start the next chapter with The Amazing and Somewhat Sarcastic philosophy of the four different types of girls. Don't forget!

Well, once everyone finished screwing around, we loaded Eric's crap-moblie and gathered around Pete who was armed with a bottle of cheap champagne and a stack of Dixie cups. As he struggled with the cork, Eric snapped on his incompetence and said that a barbarian such as Pete would never be able to open the thing. I guess Eric was right because when Pete finally popped the top, it shot off and hit Eric directly in the balls.

"Arrrrggggggg! Arrrrggggggg!" cried Eric, as I laughed my ass off in a, *"Gee, I'm really glad that wasn't me,"* sort of way.

The others did a piss-poor job of hiding their chuckles as Eric jumped about and shrieked in agony. Pete managed to look confused, stupid, and horrified all at the same time. I had the strangest feeling the first thing that ran across that son-of-a-bitch's mind was whether or not this would lose him the bet.

Unfortunately, it didn't. You see, the official, *"Yo, we are on vacation and you're not!"* speech had not been made and, therefore, by an altogether biased vote on the part of Dawn and Darien (the uninterested parties), Pete's royal screw-up didn't count. However, in a gesture of fairness in respect to Eric's balls, he was given the right to one last cigarette before the toast and another to be smoked at his discretion anytime during the wager. Pete bitched about this for a while, but we just called him a hammerhead, snapped on his wardrobe, and said that if he wished to be sloppy at any time during the vacation all he would have to do was let Eric kick him firmly in the family jewels. Needless to say, Pete stopped his whining. With that, their stupid contest was under way.

Now Eric, whose eyesight was just beginning to clear, generally liked to make these speeches. He wasn't very good at them, but they made him feel important, and then he would usually shut up for a few hours while he played back the glorious moment on his mental VHS.

"Attention, attention, may I have your attention?" he asked, in a voice a few octaves higher than normal. "Before I begin this toast, I would like to wish Tad a Happy Horny Birthday on behalf of all his friends."

They clapped. He continued. I seriously dislike birthdays.

"We are about to embark on a historic quest. We will search the vast and slightly soiled lands of New York and experience its natural wonders and its urban...."

"Oh, cut the shit and get to the point," said Jackie.

"Fine," said Eric, looking like a puppy that got smacked in the nose with a rolled up newspaper. "In conclusion, I would like to remind you that we are not just going away to spend a lot of money, drink silos of beer, and pass out in a field, but rather, to find ourselves in a time of utter uncertainty."

"That was one of the best speeches you ever made, Eric," I said, "and you really don't make good speeches. But you're right. This trip is an opportunity for us to reflect on life thus far. After all, we're graduated adults now and we have a lot of tough choices ahead."

"Yeah," said Dawn. "Who knows what will happen to us next year?"

"That's why we have got to plan our own future," I said. "We can't let things just fall into place like the rest of society. God(?) knows they're screwed. So, a toast:

"To the six of us! May we never cop out and lose our dreams.

"To trust! May we someday know where it hides.

"To air conditioning, blue jeans, and Diet Pepsi! May they always be cool. And finally, to idealistic views of reality. Let us try to keep them alive."

"Here here!" we said in unison.

Wait a minute. Why do those words consistently intrude on me? Do they find joy in jostling my sensibilities? Do they marvel in souring my spirit? As we ran to the car, fought for the shotgun position, and thereafter started cruising down the highway of dreams, I could not shake these questions.

The last time I had heard them I was losing a friend... and a job. Holy shit! It just occurred to me that I am unemployed. Perhaps that's why Pete gave me so much money. He felt guilty. Damn, that sucks. I can now honestly say that the words "Here, here" give me the heebie-jeebies. Come to think of it, I don't like that saying much either.

This is all too weird. Take over for a while, will ya? I need a nap, and some time to consider whether this is at all related to my black coffee theory. Good night.

# CHAPTER 6

They were chasing me again. Stalking me through time, space, and the desolate caverns of childhood trauma we all pretend to forget, but never do. I ran as fast as skinny legs could travel, but got nowhere. They were too quick for me. I fell down, out of time, out of breath, out to lunch, like the sign on the doctor's door. He never came back, did he? I gave up and calmly awaited my fate, but they held fast, electing instead to point and laugh, refusing to take the life they tortured.

I knew these creatures well for they habitually inhabited my nightmares. I was accustomed to their thick purple fur and triad of horns, which shot out of their skulls, amplifying their timeworn faces. Yes, these were the Incredible Zukes. The horribly disgusting, pitifully depressed, hopelessly psychotic, mentally irregular, evils beings who wore really expensive silk suits and chased me through dreamland in their battle-hardened, leased Volvo killing machines.

But the Zukes would never catch me for I had a hero, a personal protector who shielded me from their psychological onslaught. I never actually saw him up close, but I knew he was there. The Zukes knew it too and they were scared of him. All he had to do was step from the shadows and the Zukes would freeze. As I lay there, gasping for air, I mouthed a "thank you" to the individual I called Barley Man, for saving my life once again... just in the nick of time.

And as my dream became calmer and the Zukes went back into hiding, I would picture a wild-eyed, free-spirited, courageous individual, who loves his work and hasn't forgotten what it says in the super hero handbook.

That was the true Barley Man, the essence behind the ripped jeans, makeshift mask, plaid flannel shirt, and long red cape. He was honest, sincere, and the kind of guy who wasn't interested in merchandising little Barley Man action figures. He just wanted to follow his dreams and share them with others. You could trust him. In a world where you couldn't trust anyone, you could most certainly trust him.

I often wondered about these two beings and why they so eagerly entered my warped mental arena. Then one day, as I sat by the window philosophizing about the importance of bottled water in interplanetary gardening, I was struck, rather forcefully in the brain, with the thought that, perhaps, these creatures were a very real part of me. Yes, I decided they must have been best friends who bought a condo together after college. Unfortunately, they couldn't get along and subsequently spent the majority of their time fighting over kitchen appliances and a stupid Elvis-head lampshade in the living room.

After a trial separation they realized that neither could afford their own place in this economy, so they decided (without consulting me), to divide my brain and spend most of their time making sure the other one didn't cross onto their side of the cerebrum.

Given this theory, I assured myself that these annoying REM-like disturbances were due to the fact that either the conforming, corporate Zukes tried to use the bathroom located on Barley Man's side, or that the big B.M. tried to grab a late-night snack from the Zuke-owned refrigerator. It was annoying at times, but there are worse things to deal with, the DMV for example.

"Yawn!" I said, as I stretched in a most relaxing manner.

I awoke surprisingly refreshed given my nocturnal difficulties.

"Yo, Eric, what time is it?" I asked, looking to my beloved pilot.

"Well, well, well, Sleeping Beauty awakes," said Dawn, in a sarcastic tone, which revealed that she was still pissed. I ignored her.

"It's almost 1:00, dude. You have been asleep for about three hours," replied Eric.

"No way," I said.

"I'm serious, man. We're almost out of Florida."

"Damn," I muttered, not believing the amount of laziness within me.

"Why don't we stop and grab some food?" asked Jackie.

"Yeah," said Pete. "I got to take a leak."

"Fine, there's an exit just ahead, but if we keep stopping we're never going to get anywhere," bitched Eric, as he made for the exit ramp.

Hold on a minute. I just remembered something. Didn't I ask you (yes, you, the person reading the book) to take over for me while I took a nap? Well, nice job, dick-head. You really screwed up. Not only did you let me oversleep and have a truly crappy dream about the evil Zukes, but you also forgot to remind me to explain my Amazing and Somewhat Sarcastic Philosophy of the Four Different Types of Girls.

Now I have no choice but to call you a loser and say, in a most unhappy tone, that your mother is so large she could kick-start a 747. There, I feel better. Unfortunately, I am forced to bust another one of those inter-bookular time stoppages so that I can embark on a rather interesting monologue without falling behind of the rest of the characters. Now for the theory.

You see, there are four types of girls in the world and, because of this, most men are miserable. Although they won't admit it, males cannot handle the stress involved in dealing with such variety and secretly wish there were only two forms of girls: sluts and prudes. Man knows that if these were the only two types he would finally be able to say, honestly, that he understands women. In this Utopia, if a gentleman wanted to have lots of sex, he would go out with a slut, and if he wanted a meaningful celibate relationship, he would date a prude.

What happens in the real world, though, is that men, being the naturally greedy scum we are, want it all. Therefore, we go out with the third type of girl, the tease, because she is able to give us the security of a relationship without banging every other guy in sight. And yet, while being completely aware of her anti-sex attitude, we are positive that she will also provide us with the physical pleasures we desire because of our overestimated sexual prowess and the way in which she handles herself.

Unfortunately, a tease never gives in because she is only a flirtatious prude who has forbidden fantasies about becoming a slut, which her conscience will never let her actualize. By the time the poor schmuck figures this out, he is usually too deep into the relationship to back out. In turn he convinces himself that if he stays with her just "a little while longer," she'll give him the booty and he won't look like a complete fool in front of his friends. Of course, the booty never comes and the loser is destined for a life filled with bad porno and masturbation.

I know, it sounds bleak. But there is hope. You see, there's a fourth type of girl, who, in fact, is no girl at all. This is the true woman. She knows when to say "yes," when to say "no," and how to drive you crazy while she makes up her mind. Of course, there aren't a whole lot of these creatures running around, but most men are confident that they will find their princess. The fact that the greater majority of them wind up with psycho bitches is another story and is precisely the reason why I do not want to get married and have children.

Wait a minute. You are about to experience on-the-spot, non-rehearsed Philosophication. From this moment forward, the above-mentioned bitch will be incorporated into the newly named Amazing and Somewhat Sarcastic Philosophy of the *Five* Different Types of Girls, as the first amendment to this fine constitution.

The bitch is like the dark side of the Force to the real women. Men fear this last and most dangerous type of girl because they have the incredible ability to assume any form. Yes, gentlemen, even your girlfriend. They can effortlessly possess their bodies and give them the power to achieve flight with a normal household broom.

There is no defense against these creatures and no telling

when they will strike. So if by some strange coincidence you are burdened with the horrible responsibility of dealing with a bitch from time to time, just try to hide as often as possible, and when cornered, simply nod and smile a lot. Oh, there is one more thing I should tell you. If you have trouble distinguishing a bitch from an evil slut, just remember that a slut will bang everybody, while a bitch will bang everybody except you.

With this philosophy explained and the amendment added, I jump-started the universe and anxiously awaited the forthcoming meal.

As we pulled off the highway and drove down the street in Eric's dilapidated crap container, I noticed a rather interesting restaurant set to the back of the road.

"Hey, there's a place!" I shouted, even though I really didn't need to shout.

"That shithole?" asked Eric.

"Yeah, why not? It's probably cheap."

"Oh great, I can see the headlines now, 'Six Teenagers Get Shot in the Skull While Trying to Find Themselves…. Family members say they should have gone to Wendy's,'" reported Darien, in a rather whiny tone.

"Well, here's the deal, Darien: either we stop there or I'm going to take a pretty powerful leak right here in the car," said Pete.

"The hell you are, trash-monster. You do that and I win the bet," said Eric.

He hung a severe "Ueeeeee" into the previously happily self-adjusted, and rather unsuspecting parking lot. When the dust settled and Pete came to terms with his internal organs, we got out of the car and walked toward the dining establishment.

# CHAPTER 7

The eatery's empty parking lot and deteriorating exterior led me to believe the cafe would be similarly desolate. However, when I opened the incredibly squeaky door that, in my overactive imagination, surely hid some psychotic killer, I was surprised to find it quite busy. Waitresses were be-bopping around and at least a half-dozen cooks were yelling orders to be brought to some fifty-odd customers.

Once Pete returned from the bathroom, the hostess led us to our seats and graciously distributed menus. So far the experience had been completely cool. Of course, right when Mr. Comfort was going to overcome his shyness and introduce himself, the whole thing got weird. Yes, this is where we met Yolanda.

The three hundred and fifty-pound piece of anal mucus with a head cold oozed over to our table with a look of disgust for the world in one eye and contempt for the universe in the other. When the slithering slob of cellulose finally parked herself in our general area, we were fairly famished. We patiently watched her fondle her order pad for about five minutes. Then Pete, no longer able to withstand the hunger pangs emanating from the far reaches of his belly, decided to place his order.

"I'll take a double order of pancakes, three eggs, two slices of...."

"I didn't ask you all anythin'!" thundered the blob as she continued to fumble through her notepad.

"I just thou..." Pete continued foolishly.

(Note: The following "destructivication" of the English language will not be facilitated via the use of Altogether Amazing and Somewhat Enterprising "Tad Words," but rather through a pitiful display of the deteriorating educational system and its effects on the lower class, overweight, underpaid, Southern waitress population. To help you understand the following conversation, please keep a few things in mind. First, the word "I's" can mean "I have been," "I am," "I really cannot," or "I generally think bulls are quite sexy and should be mounted in the upside-down formation while eating a side order of grits." Secondly, there will be a good deal of slang in the following conversation, some of which you may not understand. But don't worry. It's not too important. I just threw in the disclaimer to avoid any dispersions that might have been wrongfully cast at my poor little Tad Words. And now back to our program.)

"Look, boy, I's can't take your food orders 'till I's take your drink orders and to the best of my's recollection, I's can't recall rememberin' takin' y'all's drink orders. So why don't you hush on up? I's know what I's doin'. It says so right here in my waitress handbook. I's followin' this here handbook since befores you is been born, and its worked jus' fine. So don't you start givin' me no troubles, or I is gonna give you a whoopin'. You hear me?"

Pete swallowed hard and fell silent. Yolanda pressed onward.

"Besides, any ol' fool should know that when you is takin' an order the correct way you always start wif' the customer sittin' on the left, seein' as how readin' left to right follows the natural order of thin's."

"Well, what if we were in Japan?" I said, unable to shut up.

"Don't you go bustin' my britches, pretty boy," bellowed the beastly one.

"Whoa," said Dawn with a confusion-causing wink, "she has you pegged."

The large one turned toward the right-side sitting Darien and shook him from a daydream.

"Okay honey, what will you be havin' this mornin'?" asked the grammatically destructive waitress.

"Oh," stalled Darien, as he tried to determine the sex of the Klingon before him, "ah... I'll have two eggs over easy, some pancakes... ah, no syrup, and a couple of slices of toast, no butter."

"You wan' your yellers busted?"

Darien was confused. He was terribly, awfully, horribly confused. He looked to us for support, but we had no clue as to what the hell she was talking about. Moments ticked cautiously by and Yolanda began tapping feverishly at her notepad. She asked the question again, but it was like shouting at a loaf of bread. She grew tired of the waiting game and commanded an answer.

"Listen, boy, I don't know what kinds a tomfoolery you is

tryin' to pull here, but I's got more important thin's to do than to stand here jawin' away with some stupid yanks. So either stop messin' around, or I's gonna call Tommy-Luke from out the kitchen and he is gonna kick y'all the hell outa here. You got that?"

"Listen bit..." shouted Jackie as I kicked her quiet.

I knew that bit of hostility wouldn't do wonders for our relationship, but I had to safeguard my potential bed buddy.

"You wan' your yellers busted, or not?" asked the creature for the third time.

The table grew silent and little beads of perspiration began to form on Darien's forehead. For once in his life he would have to make a spur of the moment, command decision. After a minute the air grew cold and the familiar tapping of doom began to echo in our ears.

Suddenly, a spark appeared in Darien's eyes. Granted, it was a tiny spark at first, but it quickly ate some Flinstones chewables, began to grow, and ultimately blossomed into a light like I had never seen. It was a highly improbable, transparently clear, blinding light, which strangely allowed the viewer to see right into the mind of the host. All at once I saw the inner working of his brain. I admired the plush carpeting and the well-organized cerebral library. I must admit, it was a pretty good set-up for an otherwise anti-stylish kind of guy.

At this point, he was using most of his intellectual capacity to decide whether the above- mentioned question required a simple "yes" or "no," or demanded an answer of a more elaborate nature. The gears in his cerebral Commodore 64 began to turn with chicken-like speed and then, from behind the shadows of that confused, frustrated, *"I can't believe Tad brought us here,"* face, emerged an expression of total self-confidence. His twisted mentality was replaced by a proud smile, his shoulders flew back, his hair began to blow in an imaginary breeze, and then it happened. He let out his first, *"God(?) damn it, I know I'm right about whatever the hell it is we are talking about and I really don't give a shit what anyone else has to say on the subject!"* manly proclamation.

"Noooooooooooo! I don't want my Goddamn yellers busted. You want your boobs blown off? Well, do ya? And another thing, I really don't want pancakes. I hate those things! All my life people have been feeding me pancakes and I kept on eating them because I didn't want to hurt anybody's feelings. Well, no more. Do you hear me? No more! Just bring me my Goddamn eggs, whatever the hell those unbusted yeller things are, and a shit-load of sausage. I love sausage, and damn it, for once in my life I'm gonna eat them. Now move it, bitch!"

Needless to say, we were all a bit shocked. I mean, let's face it, the lady was a Bates Motel reject if ever I met one, but I think Darien, in his quest for manhood, went a little too far. Nevertheless, it was a good show of balls and I mentally congratulated him for his well-deserved silent victory.

Anyway, the, *"Gee, I bet Richard Simmons could have a field day with me,"* lady regained her self-esteem, took the rest of our orders, and returned to the kitchen. Eavesdroppers reverted to their conversations as the atmosphere regained its previously described, yawn-inducing quality.

A few moments passed and then, out of nowhere (well, actually, out of the kitchen) came the hulking mass of slobbering Jell-O. She slithered ever so fluidly toward an unsuspecting Darien and, upon her arrival, bombarded him with another thought-provoking and slightly stress-inducing question.

"Honey," she said softly, as if her few moments in the kitchen had magically created a loving connection between the two, "now abouts those there sausages you seem to like so much, would you like em 'picey or miaaaaaaaaald?"

Darien didn't even bother to answer. He just turned white as a Scottish ass, rolled his eyes in a, *"Jesus Christ (?), I don't believe this planet,"* kind of way, and fell to the floor in a most unconscious mode.

"I got dibs on his sausage," said Pete, the savage Popeye impersonator.

"You're a pitiful slob," said Eric.

"Why don't you have a smoke and smile?" suggested Jackie in a way designed not so much for the question/answer thing, as the whole, *"Look, Eric, don't go snapping on contestant number one, because I can diss people just as hard as you, and besides, condom nose, casting aspersions at fellow homeboys isn't exactly polite,"* new woman, self-actualizing, I can give birth and you can't even make cereal kind of statement.

"Chill, Jackie," I said. (What? I couldn't help it.) "You're just pissed at Eric because you know that he is gonna win the bet."

"What are you talking about, Tad?" asked a confused Pete, as he began to question why I had bet against him in the first place.

"Clamp it, Pete, this is between me and the bimbo," I said, while giving him a sly wink that harbored a dual message.

(Note: I realize this is a book and you probably didn't see that wink, and, even if you did by using your inter-bookular wink-searching device and now consider yourself a rather inventive individual, you probably didn't understand it. Therefore, in a pitiful attempt at niceness, I'll explain the hidden messages.

The first of course was the, *"Yo, loser, under normal circumstances, I would have taken your side and bet my junior Mafioso training fund on you, but in light of my amazing and somewhat hard to explain plan, I had to change things up,"* message.

The second piece of information was the, *"and another thing, don't go bugging out in the highest form about this stupid bet unless I bring it up because, to be honest, I, The Amazing One, have facilitated a most creative plan for booty acquisition and will need to use your stupid bet to ensure its success, okay?"* section.

Upon consumption, digestion, and subsequent excretion of this information, Pete gave me a sarcastic wink of his own. He said, *"Look, Tad, I'll help you with your plan if you really want to get in Jackie's pants, but to tell you the truth, you're a slut. And another thing, I really wish you would cut out all this Amazing and Somewhat Sarcastic Tad shit because it is really getting on my nerves. Now if you don't stop jerking off these poor little readers with your philosophized feces, I'm going to tell them all about the time you got drunk and hit on that four hundred and fifty pound roller-derby chick."*

I never understood how a best friend could bypass your bullshit sensors and see through your, *"Please don't get too close to me because I might get hurt,"* smoke screens. It was a talent I possessed and often used to make others feel more comfortable, but I never liked playing the reverse role. It was that fear of closeness that destroyed most of my relationships. Fears and doubts aside, I thanked him for being so damn intuitive.)

Oh no! I am suddenly overcome with the undeniable feeling that I am in some deep crapola. A few paragraphs back, I called Jackie a bimbo and then proceeded to anger her further by putting her and the story itself on hold while I went on one of my, *"Gee, I wonder what this philosophy means in the greater scheme of things,"* tangents. Now, with the realization that every moment I delay this upcoming confrontation will only add to my ultimate suffering and humiliation, I, The Amazing One (Oops, sorry, Pete) will reenter the story.

"Who are you calling a bimbo, you egotistical, hypocritical

piece of used, ragged-out toilet tissue?"

Realizing that any argument at this point would do nothing more than produce further shame to the male population, I broke down, gave in, wimped out, kissed her butt, and said, "I'm sorry". I know it's pitiful and I apologize to the Harley-riding, non-sensitive, Meister Brau drinkers of the world in a most sincere form. I ah....

Wait a minute, this is a book and, in being such, it provides me with the ultimate power needed to win a conversation with a female. Yes! I have a computerized memory. No longer will I have to stutter around for an answer as she utilizes her feministic brainpower to call up arguments from years gone by. No more will I have to sit by and appear idly stupid while she destroys my logical points with sentimental rebuttals. At last we (meaning the men and women at large) are on even terms. And if that doesn't work, I'll just cheat and give her some really crappy lines and all the wrong answers. Authors can do that you know.

"Look, hon," I said, in a rather cool tone as I reentered the conversation. "I may have been out of line calling you a bimbo and I'll even go so far as to apologize for telling you to shut up. That was both rude and uncalled for."

"Oh God, here it comes," said Dawn, in a barely audible whisper.

"Go on," said Jackie, batting her eyelashes.

"However," I said. "You cannot deny that my man Eric is gonna kick Pete's butt in a most honorable manner."

"Doubt it."

"What, you don't think I see that fear in your eyes?"

"What are you talking about, retard?"

"Damn, Jackie," said Pete in a dutiful fashion, "You're getting soft. Dude snapped all over you and you're not going to do anything about it."

"Not doing anything?" she asked with some surprise. "Let's double the bet."

"Fine!" I said, hoping to call her bluff.

"Hold on, Jackie," pronounced Pete. "You know Tad can't afford that kind of cash. Besides, money is boring."

"Well, what then? This loser doesn't have anything worth taking."

"Screw you," I so eloquently exclaimed.

"You wish, boner-breath."

"Wait, that gives me an idea," said Pete. "You should bet for sex!"

"That's disgusting!" said eccentric Eric, which kind of caught me off guard. I figured he would go along with the plan, seeing as how he also has the power to read the magical winks.

"Well, how about it?" asked Pete.

"I'm game," I said. "But what do I get if *I* win?"

As you can imagine everyone had a different reaction to this ironically hilarious statement. The guys were on the floor (next to the unconscious Darien) laughing their asses off. Dawn gave me a kick in the shin and a look that could have turned my father to stone. Jackie just went berserk.

"That's it you stupid son of a…and your mother was a hairy… You wish you could have…. And another thing, as far as your dog goes, that is the… I've ever seen.

"Guys," I said, totally deadpan, "do you believe what she said about my dog?"

Pete, who had recently regained control of his personalized giggling mechanism, was back on the floor in a pit of hysterically humorous laughter.

"That's it," said Jackie in a voice that, for the first time, sounded as if she had lost control. "All bets are off. I'm tired of your crap. You're so immature."

"Hey, look, Jack," I said, "if you want to forget the whole thing that's fine by me. I won't hold it against you. I mean, we're here to have fun, right?"

Now, most of the guys actually bought this fermenting piece of feces as an honest example of feeling-oriented discourse. Jackie however, who by the way should be commended for her overabundant intelligence, was able to see through this tactic.

"There is no way I'm backing down. I'll take your stupid bet, but if Pete wins then I get your middle chain. Deal?"

Now before I let you in on my decision, I would just like to make sure you know what's at stake. On one side is booty with the approximate value of a perfect guidolopiousness body, times ten to the caring factor of six. On the other side we have the above-mentioned gold chain. While it is not the largest or most valuable of the three necklaces currently residing around my sparkling white "Giny-T-shirt," it is my favorite and the one I have had the longest. Weighing these two treasures I ah... go for the booty of course!

"Yeah, you got a deal, babe. Now let's pay the check and get out of here."

I gave Pete a mental thank you and a sarcastic smirk in exchange for his, *"You disgust me, but I like it,"* wink. After this silent conference, we split the check, said good-bye to Jabba-the-Waitress, scraped Darien off the floor, and piled into the car.

As we drove down the dusty road and said our silent good-byes to a place better left for the memory to euphemize, I reflected on the utter good fortune brought on by Darien's complete state of unconsciousness. You see, he is a simple, good-natured, value-oriented individual, who would have been disgusted if he knew the change in our bet. Therefore, out of respect for the warped *Little House on the Prairie* attitudes he holds so dear, we decided that it would be for the best if we kept it from him. This didn't seem too hard to accomplish, considering that he looked like shit and would probably stay asleep for a long while.

"Jesus," said Eric as we approached the entrance ramp to the highway, "it's almost three o'clock. At the rate we're going, by the time we get there we'll have to turn around and come back."

"Well, maybe if you drove a little faster we would get somewhere," said Pete.

"Don't even talk about driving. I...."

"Are you kidding? I could drive circles...."

"You're the one who's always got to take a leak...."

"If yours was any smaller...."

"Well, maybe if you used it...."

"Oh yeah?"

"Yeah."

"Oh yeah?"

"Yeah...."

And so the never-ending argument between the eccentric Eric and the perplexing Pete raged on. I don't think either of them cared who won. Perhaps they just liked to talk and stir up hard-to-handle emotions. Maybe arguing was the only way they could do it without feeling like a couple of fags.

I tried not to think about it. I failed. You see Pete had a way of getting inside Eric's head that I could never match. What frustrated me was that, although I could achieve this trusting state of rapport with most anyone else, Eric was out of my range. I honestly believed he had some serious issue that he wouldn't tell anyone about and Pete was the only one who could help. Naturally, I wanted to be a part of this healing process. After all, he was my friend. But I'd respect his privacy. The way I hide my feelings, to act any other way would be hypocritical. And I hate hypocritical stuff. Besides, as long as he got what he needed, it didn't matter who gave it.

With those thoughts in mind I followed the rest of my companions into a deep, fulfilling slumber, counting the argumentative rebuttals of my friends instead of sheep. It was an interesting change.

# HALF-TIME

You're still here? Wow, that's pretty pitiful. I guess life in The Do Nothing Generation must be even more boring than I initially estimated. And seeing as how I always estimate on the lowest of low spectrums in order to avoid disappointment, I think you need to rent a life.

But fear not, my idealistic dreamers, my, *"Gee, I can't believe I'm getting snapped on by a guy in a book,"* worriers, and my mental rejects from the intellectually deficient society. I, the king of moronically interesting stupidisms, will guide you to the takeout window of amusement, and let you feast from the "all you can eat" buffet bar of literary coolness. (As long as it doesn't cost more than five dollars and thirty-six cents a pop, which it shouldn't given the previously mentioned fast-food price law.)

In any event, the reason I've paused this incredible story is extremely complex. You're probably thinking I just got pitifully lost, and in a desperate attempt to avoid a much-needed, humility-inducing, embarrassing episode, came up with this rather brilliant half-time excuse to create a diversion from my stupidity. Perhaps, but it's more than that.

Look, I don't know about you, but even I—member of the lifeless class, a nerd in the highest form, the kind of guy who asked his cousin to the prom and got stood up—am fairly busy. I have work, school, an occasional indulgence in the fine art of intoxication, homework, chores, and a seemingly futile, never-ending booty quest. I just don't have time to read a piece of stupendous literature like this straight through. So when I actually take time to educate myself in the finer points of life via the printed page I have to read it in chunks. Unfortunately, by the time I come to the end of the book, I don't remember a God(?) damn thing about what went on in the beginning. Of course, being an amazing moron, I set out to read it again, but by the time I get to the middle, I forgot what goes on at the end. Ultimately, I wind up reading it about a hundred times without ever actually remembering a word. I, The Amazing One, acknowledge this horrible problem that has been plaguing the real would-be intellectuals of society and, in a most altruistic fashion, developed this improperly placed half-time report as a remarkably creative cure.

I'll begin this report with a brief synopsis of the major events that have taken place in the first half…ah third of this Pulitzer Prize-begging novel. After I rekindle the imaginary fires burning in the depths of your brain (I say imaginary because a real one would hurt and, now that I think about it, be a monumental pain in the ass to light.) I will turn the show over to a bunch of pathetic losers who have been begging me to be in this book.

While I rest my weary fingers and soak my brain in that ever-popular thought-inducing stupidity juice, they, being the fame-seeking monsters they are, will keep you abreast of the happenings currently going on in Book Land. They may even go so far as to cover the major news events you may have missed while being mentally seduced by this attention-arresting book.

To keep the show running smoothly, I have selected (she made me do it) my wonderful (pain in the ass) Aunt Judy to be the beloved (altogether annoying) announcer (fame grubber), due to her amazing ability to organize events (drive people crazy) and the fact that she made an important contribution (gave me food) to this wonderfully creative (he's full of shit) intellectual cause. With this said, let's get on with the program.

For those who haven't figured it out yet, I am a "contrarian." Due to my unyielding desire to piss off the general population by doing exactly the opposite of what everybody else thinks is so great, I have chosen to tell this story in an unusual way. Yes, it's that break the fourth wall, conversational style that never seems to sell too well (mostly because the people conversing usually don't have anything interesting to say) but always arouses the interest in a select group of individuals. I wanted to make this selection clear from the get go. Therefore, if you recall, I politely told the rest of the world to scram while those who still had a cup full of questions and a distant image of a dream hung around to see what a maniac like myself had to say. And so you stayed and I am pleased.

Nevertheless, there is an "almost true" story to tell. You know, that little thing I try to slip in between philosophies. So why don't we take a look at where we are and what the previous pages have meant in the greater scheme of things.

You're traveling with a rambunctious group of confused

individuals who must confront the horrible problem of having to deal with life alone. Yes, this is the first time Mommy and Daddy can't make it all better. Their eyes are opening and the cycle of destruction or creation has begun.

You've got Darien, a simple, *"Why did the world have to change on me?"* kind of guy, who is struggling to fit into is father's shoes, even though they are two sizes too small. There's the, *"I'm sorry I can't let you in on this one,"* Eric, who chooses creative insanity rather than motivated creativity to deal with a world so strange. Then there's Dawn, who throughout the book (or at least when I let her talk) openly emanates the feeling of confusion to the rest of the cast. Decisions don't come easy for her and she knows it.

Next on the hit list is homeboy Pete. He of course must deal with the whole, *"Dad, get out of my face,"* thing, but more importantly, he must decide if he can continue the journey. You see, his decisiveness gives the impression of understanding and direction, but don't be fooled. He too is confused. He's just hiding it a little better than the rest of us.

An idiot once said, "Show me a man who follows a plan and I'll show you a man who is a success." I, the teenage philosopher, say, "Show me a man who follows anything but his heart and I'll show you a God (?) damned liar."

*Well, now we're up to Jackie,*
*and wow this one is tough.*
*I'd like to say something useful*
*but I don't know her enough.*

*She tries to be independent*
*and she tries to muffle her fear,*

*but in those eyes, I would not be surprised,*
*if somewhere waited a tear.*

Sorry for the Edgar Allen Poe routine, but when I was writing I noticed that the sentences were of the same measure and I just had to go with it.

Well, I'm next. You know I'm an artist at heart. However, since I have no desire to psychoanalyze myself, and I just used up all the blather I got from PSY 101 last year on the other guys, I'll leave the whole, *"What do you think Tad is really like?"* routine for you to discuss with your friends in homeroom. Please do me a favor and leave the book in plain view so I can piss off your teachers and become quite famous in the process.

As far as the story goes, I haven't made any incredibly challenging plot moves yet so you should be able to follow easy enough. But just in case you're a complete moron (which isn't such a bad thing, mind you), I will go over the events and rank their importance.

On the most basic level, which by the way is all you're going to get from me now considering I just ran out of Diet Pepsi and am rather pissed off, I, The Amazing and Somewhat Sarcastic Tad, awoke, bathed, humored my father (Ah, I bet you forgot that part.), had an interesting conversation with my boss (could develop), grabbed some food (nothing important there), met my friends (ditto), and subsequently drove, ate, and drove again.

These are the initial occurrences that will act as a foundation for the most incredible, amazingly funny, almost-totally true, somewhat sarcastic, stupendous book. I must warn you though, that from here on things get a little more tense (unless of course I forget what the hell happened last summer and start talking about my uncle Fred's dirt collection). In fact, you may find yourself needing further half-time reports. Well, sorry dude and dudettes. That's tough shit. Only one sarcastic status report per book. It's one of the newest Tad's laws in this galaxy and must be obeyed at all costs...less than a buck three eighty. (Run out and buy a copy of Billy Joel's *Glass Houses* if you don't know what "a buck three eighty" means.)

Well, I guess that's all I really wanted to say. I hope you know what's going on now and can follow this psychotic piece of insanity to its completion somewhere on the last page. If you have any other questions, you're an impatient fool. And unless you revoke that, *"I don't understand if the story is the story or the...?"* question you just tried to form, I'll cancel your cool license, forever dub you a penis invertebrate, and forbid you to read this book. And so, I give you over to my pain-in-the-ass aunt, who will try to amuse you until I return from the mountain of pasta and river of relaxation that await me. See you later!

Hi there, people in Book Land. Isn't this cool? I always dreamed that someday I'd be worthy enough to be put in one of Tad's books, but I never thought I'd be hosting a half-time report. I don't know what to say. I guess it just goes to show that people with no talent can still become famous. All you have to do is find some soon-to-be-popular poor person, tell him how great he is, give him lots of food, and then "bango," before you know it you're right there on top, basking in his glory.

Oh my, how terribly embarrassing. I forgot to properly introduce myself. I'm The Amazing Tad's wonderful, and of course, favorite Aunt Judy. I live in Hartsdale, New York, in one of those Yuppie-infested co-op buildings Tad detests. At first I didn't want to buy it because I was scared The Amazing One would boycott my existence. (He can do things like that, you know.) But then I realized that by the time this book is published, he would have gone to college and be faced with a four-year, food-excluded, academically oriented prison sentence. He will need me!

Isn't Tad the greatest. (No need for a question mark there editorial staff.) Why, I remember when he was just a baby, he looked so cute. I've got some pictures I've been dying to....

"Wait a minute. What the hell is going on?" asked Tad. "I thought I told you not to talk about my childhood and not to show any of those stupid pictures."

"Oh, but Tad. You're so adorable. Look at this one with the little flowered bell bottoms."

"Enough! I've had it. No more pictures, no more amusing antidotes, and another thing: What am I doing in quotation marks when I am not speaking directly to a particular character? Whoa, this is too weird. I shouldn't even have to ask you that. I'm the author and only I have that omniscient attitude."

"That's not entirely true."

"What do you mean? Again I have to ask. I bet I couldn't even bust one of those inter-bookular time stoppages and go off into a deep philosophical discussion."

"I'm afraid that's correct, my sexist little scoundrel. You see, when you let me host the second part of the half-time report, I became the official stand-in narrator, who, in some states, has exactly the same amount of power as the author himself."

"Where are you getting this nonsense?" asked the confused, but case-building Tad.

"Hey, cut that out," warned an angered Tad. "Stop reading my mind. How am I supposed to win an argument if you know everything I'm going to say before I say it?"

"What, you think it's unfair?" asked Aunt Judy.

"Hell yeah!"

"And do you agree that only the worst kind of trickster would use this power to gain an advantage over a situation?"

"Of course."

"Then why don't you call off the bet with Jackie or at least lower the stakes to something more reasonable? Really, Tad, betting for sex? That's terrible. Grandma would be ashamed."

"Look, I can't call off the bet. It will ruin the whole plot."

"Don't lie to me. I know the end of the story now and that has nothing to do with it."

"Quiet! These dudes scraped together some hard-earned cash to pay for this book. Don't spoil the ending."

"Then promise me."

"Promise you what?"

"That you'll call off this bet and stop being so darn sexist and controversial all the time."

"All right, all right, you win. But before I promise anything, tell me where you read all this narrator hostile takeover stuff."

"On the check-out stand in the supermarket."

"What?"

"Yeah, the magazine said this lady from New Brunswick took over a certain televangelist's mind and turned his would-be self-help novel into a sexual Twister game for the intellectually impaired."

"Well, well. And I bet you read this article and then sent away for a, *How to Overpower Your Obnoxious Nephew's Mind and Make Him Write a Decent Piece of Literature*,' book."

"How did you know? Wai* a minu*e. Why am I the one asking *he ques*ions now? And why am I *alking so funny?"

"Because, my over-motivated aunt, my power is coming back.

I know you got ripped off and paid fifty-nine dollars and ninety-nine cents for the damn thing, and because of this vital piece of information I so cleverly abducted from your Napoleonic brain, I can now fairly state that your claim to my throne is pitiful at best."

"I don'* unders*and."

"I didn't think you would. Ha, ha, ha! I'm a genius. You see, my ambitious supplier of savory food-like substances, because the seller of your magical stun spell was a phony, you are a phony and therefore have no power over The Amazing Me."

"Bu* you said any*hing can happen in books?"

"Of course it can. That's why I changed three fundamental laws of the universe while you were gloating.

"The first thing I did was amend the New York State Book Power Law so that in order for a pitiful dweeb like you to take over the show, you would not only have to attend one hundred and fifty-seven years of special stupidity classes to upgrade your narrator license to that of an author, but you would also have to get ninety-eight point six percent of the reading population's approval to nominate you for a grueling thirteen point five million years of primary governmental elections in order to be worthy to run against me.

"Once my power had been fully restored, I strung you along, asking pitifully stupid questions to make you believe you had control. After lowering your guard, I stole all your 't's' and made you totally incapable of continuing your present job."

"Well... um.. ah... Wha* was *he las* *hing you did?"

"Why, I turned you into a toad and banished you for all eternity into the land of the upside-down, bone-headed, nerd's society of hopeless dweebs."

"You mean..."

"That's right. Good-bye."

"Poof," said the magical cloud of smoke as it colorfully burst into the air and took the ever-annoying Aunt Judy to her place of rest.

Look, it's getting late, so if you don't mind I'm going to skip the Book Land stories and focus on the outside world. So what's happening in 1988?

Recession, repression, cutbacks, condoms, alcohol, AIDS, drugs, depression, war, and wastelands of words like these wearily wear upon our minds. Lately, it's becoming quite hard to dream.

More news after these messages....

"Say, Mom, do you ever feel, you know... not so fresh?"

"Sure, honey, that's why I use...."

Then, out of nowhere, came a small white creature on a hidden pair of roller skates. He looked menacing, armed with a huge white cylinder and two rather large sticks. He was about to attack. There was no stopping this fiend from invading the frames of this already disgusting commercial.

"Still going."

Oh no, I couldn't bear to watch the destruction of an awkwardly inappropriate feminine hygiene TV commercial any longer. I had to run.

"Nothing outlasts the Energizer."

It was him, the amazingly rude, yet somewhat cuddly bunny. What is the Energizer Bunny doing in the world's coolest book? Ah well, I might as well do the fan thing.

"Excuse me, Mr. Bunny, sir, could I, The Amazing Tad, have your autograph?"

"Amscray, kid, you bother me."

"Wow, the Energizer Bunny actually insulted me. What an honor. He never talks to anyone. Bye, Mr. Bunny, sir."

Well, folks, we sure beat this to death. Let's get back to the story. But just in case you have absolutely no clue as to what's going on in the world, let me refresh your memory. People are still being royally shitty to other people for no apparent reason, most of the population is being grossly underpaid to perform jobs they despise, and if the above-questioned supreme deity doesn't do something quick, the world may very well lose their minds and turn to Elvisism.

# CHAPTER 8

As the winds of reality rolled gently across the fruitful field of my imagination, I stared longingly at the Barley Man and tried to fight the waking sensation that was calling me back to a world I so frequently questioned.

He saved me again and I was thankful. So as I departed his land and bid goodbye to the yellow mountains and the deep green sky, I made a silent promise to a hero who needed not his hearing faculties to comprehend my intentions.

I swore most solemnly that I would someday release him from his duties and accept the role of a grownup like the man I wished to be. I wasn't sure when someday would appear, but I had the feeling it was not far off. Therefore, in the fleeting seconds that so thoughtfully provided the barrier between my hidden world and the reality of the masses, I quickly located a

Zuke about a hundred yards away, looked him firmly in the eye, and told him to go screw himself. Of course, being the chicken-hearted fool I am, I made little haste in presenting my inter-dreamular passport to the friendly customs officer, and, once cleared, dispersed with Road Runner-like quickness.

The Barley Man saw this and smiled.

I was pleasantly surprised to find that I woke ahead of my companions. Eric, who normally refused to let anyone drive his Geritol-mobile, was busy fumbling through the junk in the glove compartment while chatting in a commendably quiet fashion with my homeboy Pete.

Judging by the ever-familiar, but never actually missed, horribly disgusting stench that was assaulting the atmosphere, I concluded that Eric must have sneaked through approximately a half pack of Marlboro Lights, while his partner in crime likely littered the entire state of (damn, where the hell are we?)...South Carolina.

Ah well, the way I see it, I'll come out ahead either way. If I win the bet, I'll tell Jackie all I want is a dinner date. That should sufficiently melt her heart and make her mine. And if I lose? Well, I can't think of anyone I'd rather have wearing my chain. I'm not sure when I fell for her, but I did and it's great. I know that sounds corny, but sadly enough, it's the truth. Too bad I can only say this sensitive stuff when everyone is asleep.

I slowly stretched my lower appendages and upon completion of this, *"Gee, that was a fairly useless attempt at comfort,"* relaxation maneuver, gazed out the window and caught sight of the, *"Now I realize I'm still hopelessly flat and boring, but I'm drinking milk and someday I'll have strong rocks and trees, with interesting curves running through the vast reaches of my geography,"* landscape.

I admired its youth and undying faith in the universal advertising industry for a second or so. Then, in a rare moment of cruelty, I informed the geographically deficient monstrosity that it was lactose intolerant and was subsequently doomed to an eternity (or at least however many years the boils of humanity allow it to survive) of puberty avoidance. This misfortune would expedite the endless stream of comedic aspersions that would be pitifully placed upon its brow and cast a life of miserably unfortunate uncoolness to all the barbarians that inhabit the overly dissed area.

Well, after thinking myself into another one of those maniacally depressed, *"Gee, the world really swallows,"* kind of states, I had no choice but to look to my traveling buddies for some anti-thought discussion.

As I turned to harass Jackie with some useless chatter about the weather, I noticed an interesting amount of hand holding in Darien and Dawn's unconscious arena. At first I was surprised to see this affectionate display whose utter existence snapped on my previously overestimated manhood. However, upon further examination and a perfectly placed feeling detachment mechanism, I realized this presentation was beyond justification or philosophical reasoning and, therefore, became worthy of my uninvited blessing.

After playing a mental version of a certain Stevie Wonder song on my intellectual eight-track player, I witnessed the day's second startling revelation. Jackie was shivering and had her hands over her eyes.

Now, if there were an incredibly disgusting horror movie playing, or a certain magical snowman were molesting his favorite season, I would have bequeathed this display no continued attention. But considering the fact that Eric's mobile shit container was devoid of VHS capabilities and the closest thing I had seen to snow in the last two years was the inside of a neglected freezer, I chose to stand guard over the curiously strange event and report anything out of the ordinary to my correspondent, Peter, *"Ha, ha, Amazing Tad, even with this overly obvious hairpiece and the denial of a recently removed, by unnecessary budget restraints, power tie, I still get laid more than you and I didn't even have to write a psychotic book to do it,"* Jennings in Washington.

Moments passed and I kept watch. Then it happened. Jackie called for her mother and reached for my hand.

How strange! A girl nobly goes to great lengths to convince the world she is rough, strong-willed, and independent. Yet, when she least expects it, her thoughts betray her, and let all those within hearing distance stumble upon her innermost secrets. What a horrible thing sleep talking must be. Unless of course you sleep alone and own a tape recorder, but that's another matter.

Luckily for her, and just as unlucky for me, Pete and Eric's arguing deprived them of Jackie's disclosure. Due to this hopelessly stupid coincidence, I had to handle the situation alone. As you know, I suck at feelings, so I decided, in a most procrastination-prone way, to ignore the event. I thought it was a pretty good way to deal with the situation, but then the above-assumed and highly questioned deity of the week, (who probably only pretends to exist in order to keep the miserably dependent masses on their toes and to piss me off in the highest form) sprung to "after" life, positioned himself haphazardly in his God(?)-like La-Z-Boy, and, once relaxing comfortably with a beer in one hand and the remote control of destiny in the other, proceed to edit my story line into an incredibly screwed-up and otherwise unsure-of-itself, friendly piece of rotten, fermenting goat cheese.

Yes, that's right, my devoted readers, the Jackmeister woke up while still holding my hand. I was convinced that when our eyes met and she realized that she'd been using my shoulder as a psychological Linus-like blanket she would go berserk and quite possibly kick the crap out of me. Much to my surprise, however, when her head cleared and our eyes entered a mutually owned atmospheric parking space, I experienced a look that both frightened and comforted me.

She was helpless. If just for a moment, she was dependent on another person. Sure, she was scared that she had to trust somebody, but at the same time, the fear that she would never learn to accomplish this task subsided. Was it an even trade? I don't know. But it seemed to me that the warm glow emanating from her slightly softer than previously admired, fiery brown eyes was enough to make the exchange worthwhile. She was truly beautiful. But alas, I was me.

I desperately wanted to pull my hand away and shift my eyes to a safer altitude, but the chilled air of openness froze my once-scrupulous faculties and forced me to act a lie. So, when she closed her eyes and waited for that special someone to grace her lips for the first time, I allowed the stranger within a rent-free moment to entertain her foolish dream. You know the one I mean, the one where Prince Charming leads the girl through the toils of everyday, to a cottage with a white picket fence somewhere in Never-Never Land.

So I lied and we kissed, a wonderful, timeless, perfect kiss. Still, there was guilt. So as the stranger slithered back to the Zuke-owned side of my psychological time share and the beautifully betrayed Jackie drifted back into her own land of dreams, I tried to come to terms with the whole affair.

# CHAPTER 9

Moments past as we rested. Then hours, being much larger and more physically able than minutes, realized their formerly ignored agility, did a couple of rather interesting toe touches (interesting only because the hours of time have no toes), and began to pass as well. In fact, it appeared, for an undefined portion of the greater scheme of things, that the hours were flying by much more quickly than the minutes. They even went so far as to steal the minute's time-cherished position in the Three Minute Egg in order to benefit the customer and further its own acting career.

At first I was shocked that the hours of eternity would perform such a hostile takeover. But after further consideration, I decided that seeing as how the consumers were getting royally screwed on a daily basis by governmental institutions who really couldn't give a flying fa' un culo (pardon my English) about the hopelessly stupid, recession-infected, ignoramousses of the world, I should support this final attempt at whatever the hell I just spent the last paragraph explaining. Peace signs in hand I marched down a crowded Albany street and shouted rhythmic slogans at my invisible enemies.

Given the state of stupidity that was currently funneling a few dozen cases of, *"I realize I shouldn't be drinking this because it will probably render me horribly catatonic for the next few millennia and even put a good deal of hair on my tongue, but what the hell, it was cheap,"* beer while doing the wave at an imaginary Lakers game, I should have ignored the antisocial, *"Yeah, fight the power!"* time forms. I tried to, but sadly enough, they would not ignore me.

I looked around the car. Everything seemed normal. Those in the back of the transport were unconscious, while Pete and Eric were busy playing Monopoly. Pete had just landed on the Eric-owned Boardwalk and was about to fork over a shit-load of cash due to the recently built hotels that inhabited the area.

Monopoly? Wait a minute. What's going on? Who is driving? Oh, I get it. They're probably just waiting for somebody to wake up, notice the Monopoly board in the middle of the seat, and freak out. Well, I'll show them. No one takes advantage of my pitiful laziness.

"Hey, guys, that's a cool way to pass the time. Who's winning?"

They must have been fairly annoyed that I spoiled their joke because they didn't even turn around. Pete just grunted and started to count out his money.

"Wouldn't you guys rather be bowling or something?" I asked, in a most sarcastic tone.

"Grunt roughff yak unoslap grunt onogrunt," said Eric, to a

seemingly understanding Pete.

"What do you mean, that's a good idea?" I asked. "We're nowhere near a bowling alley and, even if we were, we don't have the time to stop and screw around."

"Huh?" I questioned quietly. "How did I understand that? It sounded familiar but I.... Oh my God(?). It can't be them. Not this soon. Not here!"

"Zapf onk uongrunt sleroloious two!" said Pete as he slowly morphed into a Zuke-like creature. My knees knocked as his horns sprang out arrogantly over newly arrived purple head fur.

"No!" I pleaded. "I refuse to play Zuke bowling again, you rat bastards."

"Urkoladus xoralptis uno gruntifus?" asked the Pete Zuke of the Eric Zuke.

"Giuno, retufus zapmanditrone," replied Eric Zuke.

"Oh shit!" I said, as the front of the car shot out sixty feet to form a three-lane bowling alley complete with an overly flirtatious, underpaid, stupendously ignorant counter girl named Emily; four fat, beer-sucking gentlemen dressed in "Carmine the Big Ragu's Wonderful World of Watermelons" T-shirts; and a lopsided pool table, which had the audacity not to accept dollar bills.

I turned to my formerly friendly backseat associates only to find the sea of hospitality had evaporated and had been subsequently replaced by that ever-unpopular, purple desert of green Zuke dust. Yes, that's right, even the newly sweetened Jackie was lacking some of her usual lustrous brilliance due to the freely flowing, sloppy Zuke saliva cascading down the corners of her once-petite mouth.

In the recently written Amazing Tad Dictionary of the Universe, this event most accurately illustrates the phrase "scared shitless." Acting on this creatively devised denotation of an otherwise pitifully sad and slightly overused pair of words, I tried to "jet" (that's "run real fast") in the highest form out of the Zukeably stolen, Bowling Mo-Buick. Unfortunately, due to the surprisingly fastened, Incredible Zuke steel-belted horror strap that so antisocially constricted my favorite set of kidneys, I decided it would be most beneficial to stay where I was. Yes, I was in some deep guacamole. And I mean that literally. They had the stuff spread out all over the back seat and started making those little Zucko-guacamole-ma-fritters I hate so much.

All at once, the engine bellowed a satanic decree of historically evil proportions. It raced down the undefined highway at a ridiculous pace, ignoring all of the imagined and not-yet-imagined Inter-Stupidic Highwayolopous Laws of traffic safety as it went.

I began to feel incredibly dizzy. My head was spinning at about one million miles an hour (or is that minutes now, seeing as how they are longer?) and I felt about as socially acceptable as that wilting chunk of green fungus growing in the bottom-left drawer of your refrigerator.

I tried to keep conscious while the Zukes warmed up their bowling arms by eating some imaginary spinach and reciting a few hundred choruses of, "I think I can, I think I can." Unfortunately, the force currently playing Twister with my internal organs was just too powerful, and I blacked out.

"Owwwww!" I yelped as my subconscious caught a swift construction boot to the torso. "Watch the shoulder, will ya?"

(Oh, in case I forgot to mention, I have a bad shoulder that tends to dislocate for no apparent reason. It first happened about three years ago on the fourth of July. I was just standing around waiting for someone to feed me, when my little brother

T.J. (only six at the time) ran past me and waved in a, *"Wow, Tad, you're really my hero,"* kind of way. When I tried to wave back, my God(?) damn arm fell off, and ever since it tends to dislocate at the most inconvenient times.)

"Zork unabopilozzi!" said the irritated Eric Zuke, as he lifted me by the neck.

"What did you say about my mother? You big, ugly, nasty, couldn't-get-a-date-with-Medusa's-ugly-cousin's-former-roommate piece of decapitated...."

The above ellipsis was not implanted there because I ran out of insults for the incredibly evil ones. In fact, they—the insults I mean—continued all the way down the alley. I even managed to get in a final stupendously historical aspersion about his homosexual Uncle Chester before I crashed ever so harshly into the pins.

As I lay there on my back, humiliated to the finest extreme, I came to the pitifully depressing conclusion that not only had my shoulder dislocated on impact with the pins, but also, as if to add further insult to an already impressive string of injuries, I had a rather large Zucko-guacamole-ma-fritter shoved up my nose. Feeling lower than an anorexic mole's herpes infected toe jam, I pulled the Zucko-guacamole-ma-fritter from my violated nostril area, hurled a few antisocial remarks in the general direction of no God(?) in particular, and then, respectably, in a pathetically defeated manner, passed out.

I awoke smelling of sweat and anxiety. I wanted to keep my eyes closed, for fear that some new horrible habitat would play uninvited host to my disillusioned schemata, but they opened of their own accord.

Slowly, I gathered the strength and humility to rise. I collected my troubles and tossed them into a ratty, sticker-ridden, emotionally scarred suitcase. And so I sat, butt pressed against the overstuffed container, trying hard to force it shut. Sometimes it's the little things that can get you down. I clicked the case closed and tossed it over an imaginary bridge. Sadly, it bounced back as if held by a bungee cord. Where was a knife when you needed one?

I was about to cry when I heard a voice. Constructed from the tones of testosterone the siren-like sound's powerfully gentle rhythm dulled my senses and commanded my attention.

Cautiously, I climbed out of the vanishing Zuke gutter and began my descent down a road called Boulevard Street. (Now that I think about it, the climbing was rather idiotic since the previously painful place was in fact disappearing. Thus, the above-mentioned act of strenuously trying exercise could have been avoided with a little patience).

I had no idea where I was going, but I was sure it had a purpose and that comforted me. Besides, I could still hear the magically pleasant voice in the distance and I figured I had little to lose by investigating.

Surprisingly enough, the walk wasn't so bad. Hell, if you disregarded the ever-changing planetary color scheme and avoided noticing an occasionally flying Freudian sexual device, it was actually kind of pleasant.

I traveled on.

When I reached the corner of Boulevard Street and Avenue Court I noticed a living painting of a dead actor standing on an invisible platform. He was performing nothing, but he was indeed painting nothing also. I watched him for an interesting group of seconds, and when he finished doing nothing to nothing (which was kind of hard to tell), a group of Nobodies, who swore they were Somebodies, neglected to clap or call for an encore simply because they weren't there. Feeling sorry for the obvious boycott of the Somethings in the world, I quickly began to do anything in hopes of rectifying the situation.

Unfortunately, The Intergalactic Committee of Treaty Regulators for the Overlystupidic Something/Nothing Wars appeared out of nowhere and everywhere simultaneously and handed me a great deal of nothing and a little bit of something. They appeared painfully confused for a moment and then declared to the ever-present Somethings and the nonexistent Nothings that the Amazing Tad recently performed "Anything" would not violate any of the incredibly important and horribly useless Society Reorganization Documents.

It seems that many, some reference to time, ago, the Nothings took over the Somethings with their world-famous, top-secret stalling techniques and drove the so-called, evil Somethings out of Somewhere Land forever. When I, with all of my impatience, tried to create something to relieve my sense of boredom, through the use of Anythings (which are far more evil than the Somethings, that is, if you're looking through the eyes of the Nothings) I created an imbalance, due to the lack of specification. This batch of ethnocentric stupidity almost caused the galaxy's second round of Inter-imaginary Something/Nothing Wars. Fortunately, my ignorant disruption only facilitated a slight change in the Nothing World agriculture system. It seemed that now, the cows of the land laid the Nothing eggs, while the chickens, if in fact they actually did something, which they didn't, would have taken over the job of giving milk.

Feeling like a complete shit-head, I invented a bar on this

historic corner of Nothing Land (which just pissed them off further because it wasn't supposed to be there), affectionately named it, "The Guy Who Screwed up Your Entire Planet's Place" and entered.

Realizing that I might never wake up, I came to the conclusion that the most appropriate thing for me to do was to get blasted out of my skull and yodel some old Swahili rap songs until I aggravated even the most patient Nothings in Nothing Land. This aside, a recently invented bar tender conveniently appeared, so without a first thought, I started a conversation.

"Hey, pal, what do you say?"

"I kind of figured you'd get here sooner or later," said the same amazing voice originally cited in previous pages. "What'll it be?"

"It's you!" I said in much the same tone as Mr. Howell probably used when he finally got off the island and saw his first C-note. (Do you think that the Professor or Gilligan ever nailed Ginger or Mary Ann? I mean let's face it, they were on the island for fifteen years.)

"Stop mentally fornicating with women as old as your grandmother, Tad," commanded the Barley one. "We have some important business to discuss."

"What do you mean? And what's with that Zuke bowling crap? I thought my summit with puberty was going to be a slow, evolving process. But two minutes out of the dream and I'm getting the crap kicked out of me while spending the greater portion of my recovery time bullshitting about certain time disturbances with a group of individuals so utterly pathetic they don't even exist."

"Don't blame me. It's your dream."

"But how...?"

"Let's just say that you have somehow altered your destiny and are in for a serious amount of crapola."

"What are you talking about?"

"I can't say, Tad. You need to sort this alone."

"Well, what about the Zukes? They kick my ass when you're not around?"

"Don't worry about those guys. You stood up to them, and they respect you now. Granted, they still don't like you and could quite possibly get a bunch of their friends to tie you down with their industrial strength Zuke-o-liptus leaves and make you eat those nasty Zucko-guacamole-ma-fritters until you puke. However, it's safe to say that there is only a fifty-two point fifty-seven percent chance of that happening this week."

"Oh great. That makes me feel much better."

"Good. That's what us superheroes are supposed to do. Now get back to reality and kick some ass, kid."

I started to drift away on that, *"Damn! Do I have to go back to Kansas now?"* balloon, when I suddenly realized I wasn't given any of that incredibly inspirational theater-like advice, which is so often present in books of this nature.

"Excuse me, Mr. Barley Man?" I said ever so cautiously, as I slipped past the twelve sleeping security guards and into his dressing room.

"Came back for some motivational words of wisdom that will supposedly give meaning to the universe, did you?"

I didn't answer.

"Fine," he said, while removing the make-up I wasn't aware he wore. "For this mission you will need to know three things."

You notice how it's always three things with these guys? Just once I'd like an imaginary superhero to come up with a different number.

"Stop philosophizing and close your eyes, damn it!"

I did, without further hesitation.

"First: When you gaze into a mirror, really consider who is looking at whom. Second: When you find that person, ask for a cup of tea, a package of Pringles, and a little sympathy. Third: If this goes well, introduce yourself and realize you have not been paying as close attention to life as you would like to believe. Open your eyes."

I did. I opened them an instant before I woke and I saw him for the first time.

Reality returned.

# CHAPTER 10

My dream created a lasting memory that would forever sit atop the highest platform of my imagination. However, with consciousness regained, I noticed that, in the real world, it was I who was clinging to Jackie while she debated her possibilities of escaping such a position of responsibility.

I always hated falling asleep in front of people. First of all, you look like an asshole. Secondly, you have to go through the whole, *"You snore. No I don't. Yes you do. No I don't...."* routine. But what scheeves me out to the utmost plateau of "Eeewwww-ness" is that you are forced to believe whatever your comrades tell you.

The only thing worse than public sleeping is public drinking, because you're not only stupidly unconscious, you're mobily, stupidly unconscious with a never-ending sex drive. Friends can tell you that you sucked down a bottle of Absolute, mounted a nine hundred-pound bisexual named Bubba Luu and returned home two days later on the back of a beat-up Harley wearing nothing but a French racing cap and a cock ring.

On a personal note, all I had to do was nip too much of the sauce one night and envision myself running through an imaginary, rain-soaked field being chased by bugger-flinging Yuppie warriors from Scarsdale and I quit drinking. Hey, but, kids, if you must drink (everyone together now), don't drive! Now you can tell your parents there was a message in this insanity, which might make up for all the cursing and hopelessly pessimistic views of the universe.

Anyway, lucky for me, none of the guys decided to draw penises on my forehead. In fact, it appeared that no one noticed any of my alleged disclosures. Feeling satisfied with my manly status, I reopened the story line.

"Psst, hey, Jack," I whispered, hoping to avoid waking Darien and Dawn. It was obvious that if Eric and Pete, who, by the way, have been arguing since the end of chapter six, didn't wake them with their constant bombardments of bullshit, they could sleep for all eternity. I was just being polite.

"What?" asked the sleepy, sexy one as she consciously used my shoulder as a pillow.

"What time is it?" I asked of the general listening audience, once realizing that Jackie's instant slumber relieved her from any further conversational duties.

"It's 8:30, jag-off," said Eric who was surprisingly found in the passenger's seat.

"8:30?" I asked. Amazing, I was an insomniac ninety-nine percent of the time, but you put me in a car and I'm Rip Van Winkle.

"Yes, shit-head," said Eric. "You've been sleeping since 2 30 this afternoon. Before that you went to sleep at 8:00 in the morning and stayed that way until 1:00. The only reason you woke up at that time was to take a leak and lead us to that psychotic restaurant."

"But I thought...."

The three dots represent a futile attempt at diss avoidance.

"Don't even 'but' me," said Eric, as Pete muffled his laughter with a cigarette. "I'm nowhere near finished. After we escaped that hellhole, not only did you fail to apologize, but you also went back to sleep until the present time. Do you realize what that means?"

"Jesus(?), Pete. How much coffee did you give this guy?" I said, ignoring the hell out of Eric.

"Don't look at me," said Pete. "See that humongous Thermos on the floor?"

"Yeah."

"Well, that crazy son-of-a-bitch tried to down the whole thing so he wouldn't have to let anyone else drive."

"Excuse me," said Eric, hoping to be noticed.

"You're kidding?" I asked.

"Naw, Tad, I had to stop him after the fourteenth cup, when he started singing 'A Hundred Bottles of Beer on the Wall' in French."

"But he doesn't speak French," I said.

"You'll be surprised at what you know after fourteen cups of coffee."

"Well, did you let him drain the inch worm?"

"I offered, but, even when we changed places, he said he didn't have to go."

"My man's back teeth must be floating."

Now Eric, who, by the way, looked as attractive as a sheepdog put through the old wash and spin cycle, was getting tired of being treated like a deaf seventy-five-year-old. Suddenly, he exploded into a slightly confused, bug-out frenzy.

"Gentlemen? Tad. Pete. Do you mind if I make a small request?

We looked at each other and smiled. The evil smile is important.

"Yes. Yes we do."

"Arrrrg!" screamed the eccentric one. "Shut up! Just shut up! And for God's sake, stop talking about my bowel movements like they're last night's Met's game. That is really sick. Just answer me, Tad. Do you realize how long you've slept?"

"Well I...."

"Twelve hours! You've slept twelve hours today."

"Twelve hours and thirty-five minutes to be exact," said Pete.

"Don't you even start, shit for brains, or I'll cut off your balls and feed 'em to a squirrel."

"I seriously doubt it," said Pete, as the train of hostility returned to its familiar track.

"Oh you think so, huh?"

"That's Goddamn right, you...."

Being the only conscious person in the back seat, I took advantage of the opportunity and utilized the moment of privacy to adjust Mr. Penis into a more comfortable, upright position. I realize this my seem crude, but when the closest thing you've had to sex in three months is a late-night Showtime movie, it doesn't take that much to stir the one-eyed sea serpent's curiosity.

Anyway, as I searched the window for signs of the Tri-State area I couldn't help noticing a strange sound emanating from the bowels of the beast-mobile.

"Hey, Pete," I said. "Do you hear that?"

"Hear what?"

"I don't know what. If I knew what it was, I wouldn't have used the non-descriptive word 'that.'"

"Well, what did it sound like?"

"You're really dense. You know that? If I knew what *it* sounded like, I could say, 'Hey, Pete, did you hear the noise that sounded like a whatever?' Got it, dick-head?"

"Oh yeah, that kinda make sense, now that I think about it."

"Well?"

"Well what?"

"Did you hear that?"

"Hear what?"

My readers, let's talk frustration for a moment. Do you see what I had to go through? All this and we didn't even get to the dangerous part yet. I started to get a tremendous headache in my left eye, but the shit-mobile soon stole my attention. All at once the engine raced and stalled, counted to five in German, then raced and stalled some more. I wanted to say a big, loud, "I almost told you so," but given the decibel level of the already horribly mind-numbing screeches, I realized my contribution would be meaningless.

I freaked. Granted, everyone else was now awake and probably frightened as well, but at least they didn't have to worry about the rest of the group transforming into highly arrogant, psychopathic mutant creatures whose sole desire is to beat the crap out of you. My insanity soon spread to the rest of the travelers. Fortunately we didn't crash, but a certain unhappy spark plug decided to run away from home and use the top of the hood and about six million pounds of pressure to facilitate his escape.

We sat parked on the side of the road and watched in disbelief as an amazing amount of oil rocketed up through the newly formed hole in Eric's hood. I could only imagine what was going through each of their heads. Well, to be perfectly honest, I am the all-powerful author and if it meant that much to you, I could put some crap in their heads and eventually run it through, but that wouldn't be quite the same, now would it?

Since we agree, let us just sit here and admire the endless stream of imitation Slick 50 as it cascades in a fountain-like fashion and comes to rest on top of Eric's car.

Beautiful, isn't it? Why don't you go on to the next chapter? I'll be over in a few moments to continue the story. That's a good bunch of fellas...and chicks—damn I always seem to forget saying chicks. My bad. I'll see you in a little while.

# CHAPTER 11

I must confess, folks, that during the course of this "almost true story," I bullshitted the hell out of you from time to time. I didn't mean any offense. That's just what I do. You see all writers are egotistical maniacs who are full of a great deal of crap. Of course, when they're not full of feces, they're usually full of booze. And while these substances may appear different on a scientific level, they both indubitably increase the writer's general pain-in-the-ass factor forcing their unfortunate friends to ask an unknown deity that the annoying imbecile be shown another career.

In light of this, I genuinely feel that most writers, especially the ones who drink, are huge assholes who are so monumentally bored with the systematic society that they can't stick to a previously written story line without ad-libbing here and there...

mostly there.

Just look at the Bible. Can't you picture a couple of recently self-actualized monks sitting around in the Dark Ages saying things like, "Naw, man, I think the point would get across much better if it rained for forty days instead of forty minutes. And what's with all this Greek crap? Hey, Caesar, you know what that word means?"

"No. I've never seen that one before. Why don't you just throw in a story about a couple of sheep and call it a done deal."

"Good idea. Now how old did you say Moses should be...?"

Anyway, the point is that all writers, myself included, tend to get off track. For example, when I finished the last chapter and went to reach for my newly opened can of Diet Pepsi, I inadvertently glanced at my faded, scribbled-on-the-back-of-a-history-textbook outline and noticed that I was way off course.

After further inspection of this previously jotted memory-enhancement device, I came to the not-so-startling recollection that, in real life, Eric's car had broken down much closer to our destination. In fact, now that I've adjusted my mental rabbit ears to their ideal antenna-like position, it has become overwhelmingly clear that in the initial, story-inspiring journey, we were incredibly pissed only twenty-eight point seven miles from my grandfather's country house.

Given the fact that I did considerably more philosophical chattering on this trip than the previous one. And given the bonus fact behind curtain number one, that Eric drives slower than a three-legged turtle with a bullet in his balls, it's easy to see, or at least to imagine, the reason we are so far behind schedule.

As you must know by now, I'm an incredibly lazy fellow and there is no way I'm going to go back through all the crap I've just spewed out in order to decipher where I went wrong. So for the sake of convenience, let's just assume I've recently busted one of those inter-bookular time alteration/displacement jammys and therefore, it is much later than it actually appears to be. (Let's face it, given the previously discussed minute/hour time distortion theory, it very well could be.) And let us also assume that we are sitting, miserably sad, only twenty-eight point seven miles south of a little town called Pine Plains, New York at the exact same hour we would have been sitting in the same mental state, much farther away.

What the hell, as long as we are assuming so much, let's assume that my friend Cathy (who is not at all in this book) has a life, and that I have lots of money and get laid quite frequently. Or for convenience's sake, let's just assume that I'm banging a rich girl named Cathy with a life three times a day. Yes, that's much better, don't you think? I love convenience.

And now back to our stupidity....

This was a glorious moment for people watching as most of the major emotional states were represented in the Eric's Screwed-up Car Summit. Darien was awake and looked as appealing as a hairy rat's ass, but at least he was awake. I was surprised. Pete was laughing. Dawn looked confused. And Jackie appeared frightened. As for Eric, well, he managed to grab the rest of the emotions known to man, roll them into an interesting configuration much like a ball of stale bread (the crustless kind, of course), and successfully smash this horribly stupid whatyamacallit into his skull.

"Jesus(?) Christ!" I started.

Well, somebody had to start and, since I do most of the talking anyway, I figured it might as well be me.

"What's going on?" asked Darien.

"Dude, I have no clue," said Pete, as Eric looked to the newly discovered cows for some sort of an explanation of life in general.

The cows were of an anorexic breed, well fed, but somehow anorexic. Eric loved cows and often wondered if, in a former life, he was one of them. You see, he didn't believe in the afterlife and he really didn't believe in a God(?) of the conventional sort, but he did believe, very much actually, in cows. They were simple and stupid, which were two of his favorite characteristics. So as I watched him watch the cows, I pretended he was imagining he believed a little more in an afterlife with cows than in cows themselves with no afterlife. Don't ask me why.

A few moments passed. A few more moments passed, and then, as if it were the natural thing to do when your favorite auto-mo-Buick bites the big one, Eric got out of the car and shined the left front headlight with a portion of his no-longer-white, button down shirt. Upon completion of this seemingly useless but somewhat affectionate task, he walked two steps in the direction of his beloved cows, and took the most mind-boggleinglynest, incredibly non-small, major leak I have ever witnessed.

Given the stupendously false but equally well-accepted Girl Scout adage, which states that the boy who walks the farthest away from the campsite to shake his lizard has the smallest tool, we all noticed ourselves carrying a new-found basket of respect and awe for Eric's shlong.

Needless to say, we tried to fix the car. Well, at least Pete, Dawn, and Darien tried. Jackie and I were about as handy as a Velcro rubber, and Eric was too busy becoming one with the cows.

After a good deal of cursing and banging, a horribly depressing, *"Hey! I think I know what the problem is.... Aw shit, that's not it,"* exclamation by Pete, and another large amount of cursing and banging, we came to the horrendously pitiful realization that, not only had we eaten all of our emergency food, but we were also twenty-eight point seven miles from a somewhere that was intentionally fifty miles from nowhere.

"Well, I guess we better get going," said Pete as he grabbed his recently pressed, but formerly disgusting, puke-green duffel bag that was filled to the brim with neatly folded, dirty laundry

"What? Where are we going to go?" asked Dawn in a tone of disillusionment.

"We can't stay here all night. We're going to have to catch a ride or something," said Pete.

"No way," said Darien. "I ain't hitchhiking nowhere. I heard too many stories about people getting killed by crazy New Yorkers. And besides, what about Eric's car?"

"Forget it," said Jackie.

"What do you mean, 'forget it?'" asked Darien, obviously concerned. "We just can't leave it here."

What a pansy! I tell you, if he weren't my friend, I would've smacked the dirt off of him.

Annoyed to the finest extreme, I was forced to show these two feeling-oriented morons that this would not be such a dramatic loss for Eric.

"Yo, Eric, how much did you pay for this piece of shit?" I asked.

"About two seventy-five at the auction," he said in a voice surprisingly devoid of feelings.

"And how many miles were on the thing?"

"About, oh I'd say... one hundred fifty-four thousand seven hundred and thirty-two and six-tenths miles."

"About?"

"About."

"And when you made the purchase, what did the guy tell you?"

"He said it probably wouldn't last too long."

"Please, now, Mr. Shibly, tell the court exactly what the man said."

God(?), I felt like I was guest staring on one of those unbelievably popular courtroom dramas, so much so that I called my homeboy Pete to the imaginary stand just for the hell of it.

"Mr. Dempsey, you were there that day. Were you not?"

"Yes, sir. I was," said Pete.

I could always count on him to play along.

"And, dude, or rather, Mr. Dempsey, do you not recall what the salesmen told Mr. Shibly about the above-mentioned car on the date of its purchase?"

"Yes I do."

"Would you please tell the court?"

"His exact words?"

"His exact words."

"The guy said it was the cheapest pile of horse droppings he had ever seen and would be honestly surprised if the damn thing started at all. Furthermore, and I'm still quoting mind you, he said that he was going to find the stupid son-of-a-bitch who bought the monstrosity for his lot in the first place and have the idiot shot several times in the groin with some rather large bullets."

"Thank you, Mr. Dempsey."

"You're welcome, counselor."

"Therefore," I concluded, "based on the relative and not-so-relative facts in this case, I challenge anyone who further disputes the opinion that Eric's car is fundamentally dead and we, being the former riders of this deceased shit-box, are equally, if not more so, fundamentally screwed.

"In light of this knowledge, I propose that we follow the Pete-placed point of our utter strandedness and jet from this roadside in the highest form."

The disputes came, but they were trivial. And seeing as how I was in of those, *"I feel incredibly unbeatable at the moment, while you, on the other hand, look rather like a bucket of shit,"* kinds of states, the objections were countered with un-rough-like smoothness.

Darien helpfully noted that if we didn't get to some serious shelter within the next few hours we'd all freeze our favorite genitalia off. So we conducted one of those ever popular Inter-stupidic automobile funerals, grabbed what we could carry, and proceeded to follow the Yellow Brick Road to what was sure to become the most interesting event of our lives.

A while into the walk, I rechecked the whereabouts of my junior spy envelope and attempted to estimate our progress. Interestingly enough, when I finished the not-so-intellectual calculation, which, by the way, was even less effective than intellectual, I looked back toward the car and noticed two things. The first was we hadn't walked nearly as far as I had hoped. And the second, more interesting, thing was that Eric looked upset. Whether this sadness was brought upon by the death of his automobile, my psychotic Matlock impersonation, or the highly rude interruption of his cow conversation, would never come to light. What remained irrevocably clear, however, was that I acted like an amazingly stupid hunk of Cheez Whiz, who accounted for the feelings of no one but himself. Perhaps it would be better if I remained where other people were not?

Time and distance past.

# CHAPTER 12

"Beans a beans, they're good for your heart.

"The more you eat, the more you fart.

"The more you fart, the better you feel.

"So have your beans at every meal.

"Beans a beans...."

Yes, that's right campers, we skipped over the whole, "A Hundred Bottles of Beer on the Wall" thing and went straight for the classy stuff. I tell ya, it just doesn't get any better than this. (Please note the overflowing sarcasm.)

Just to keep you up to speed, it's about 9:37 p.m. here in Book Land. How is that possible, you ask? Well, assuming that the car went to hell around 8:30 p.m. and that we subsequently spent the following five minutes formulating that amazing inter-bookular time distortion-disruption thing-a-ma-jig, the next two enacting it, and the previous hour walking and singing stupidly silly songs, it's not so hard to digest.

"Jesus!" said Pete. "I can't believe that no one has come by."

"Yeah," said Darien, "I wouldn't even mind if they didn't stop. Just knowing there are other life forms out there would be comforting."

"Oh, stop bitching. Let's look at the bright side," I said in one of those painfully fake, *"Did you ever notice that all the people who believe they are so smart because they walk around thinking positive all the time expend most of their mental energy on this completely foolish reevaluation of a society gone astray and, therefore, have no intellectual capacity left over to actually deal with the problems they've euphemized. This, in turn, produces the direct effect of making them appear incredibly plastic, stupid, and so monumentally full of shit, but in a nice, cute, friendly way,"* Amway tone of voices.

"Oh shut up, Tad!" said the group in unison.

It was my kind of crowd and I gave them a silent thank you. I also gave Jackie one of those, *"I really want to get you naked, tie you to the top of a mountain, and throw little pickles at you until you beg for mercy,"* winks. Unfortunately, Jackie bent down to tie her shoelaces at the exact second I let the wink loose. So while I paused for a moment to admire her lower features, the un-piloted wink, harboring the secretly sexual message, smashed Pete right under the chin. It was a pretty potent wink if I do say so myself and, by the time Pete adjusted his mental alignment, Jackie and I had caught up to the others.

The first thing Pete saw when he opened his eyes was a nasty, dirty, country-kind-of-funky, seventy-year-old skunk named Elmer. He looked at the group. He looked at the skunk. Then he switched things around so he looked at the skunk and then looked at the group. Finally, he managed to look at the skunk, the group, and hopelessly confused all at once. It didn't look too good.

The conclusion of this incredibly idiotic event was me getting kicked in the shins and called "a maniacally twisted sexual perversion of anything remotely reasonable" for, at the time, no apparent reason. We traveled on.

"...Alaska."

"Allentown."

"Nevada."

"Jesus Christ, another 'A?' I really hate this Goddamn game," said Pete as the cycle of silliness rapped upon his psychological screen door for what could have easily been the three hundred and seventy-forth billionth time.

"This sucks," moaned Eric. "How long have we been walking?"

"Oh, I'd say about three or four hours," said Darien, after looking at his horribly broken watch.

He was the only one of us who wore a watch. It wasn't because he looked tremendously good in hopelessly fake leather and imitation gold, mind you. And it wasn't because his ancestral line could be traced back far enough to prove he was a direct descendent of a gentlemen named Fenmoore Gilbergot, who, by the way, was known throughout the land of amazingly primitive, yet eventually to be called Switzerland, not for inventing watches, but for liking them very much and wishing all the intellectual philosophers of the day would stop working on miserably useless medical chants and get to inventing watches. No, he wore a watch for the same reason he did everything else, out of a sense of duty.

We all knew this rather interesting and yet highly useless piece of Darien's family history and that made him extremely nervous. We also understood that most of his family cared a great deal about time and, in turn, hated those confusingly annoying, miserably hopeless medical chants, which currently continued to assault his family's senses through certain PBS shows and *National Geographic* specials.

Sadly enough, Darien didn't take pride in his family history. In fact, he really thought the whole affair to be quite foolish. Therefore, in an interesting attempt at teenage rebellion, he liked to sport a broken watch, hum ancient medical chants tremendously off key, and misquote people the time on every available occasion. We knew of this also and that had the direct effect of making him increasingly more nervous.

Still not knowing the exact time, but realizing it was nowhere near as long as Darien had originally calculated, I tried to initiate another, *"Gee, I wholly believe that a good-sized root canal would be far more amusing than this incredibly boring piece of donkey dung,"* game. But just as I was about to utter the mostly horrible words, "I'm thinking of an animal..." something truly amazing happened.

At first I wasn't quite sure it happened. After all, it was fairly far away. But then, the truly amazing something continued to happen. We were stunned.

The six of us saw the headlights approaching our more-than-general direction and watched in amazement as the ant-like figure metamorphosed into a huge cow-like figure that closely resembled a truck. After a more detailed inspection, we came to the apparently correct conclusion that the figure was indeed a truck (that relieved us), with a large dissected cow painted on its side. (That made us horrendously insecure.) What made us increasingly more horrendously insecure was that, blasting from the truck's cabin, was the most antisocial death metal I've ever heard. With the sudden, overwhelmingly clear realization that we were stranded at an hour of the evening much closer to twelve than eight, on a pitch-black country road in the upper-left-hand corner of nowhere, we were all simultaneously presented with a totally consuming desire to shit our pants.

Fortunately, having recently relieved our beloved bowels, we were left with no other alternative than to do a quick, *"Oh look, that poor little squirrel is frozen in the headlights and, if he doesn't stop running back and forth in the road like an overly stupid simpleton, he is sure to die a rather gruesome, perfect-for-a-high-school-driving-course parkway death,"* impersonation.

It was clear from the truck's speed and trajectory that we were doomed. I panicked. Thoughts were orbiting my cranium and landing upon my cerebrum without the proper paperwork. Small groups of bearded individuals invited themselves into my schemata and decided it would be a nifty idea to play Gripto-Gamma in my living room. (Gripto-Gamma of course, is a highly stupid form of Steponaball.)

Then in a moment of heated anxiety, I repossessed my mental faculties, grabbed Jackie firmly by the waist, and shoved her to the ground. I glanced to the right and noticed the truck parked ten yards to the north. Its brakes were smoking like the devil in a pool hall, and the formerly annoying music had been replaced by the constant bellowing of an overenthusiastic horn.

"Shit, that was close," said Pete, struggling to his feet.

"Jeez, bud," said Dawn, "if you wanted to jump her that bad, maybe you should have asked."

"Yeah, it looks like he's not even waiting for the results of the bet," said Darien, as he noticed Eric nervously lighting his only allowed cigarette.

"I wanted to save this for later, but... 'puff, drag, puff'... I just can't hold out anymore," said the eccentric one.

I looked at Jackie, who was still lying beneath me, and mustered an apology.

She looked irritated for a moment and then, suddenly, altered her expression to one of warmth and understanding. While the rest of the group both occupied and preoccupied themselves with testing their major appendages, she noticed our faces were barely two inches apart, smiled slightly, and then mouthed a soft, "Thank you."

I tried to look confused and actually did a fair job of it for a moment. Surprisingly enough however, during the next few moments I was much too busy kissing to attempt looking confused. The funny thing was that it bore a striking resemblance to the dream kiss, only she initiated it, I was running the mental Disney movies, and nobody—I repeat nobody—turned into an Incredible Zuke.

When we got to our feet, she ran off to join the others who were checking on the truck driver. I was left alone to contemplate the recently transpired event and make sure it favored plain tea with a slice of lemon on the side (solely decorative purposes) over that mostly horrible Black Blood of the Earth.

Upon completion of this analysis I discovered three things. First, I made a step toward actually caring about and trusting a person. Secondly, I would never, so help me any supreme deity who is not playing racquetball or eating a cheese dog at the time, ever, purposely cause another horribly disgusting road kill again. And lastly, my formerly friendly sock transformed itself into a quitter. Don't you just hate that? To avoid feeling like a complete shit-head, I pulled up the lazy garment, wrapped it in a rather helpful rubber band, and quickly joined the others.

The trucker dude cautiously climbed out of his seat. He appeared to be in good shape for someone who had almost killed six mentally defunct high school graduates. In fact, he had a rather sunny disposition.

He was a thin, vertically disadvantaged fellow who, I estimated, at one point in his childhood, between the sixth and eight grades, surprised the hell out of his classmates by getting incredibly pissed off one imaginary afternoon and subsequently beating the crap out of the school bully, who, ironically enough, was to become to next heavyweight champion of the world. Unbeknownst to him at the time, this action altered the course of professional boxing so dramatically that, for years to come the world's greatest pugilists would be little white schoolchildren with sunny dispositions.

I further imagined that, weeks later, in an attempt to restore the natural order of things, the driver challenged the same bully and his entire gang of Huffy-riding Hell's Angels to a fist fight at the local hangout. Of course, he lost pitifully and was subjected to some of the most horrible name-calling in history. But at least he wasn't responsible for a tremendously stupid accident. And besides, he quite enjoyed driving his truck.

"Where you kids headed this time of night?" asked the truck driver, who was much too young to call us kids.

I guessed twenty-seven, not that it's tremendously important.

Pete explained the situation to him and, after he finished laughing at the utter shitiness of Eric's car, he shook his head back and forth a few hundred times in a disapproving way. (God(?) damn it, I hate when people shake their heads in disapproving ways. It makes me feel so God(?) awful mad. Not to mention a bit insecure.)

"What's your name anyway?" asked Darien.

"Omar, Omar T. Tannenbaum. I'm the president of Omar's Meats, Inc."

Yes, he actually said "Inc."

"Well, I'm Darien, and this is Dawn. That's Tad, Jackie, Eric, and Pete."

"Nice to know ya."

Now don't get me wrong, under the right circumstances the pleasantries would have been perfectly acceptable. But considering that we were standing in a deserted highway, (which, by the way, was conveniently located in the middle of the night) staring at a giant meat freezer, and chatting with a white man named Omar, the conversation was beginning to piss me off.

"Hey, I hate to break up the party," I said, trying to subdue the boiling bits of sarcasm that were preparing to burst from my being. "But do you think you could give us a ride to the Jackson Corners exit in Pine Planes?"

"Sure, I'd be glad to."

We all breathed a heavy sigh of relief.

"Except that only three people can fit inside the cab and they don't allow commercial vehicles on the parkway."

"Great, just great," said Pete. "You know, I'm getting really sick of this shit. You go on vacation to get rid of your problems and what happens? The problems tag along anyway, and invite three or four of their friends for the ride."

"Hold on a minute," said Omar, as the surprising voice of reason. "I know the back roads pretty well. Given a short cut or two, y'all ain't but ten or twelve miles from where you want to be. So why don't I take you in two at a time? It shouldn't take more than an hour."

Until now, my bullshit sensors remained relatively silent.

However, after noticing the double-barreled shotgun conveniently located in the truck's back window, and realizing that this man did in fact, slaughter animals for a living, my brain pointed out that it had seen enough horror movies to know this wasn't the most ideal of situations. With this in mind, I nudged Jackie, gave her one of those explanatory winks, and then, since I was winking anyway, re-described my little pickle fantasy. I think she liked it.

"I don't know," she said. "I think we should all stay together."

"Yeah," said Dawn, "the last two could get lost or something."

Omar, who wasn't quite as stupid as a person named Omar is supposed to be, knew this was a bunch of horseshit and tried to argue his point for a moment. Then, realizing he was dealing with a bunch of frightened fools, who probably went to the movies much too often for his tastes, abandoned the debate and opted for an alternate road to niceness.

"Well look, guys, if you want to pile on the freezer, that's fine with me. But I got to warn ya, these here back roads get pretty bumpy."

"I'm up for it," said Jackie.

"No way," said Darien. "At this juncture in my life I have no desire to travel down a country road strapped to frozen food container."

"He's right. We're only a few miles from the place anyway," said Dawn.

"Look, my risk-adverse, anal-retentive, *"Gee, I really wish I could get his stick out of my ass,"* compadres, this is precisely the time in your life when you need to barrel down a road strapped to a meat locker," I said.

"Wait a minute," said Eric in one of his confused yet slightly scholarly attempts at normal rationalization. "I think it's safe to say that all our parents have sufficiently grown up. Is it not?"

We grunted. We always grunted at his attempts at logic. Now that I think of it, perhaps we should have been more supportive. He continued undaunted.

"And since they are indeed grown up, isn't it is also safe to assume that they are alive?"

Even Omar looked bewildered.

"Therefore, since they are living grownups, who've never blasted down the countryside straddling a meat container when they could have just as easily walked that same stretch of road, we can assume that this above-mentioned blasting isn't vitally important for the survival of the teenager."

He smiled a moment, looking rather pleased with himself.

"He's got a point," said a relatively satisfied Omar.

"No. No. No. He doesn't have a point," I said. "He doesn't have anything remotely related to a point. Jesus(?), I can't believe we're having this conversation.

"The purpose of this adventure was to do things differently, to not fall into the same awful mode of learned stupidness as the rest of the population. Have you guys forgotten that already?"

Book readers, in case you haven't noticed, I've been going through my mid-life crisis ever since my seventeenth birthday. I really didn't expect it to come this soon or to last this long. And quite honestly, the whole experience has been rather shitty thus far. Feeling the need for a little friendly input, I explained the experience to Pete. Now, because he's so amazingly stupid, when he could just as easily be so amazingly smart, he came to the totally wrong conclusion that my misery looked like a lot of fun and wanted to do it as well.

To accomplish this, he bought three cases of beer and invited the other four idiots over to his place, where we all got incredibly wasted and started analyzing the mysteries of the universe. After recovering from the kind of hangover that could kill a brontosaurus, they discovered they had been transported to a mental state much like my own. As you can imagine, after hanging out in my brain for a while, the rest of the group got incredibly annoyed and called Pete a tremendous asshole for convincing them to participate.

Realistically it was an asshole move, but he was my best friend, so I had to let it slide. Besides, if I had to pick five people to be hopelessly confused, partially pissed, and slightly depressed with, these would be them. The way I see it is, if you're going to be miserably lost, your best friends should want to be miserably lost as well.

I continued my argument.

"Eric, let me ask you something. Are your parents happy?"

"Not really."

"What about yours, or yours, or any of yours for that matter?"

The roadway was silent.

"Well, my parents are kinda happy I guess," said Omar, even though no one was talking to him and that same group of no ones really couldn't give two shits. "They're not rich. They're not very popular with the town folk. And they really don't do much except work in the sausage factory over yonder and play horseshoes. But they kinda like horseshoes, I think. So yeah, I'd venture to say they is happy.

"Well, enough of that. I gotta get moving. You guys coming, or not?"

He offered a hopeful smile as he walked toward his truck.

"Do you see that?" I said, trying like hell to make them feel guilty. "This is what our dreams have come to. We're scared of every little thing. We're questioning our philosophies on the basis of some monkey nut of a truck driver's view of parental figures. And most of all, we're lying to each other. Don't you remember our toast?

"Frankly, guys, I'm disappointed. You can walk if you want, but I'm going with Omar. And damn it, I might just teach him a thing or two about universal Philosphication."

Whether I touched the group emotionally or they simply feared for Omar's brain was not important. What was tremendously, drastically important was that the group reunited. It was much like Germany, only smaller and incredibly different. I was most pleased with this event, but severely disheartened with the ultimately decided decision that I was to ride shotgun with Jackie.

It figures. The two people who really wanted to have the experience of riding on a meat freezer got stuck discussing the importance of the breastbone in relation to a chicken's tenderness, in the cab of the truck while the four formerly wimpy crybabies got to speed recklessly through the wilderness at near seventy miles per hour.

Oddly enough, I felt strangely like a certain boy who avoided painting a certain fence by way of a similar speech. In recollection, I think it's safe to say, his speech, which by the way was far shorter than mine, went over a hell of a lot better. Perhaps I overdid it?

# CHAPTER 13

When we arrived at the country house the sky was resting joyfully in the midnight hour. Its buddy, Father Time, enjoyed his one millisecond of sleep before his eternal alarm clock forced him back to the tedious task of transforming night into day. Sure, the total power over the millenniums; the imaginary, personal, perhaps sexual relationship with Mother Nature, and the fact that he alone is the life of the party every New Year's Eve could lead one to believe that being a deity of sorts was quite glamorous. However, if you were to analyze his position further, you'd have to agree that his job is really rather miserable, in a dull, humdrum kind of way.

Let's think about it. The guy has to keep time rolling forever, right? No vacations. No weekends on the shore. Forever is an eternity and an eternity is a pretty large chunk of anyone's time, even if that anyone is an immortal.

It's all rather depressing if you think about it long enough. The "it" here being, of course, the horror of having to baby-sit time as it heartlessly grows up and has a family of its own. Not to mention the pain of never personally entering a relationship, a conversation, or a kiss. Sad really, but Father Time spends his watching it all melt away. It's like being asleep and dead at the same time, only you're alive, not dreaming, and getting paid a horribly miserable salary; which isn't so bad really, considering that you wouldn't have time to spend it even if it was good.

Looking on the incredibly small, but allegedly present, bright side, just for the hell of it; it must be fairly stated that Father Workaholic does in fact have two pieces of time (much smaller than moments), for rest and relaxation. One is of course, the above-mentioned midnight and the other, less important nanosecond occurs at 3:47 in the morning, which by way, is a ridiculously stupid part of the day.

Anyway, after admiring the sky and reminding Father Time how ultimately pitiful his life is, I opened the door, helped Jackie out of the truck, and proceeded to check on the guys.

They looked like shit. Well, after further recollection, they looked far more like soupy diarrhea than ordinary shit. But for the sake of historical memorabilia, and the fact that I'm eating another one of those, *"I have nothing to do with a cow,"* burger-like substances here in the real world, let's pretend they just looked like regular old shit. Okay?

Hair was blown. Papers were scattered. And looks of confusion and fear were generously draped on the brows of my buddies. Plus, for a reason I couldn't quite figure out at the time, they were all vaguely blue.

"Yo, Omar, my friends are blue!" I shouted, mostly because I couldn't think of anything else to shout.

Omar and Jackie walked to the back of the truck and then, after taking a look much too brief to be able to fully analyze the situation, Omar started to laugh.

"Not again," he said.

"What do you mean, 'not again'?" asked Jackie. "Do you freeze people all the time?"

"Don't worry," said Omar, needlessly defending himself. "They'll be all right. That there shit's as funny as a bitch."

After removing our rigormortis-ized friends from the top of the meat container, Jackie helped them to the cabin, and left me to bid farewell to Omar.

He was an interesting dude. Granted, we had nothing in common and during our conversation I discovered he basically despised most of the things I believed to be rather nifty. Still, his sad story was compelling.

Apparently, in the past week he had lost his job, his apartment, his car, and his beloved Uncle Woody to a serious strain of the common cold. On top of that he had impregnated his girlfriend, assumed his embarrassing meat-delivery position, and had been forced to mourn the loss of his dog, Samson, who had been struck and killed by a supped-up 1978 Ford Fairmont.

I didn't believe a word, except of course the part about his dog, You see, my brother Jason owns a similar vehicle and has yet to see the anti-road kill light. Still there had to be something wrong in order for him to go through a line of crap that large. So, when nobody (myself, just for a moment, included in the nobodies) was looking, I made him an honorary member of the posse and slipped him a hundred, a handshake, and a fairly decent regard.

He offered to help with the suitcases, but I was rather looking forward to the evening exercise, and so I declined his attempt at restitution. We shook hands, I said the stupid little things you say to a person who gives you a ride on the back of a meat truck, and then he left.

As he drove down the street I wondered what he was going to do with my bracelet. It was worthless and wouldn't bring a dime at the pawnshop. Yes, it was, by far, something that anyone of the scantiest intelligence would have avoided stealing. He, however, being overwhelmingly stupid, had not. Ah, what the hell, people are flawed. Understanding aside, however, I mentally revoked his posse membership card. My friends don't steal.

When I finally made it up the hill and tossed the remainder of the camping paraphernalia onto the porch, I was ready to sleep my ass off, or quietly die, whatever was more comfortable. Unfortunately, this particular cottage came complete with an official camping law, which most righteously states that, before doing anything remotely resembling something of major or minor importance, the camping humans must take stroll up the mountain to greet the wilderness where they wish to be welcome.

Granted, it sounds like a pretty stupid thing to do, especially at midnight. But this is a mostly true story, and in all honesty, once I explained the tradition to the guys and they finished bitching, we did, in fact, participate in this incredibly weird event.

"Why can't we do this tomorrow?" asked Darien.

"Yeah, bud, I'm tired," said Dawn.

"Look, my great grandfather put an old Italian curse on this land about eighty years ago to keep people from coming up here and screwing with the place when we weren't around. Ever since, anyone who tries to camp or hunt on the land without following the ritual is burdened with horribly bad luck until they leave."

"So what!" said Jackie. "You don't even believe in luck."

"I realize that hon, (yes, I called her hon), but the person who put the curse on the land did and that makes it very real. Besides, you not believing in luck doesn't hold too much weight if luck, being the sarcastic piece of imaginary substance it is, decides to believe in you."

"Sometimes I wonder about you," mumbled Darien.

"Forget about it. Let's get going"

"Where's Eric and Pete?" asked Dawn.

"Well, Pete is visiting a bush and I think Eric is in the house," said Jackie.

"Come on, guys," said an excited Eric, who was heavily shielded with earmuffs. "Let's go already. Let's go."

The maniac staggered into the darkness and, after a few moments of not-too-suspenseful silence, we heard a not-too-surprising grunt. A second later Eric appeared out of the blackness with a rather arrogantly protruding bump on his head.

"You all right?" asked Darien, while the rest of the party muffled their laughter.

"Do you have a...?" asked Eric, as Dawn handed him a much-needed flashlight.

"Thanks," came Eric's embarrassing murmur.

By this time, Popeye Pete had finished playing with his little Sweet Pea, so the group reassembled its ranks and headed down the path wearing the highly ridiculous earmuffs. The walk was a short one considering that we only had two flashlights and couldn't see a God(?) damn thing. But it was enough to appease Grandpappy Niko and persuade him to lift his curse.

To be honest, nothing tremendously interesting happened

during that walk, but I just thought I'd tell you about it anyway so you can see that I come from a family of deep-rooted cultural shit.

When we returned to the house it was close to one o'clock in the morning and everybody was mad tired. We would have loved to have gone right to sleep, but there were a couple of little, itsy-bitsy, tiny, insignificant, hardly-worth-mentioning, incredibly unimportant, minuscule pieces of information that I neglected to inform my buddies about. You'll see what I mean.

"Oh Jeez, the kitchen light is burnt out," said Dawn, who was the first to enter the room.

"Try the one in the living room," suggested Pete, as I slowly melted into the wallpaper.

"It's busted too. Hey, what's going on? asked Dawn. They're all busted."

"Holy shit!" said Eric. "There's a newspaper on the table from 1984."

"Excuse me, Tad," said Darien, with a most unfriendly look in his eye. "Is there something you want to tell us? You know, like if radio was invented the last time someone camped here."

You know that face you make when you clamp your teeth together real tight, muster an obviously counterfeit smile, and suck up some serious wind? Well, picture it for a moment and then add to that expression an, *"Oh shit, I just dragged five butt-ugly people sixteen hundred miles to a place that makes Bedrock look like Beverly Hills,"* thought. This wasn't a warm moment. I had to bullshit.

"Hey, people. You wanted to go camping, right? I mean we coulda gone to the Bahamas. We coulda gone to Disneyland. But you wanted camping, so I brought you camping. And now things aren't up to par and you're flipping out. Look, man, or men and women, as the case may be, don't worry about it. Everything will be fine. So we have no electricity, no food and no water, we can...."

"No way!" screamed Jackie. "You're kidding, right? There is no way I'm going a week without taking a shower. It just ain't happening."

Suddenly a smile pole-vaulted onto Pete's face, and once again the famous Eric annoyer came to my rescue.

"Hey now, let's hold on a minute here. There's no need to get on Tad's case. If we can't shower, we can't shower."

"That's easy for you to say, you sloppy bastard," said Eric. "You don't have to smell that horrible stench of yours. Jesus Christ, you can already peel the paint off a porta potty. I don't even want to imagine what you're going to be like after a week. And, I don't know about this bet now. You have it way too easy."

"Tough luck, dude. You knew where we were going. I'll just have to find new ways of being neat."

"I think I should at least get another cigarette."

"I don't think so, guy. You just have to face the indisputable fact that I was destined to win. Now, I would spend the next few hours dissing you in the highest, but I've got to take a killer shit.

"Tad, where's the bathroom?"

A menacing grin assaulted Eric's facial features as I watched my only ally revoke his allegiance and turn against me.

"Ah... Pete," I said. "You know the water is broken, right, and that means...."

"Son-of-a-bitch. You got to be kidding. I have to shit in a field? This is not good. This is not good at all. Someone at least brought toilet paper, right?"

"Yeah, loser boy" said Eric, "there's some of that freshly-rained-on, dirty-leaf brand outside."

"Forget it! I'll just hold it till the morning and then go down to the store."

"The nearest store is three miles away," I said, for a familiar-looking reason, which ultimately turned out to be stupidity's second cousin, ignorance.

Pete growled at me. Eric growled at Pete. Pete growled back at Eric. And then Darien, who often had the feeling he was missing something vastly more important than his keys, growled at no one in particular for a reason of similar vagueness. Unfortunately, after the growling ceased, he still had the feeling.

# CHAPTER 14

- Toothpaste
- Chicken salad
- Lactose-free cheese
- Saber-toothed squirrel kabobs
- Diet Pepsi
- Peanut Chews
- Pringles, cans and cans of Pringles

# CHAPTER 15

The country house was a shit-hole. I loved it dearly, but it was, in fact, an ancient shit-hole, carved ever so carelessly from the molds of total crappiness. From the outside it appeared that a certain group of fools decided they would try their hand at home improvement. This same group also decided it would be a pretty nifty idea if they knocked down the highly regarded porch and extended the horrendously ignored kitchen, even though the highly regarded porch was increasingly more useful in the ever-popular art of wilderness baking. Halfway through the project, however, someone came up with another idea, which sounded even more nifty at the time. Thus, the project was abandoned so quickly that, to this day, an incredibly bored yet admirably patient hammer waits, frozen in mid air, for the special someone who will guide its catatonic swing to its long-awaited completion at the head of a certain nervous looking nail.

One rumor has it that the above-mentioned nail came up with that incredibly nifty idea in order to avoid being smashed to death by the presently hanging hammer. A second rumor says this nail is currently undergoing psychological evaluation for a personality displacement problem, seeing as how a nail is supposed to enjoy being smashed to death by a normal non-hanging hammer. Finally, a third rumor has it that whoever believes in the first two is a total loser. Of course this was cast into the realm of unbelievablity after it was discovered that the atrocious falsity was commissioned by a thirty-five-year-old Yuppie who wasn't supposed to read this book in the first place.

In its original splendor, which wasn't that splendiferous, the house came complete with a kitchen, something that tried desperately to pass for a living room and a hallway at the same time, a den that had recently been converted into a storage area for anything that looked important but actually wasn't, a crib room that currently housed the jilted kitchen supplies, and three working bedrooms.

Ironically enough, the three bedrooms, which broadcasted their entranceways from the northern-most wall of the living room, contained six beds. The one in the left-most corner of the right side of the room harbored a set of bunk beds and a rather inviting queen-size cot.

The guys (giving reference of course to Pete, Eric, and Darien), in a heartless attempt to boycott my being, rushed into the first bedroom and quickly closed the door. I was kind of upset because I always used to sleep there with my grandparents when I was a kid. But given my recent display of sneakiness, I figured I deserved it. Besides, what was I gonna do? I couldn't very well say, "Mom! Petey stole my bed. Na-Nu-Na, Nu-Na-

Na! Mommy's gonna get you." After all, he is an idiot and would have likely responded with, "Oh yeah, well my momma and your momma were sitting on the park bench. When momma called your momma a crazy three-legged wench."

In any event, while I was daydreaming, the girls dissed me as well by taking room number three with comfortable-looking but *"Ha ha ha. Jackie doesn't know this yet, but her bed has been under construction for the past ten years. And, given her weight, the ambient temperature, and the unique effects of wood rot, I expect it to fall apart about an hour and a half into her slumber,"* highly unstable, bed-like substance.

Of course, being a respectfully righteous, dude, I won't take advantage of her when she comes sleepily stumbling into my room, which by the way, has the most incredibly comfortable king-size bed known to man.

Hey, wait a minute now, readers. Don't look at me that way. I was going to offer them the best bed, but seeing as how everyone accosted my personality with some totally uncalled for aspersions, I felt no need to be nice. God(?), don't be so judgmental.

In any event the goodnights were said and we all tried, some more successfully than others, to fade off to sleep. Five minutes into the fading, however, we heard an incredibly offending noise. After thirty blood-curdling, wallpaper-peeling, so God(?) damn-smelly-that-you're-dog-runs-out-the-room, funky, nasty, put-tears-in-your-eyes, horribly inconsiderate, mostly miserable seconds, Pete, that disgusting son-of-a-bitch, came barreling out of the bedroom with one hand over his ass and the other over his nose.

Now I realize most authors wouldn't have gone into this much detail about an event so seemingly trivial, but let me tell you, this really happened! And furthermore it was so tremendously sickening that it must be recorded for all time in the Amazing Tad book. Besides, this infamous *shart* of legendary and historic proportions does have an incredibly influential role in the story. Therefore, to make sure no one misses a single stinky second of this plot-altering event, let us go back and relive the half moment between the altogether atrocious act and its creator's hasty exit. Of course, Eric and Darien were the first to go.

"Jesus Christ. Arrrrrg, choke, gag...."

"What the hell...? Sniff? Ohhhh? Arrrrrg."

"Quick, choke cough, warn the others. Cough.... Warn the others.... Ahhrdg."

The ghastly smog found the girls next.

"Oh my God, I don't... cough, choke...."

"Who could...Arrg."

"Pete...!"

During the final five seconds of its existence, the seeping smog made its way into my chambers. To be honest, I really wasn't in a fighting kind of mood. For all I knew, I might encounter some horribly awful Zukes during the course of the evening. So, I decided to save my strength and just pass out.

The house was still when I woke twenty minutes later. Pete returned from his shit-taking experience, but instead of recovering comfortably in his nice dusty bed, he was lying on the incredibly cold, *"You could call it a living room if you really want to,"* floor. He was considerably unconscious and looked much less appealing than any of the assorted, hairy anal moles you may have encountered in recent weeks.

It seemed that while he was giving birth to a variety of strange and unholy objects, Eric and Darien drew up some anti-Pete signs complete with a rather catchy slogan and placed them about the entrance to the now-forbidden realm. The girls would have created similar signs, but they were much too busy being unhappily unconscious to worry about such things.

I, on the other foot, had both a sneaker and a great deal to be worried about. You see, unbeknownst to my compadres, I had to complete a ritual of my own devising before turning in. I located my flashlight, threw on a jacket, and left to have historical conference with a certain something much more improbable than a nice fresh donut on Wednesday afternoon. Actually, with my manhood among me, I really shouldn't have been too worried, seeing as how the event was much more improbable than stress inducing.

The air had taken on an unseasonal chill. It was surprising and I wondered for a moment if perhaps the wind was becoming like so many other formerly accountable things, who were currently conforming to the hipness of non-conformity. Then, almost immediately, I tried to wonder about something else. Not that the something else was of any importance, mind you, but rather, because the first something was most disheartening. I failed.

Are we becoming so mindlessly robotic as a society that even the formerly consistent (let's be fair, mostly consistent) elements of nature are becoming so dependent on conforming to the ideals of other formerly consistent entities that they would consider going along with something so monumentally contradictory to their nature, as "Maverick Contrarianism," if, by some strange coincidence, Maverick Contrarianism were to become the current fad? The questions left me bitter.

A chill entered my bones so I started hopping up and down in order to get my circulation more enthusiastic about its job. After moment or two I decided that someone needs to come up with a catchy synonym for moment, considering that I hate saying minute and sixty seconds sounds awful corny. Regardless, one sixtieth of an hour later I began my walk and decided I would stick with the moments for a while.

I walked over the hill and through the woods, but just before I got to an imaginary grandmother's house, I came across something much too warm to leave un-personified – a familiar oak tree of vast personal importance. I say it was familiar, for it was the Transitional Tree, the one in your front yard.

You know the tree I mean. You rested there with your mom one lazy summer day and asked about the clouds and why some assumed deity made the grass so green. You proved your man or womanhood by climbing it. You had your first kiss under this tree and promised to love each other for all eternity. You lied. You snuck your first beer there and quickly decided you'd stick to soda for a while. Your father found you there, crying over your first broken heart, and though he couldn't make it right, he gave you a, *"Things will be okay,"* hug that made it a heck of a lot better. You fell in love, proposed, and subsequently got married. The tree was there. You questioned your role as a parent and your philosophy of life and the tree listened. You went through your mid-life crisis, launched kids into the world, and settled into retirement. The tree stood by you. You grew old and died, but the tree continued to look after your family. Friends do that.

So there I was, standing before the one thing (being... he likes to be called that) I could count on when everything else falls victim to the sins of the masses. He was the epitome of trust and would never leave me. I didn't realize how strong his commitment was until that moment. It was rather comforting. Perhaps I should explain the experience.

*I looked down at his roots and was awed by their power,*
*their will.*
*They held on, spread out, dug deep into the Earth.*
*He would not be moved.*

*I gazed at his trunk and noticed his age,*
*his experience.*
*He was armed with knowledge, wisdom, and manhood.*
*He would not be moved.*

*I recalled his branches and experienced his size,*
*his community.*
*They were determined, adventurous, and daring.*
*He would not be moved.*

*I knelt by the stump where my friend once stood,*
*once lived.*
*I watered the seedling that sprouted there and smiled.*
*He would not be moved.*

After he wished me happy birthday, we discussed at some length the more perplexing issues of the universe. He was increasingly intelligent and as far as Intergalactic Philosophication was concerned, I couldn't hold a candle to him. Nevertheless, he was touched by my efforts and trained me in the ways of Creatably Stupidic Invent-O-Philosophy, from time to time.

Most of our theories were mutually created endeavors, but he always promised that if I could somehow impress him with an interesting concept of my own, he would allow me to ask any question. Then he, the ultimate brainiac stud, would supply the answer.

I never impressed him.

However, on this highly improbably occasion called 3:47 in the morning, I, The Amazing One, explained my newly devised philosophy of the five different types of girls and accurately compared it to a bowl of luke-warm chili. It was a mind-bogglingly interesting event and, needless to say, I impressed the hell out of him. Thus, I was awarded my first question.

But what to ask? The meaning of life? My ultimate destiny? The success of this book as a teaching aid in Catholic grade schools? No, too corny for me.

"Okay, Tree, old pal-o-mine, if you are so vastly intelligent, as I know you are, please tell me the secret of sarcasm."

"Would you mind phrasing that as a question? You know, kind of like on *Jeopardy*."

"No problem. Oh wise tree…."

"And cut out all the ass-kissing. It's not like you."

"Fine, dude, so how can I become the most sarcastic man in the universe and how will this effect the formation of a happy life?"

"You realize that's two questions?"

"Is it? I hadn't noticed."

"Don't lay any horseshit on me, Tad," said the tree. "I'm not one of those mindless guidolopiouses."

"Damn, my man is even wise to the new philosophies. It's like trying to win an argument with your mother."

"Look, because I like you so much, I'm gonna answer both."

"Oh, thank you, oh…."

"Don't grovel."

"Not at all."

"Good. Now listen. In order for you to become the most sarcastic man in the universe, you must practice. I know, any idiot could have told you that, but let's keep in mind that any idiot could have asked it as well. But here's a hint. Never underestimate the power of a day-old Danish."

"A day-old Danish?"

"That's three questions. Now come on."

"Sorry."

I thought about muttering something under my breath, but after considering the infinite intelligence of my counterpart, I decided against it.

"Well, what about my second question?" I asked.

"I can't answer that."

"Why the hell not? You just said you would."

"Changed my mind."

"Oh great, an infinitely wise Transitional Tree with a tendency toward fickelism."

"First of all, Tad, fickelism isn't a word. And secondly, you don't need my input because you already know how to be happy. In fact, with a little effort, you could be quite good at it."

"What are you talking about? I'm miserable all the time. Go ahead, give me something to complain about."

"Don't get smart."

"Sorry, dude. At least give me something to go on. Where can I find this secret?"

"You really want to know?"

"Yes!"

"You're not going to like the answer."

"Just tell me!"

"You'll find the answer in a book."

"Not *the* book? Don't tell me all those Bible Jockeys were right."

"Not exactly."

"What then? What book?"

"It's called *Eating the Cheese*, the amazingly nonexistent sequel to a truly magnificent piece of literature originally entitled, *Barley Man and the Incredible Zukes*."

While I was busy bitching, the Transitional Tree's voice faded to a land not entirely unlike Eastchester and was lost for an amazingly short forever.

"That's it! I have truly flipped out this time. You hear me, world? This Amazing and Somewhat Sarcastic Asshole has finally lost his mind."

The incredibly short forever finished its job on schedule and, soon after, replaced the Tree's voice.

"You haven't lost your mind, Tad, at least not yet. Besides, there is a great possibility that your mind is really not your own and that you have just been leasing it. Therefore, if you were to lose it, you shouldn't become too upset, because you probably just forgot to make the payments and could clear the whole thing up by going down to the Intergalactic Department of Missing and Repossessed Cerebral-like Substances."

Then he faded away into a much larger forever and I, after a highly unsuccessful five minutes of trying to understand his comment, became completely consumed with the task of uncrossing my eyes. It was indeed a Kodak moment.

When I returned to the house it was precisely one hour and twenty-five minutes after a certain somebody had attempted to attain a fulfilling state of slumber upon a rickety, rackety, about-to-fall-apart, seventy-five-year-old bed. Realizing this, I jumped under the covers, pretended (quite well, actually) to be asleep, and waited for my princess to arrive. Five minutes later (I'm telling you, no horseshit this time), exactly five minutes later, Jackie came into my room. You want to talk hard-ons?

What? What was that? You want to hear the details? Why, you sick, perverted book-reading individual, I can't talk about my alleged love life. You must remember; I hate that kind of thing in books. It's so unrealistic. Look, if anything happened, 'cause I'm not saying it did, it was strictly a lucky coincidence.

If you really want to know the details of the intimate event that may or may not have molded my manliness, just use your imagination like viewers of an old Fred Astaire movie did during the fadeout smooching scenes. And as long as you're using that highly hormonic imagination of yours, you might as well make me appear sexually talented.

Well, I have to take a serious crap of my own here in the real world so I'm gonna leave you hanging. But don't worry, I'll make it up in the end. See ya next chapter.

# CHAPTER 16

It was 6:30 in the morning. Exactly an hour and a half after I had gone to bed with Jackie. A wholly ridiculous time to be cooking sausage if you ask me, but you didn't. Did you? Ah well, it doesn't matter because I'm an arrogant, over-talkative piece of wilted Gefilte fish and would have probably told you anyway.

Where the hell is my Diet Pepsi? Excuse me for a moment, would you please? I have to run to the kitchen.

Thanks. What was I saying? Oh yes, sausages. I quite hate them. I hate them more than the infamous band of Intergalactic Indian Burn Givers who irritate me considerably more than the legendary posse of Outlaw, Brotherly, Nuggie Offenders. I tremendously hate nuggies.

So why am I preparing the arteriosclerosis-inducing meat-like substance? Well, quite simply, my friends are suffering from a serious case of horribly depressing, *"Thank God(?) I'm completely unconscious for the time being. But, if I may be so bold, I would like to go out on a limb and request of the supreme dude that the above-mentioned 'time being' be made as long as possible because, the truth is, that I really have to take an enormous, Earth-shattering, utterly-confusing, butt-numbing, remarkably loud, highly offensive, possibly greasy, Pete-like crap. And, I seriously do not wish to undertake this endeavor without being in close proximity to the latest medical technology, or if unavailable due to the recent cutbacks in aid to the people who really need it, and the over-spending in an area of utter un-usefulness, at least, a healthy variety of paper products and a nice, soothing bottle of the pink stuff,"* nighttime disturbances. And... (I know this has been a rather remarkable run-on sentence, but bear with me, I'm considerably depressed)... if you think about it, there is really nothing else to do in the middle of the upper-right-hand corner of nowhere at this ghastly hour.

I sighed. It was rather un-relieving. Then I flipped the crispy sausage, more for me than the sausage itself.

As you can tell, I went sleepless again. It was becoming a disturbing habit. I must confess, however, that I wasn't completely put off by the experience. Granted, at this tender age, I could have used the rest, but being disturbed at unusual hours was actually rather enjoyable. It gave me time to think. During one of these episodes of intellectual masturbation I formulated the wholly perplexing concept of how to use the potential of incredibly upsetting lawn mower accidents to your advantage and subsequently facilitate gardening avoidance. Upon completion of this idea, I firmly decided that insomnia was the most useful of all mental illnesses if you favor personal productivity.

Schizophrenia ran a close second, but after a few days of working with some newly installed personalities, I discovered I was spending much too much time organizing events instead of actually doing them. It bears a strange similarity to corporate America, don't you agree?

When I finished cooking, I gazed proudly at my creation. But just as I settled into the comforting emotion, I was assaulted by an overwhelming feeling of being completely lost. It's funny how that always seems to happen to people when they are making breakfast. Perhaps it's the cholesterol?

I left the untouched meal on the wood burning stove and headed out of the house for no reason in particular. The feeling hesitated a moment or two, but after coming to the conclusion that it was considerably more bored than unfriendly, it followed me into the morning. We played our assigned roles. I walked and gave him a mode of transport. He projected and I got lost.

Have you ever been the kind of lost whereby you know exactly where you are, but have no idea as to how you got there or what made you head in that direction in the first place? I had that feeling then, or now, depending upon the tense in which you choose to view the story. I use both. It's reassuring.

Being lost, however, was anything but reassuring. Although I suppose if you just finished a positive-thinking course and really wanted to be reassured in your life, your relationships, and ultimately make yourself believe that the above-mentioned course was worth the eighty-six thousand dollars you paid for it, you could conceivably convince yourself that the state of being lost ultimately reassures you that there is in fact a path of life, success, and ultimate happiness. But this is a bunch of osprey organs and a truly stupid way to view the greater scheme of things. The correct way of course is through 3-D Captain Ice Planet space goggles.

As I walked, the feeling of being lost met up with its cousin

Dr. Questions, and together, they consumed me.

Should I go to college, or work, or both? Should I try to assimilate into society, or listen to rap music and fight the power? Will I ever have a real relationship? Will I ever learn to trust? What's more important, education or bullshitting skills, or is the educational system itself one big lesson in how to bullshit other people?

This one's interesting. Let's think about it for a minute. A bunch of frustrated, hibernating, over-educated morons, who couldn't get a job in the real world, charge you forty grand so they can tell you all sorts of stuff you think they know, but don't. You, being a complete asshole, go along with a system created by the very idiots who will never become a part of it or the life they are preparing you for.

Sure, you get a nice-looking piece of paper that supposedly opens the doors to the job market and the American dream, but don't you see? They are the locksmiths. They make the rules and only they decide who gets in where.

If you're like me and don't fit the current socially acceptable mold, they'll give you a long-winded, incredibly insulting, *"What, you don't have the money for a master's degree in something I think is rather nifty? Well then, I guess you don't become part of corporate America, now do you? Sorry, we realize you're an intelligent, hard-working individual, who would probably do rather well in our organization given a better economic climate. Unfortunately for you, it is much more politically advantageous for us to allocate our financial aid to people who come from more exotic national origins, regardless of their relative economic status.*

*"Yes, yes, we were given specific instructions to only admit two types of people. First and foremost are spoiled, lazy, arrogantly wealthy shit-heads, the parents of whom desperately try to convince themselves that their offspring are just as capable as the rest of the family. Of course, these same offspring*

*wear rather large nose-rings, bite the heads off little dogs at important social events, and couldn't care less about intellectual simulation if you paid them with puppies.*

*"The second type of people let into our schools are the exotic individuals noted above. They are not mentioned solely for the exoticness as such, as that would be anti-social, but rather, for the opinion that some of them take the tiniest advantage of every social program available, even if they are physically able and really don't need it. They are, of course, currently enjoying the wave of, 'Gee I realize we (the "we" here of course meaning the political, not the education system, at large and a couple of rich assholes who run that! Notice the singular quotation marks beginning at the word "Gee" which represent a different imaginary speaker) have been royally screwing over the majority of people for the last twenty years, but we really didn't mean anything by it. Honest. That sex scandal was just a little boo-boo. And the economy, well... oops. Anyway, we are tremendously sorry, so we're gonna cut all the spit, throw a couple of women and blacks—or rather Afro-Americans in office—and by golly, we'll even clean up the environment,' bullshit currently emanating from the mouths of our elected officials.*

*"I can see you're upset," continued the first imaginary bunch of rich educational assholes I was quoting, "but here's a thought. Why don't you just give us whatever money you were going to use on yourself, and help support someone who has a better chance at grubbing off society? It just so happens that we collect for the United (Kinda Racists If You Think About It) College Fund, and I would be more than happy to con you and all your friends out of their hard-earned money so I can split it between my cause, a couple of key political figures, and an overweight reverend,"* anal smoke-blowing speech. (I realize the thought within a thought may have been a confusing, but what can you expect? I was never properly ed-u-ma-cated.)

"Yo, Tad!" said Pete from a distance. He sounded excited, but then again, he always sounded excited. The kid could undergo natural childbirth through his penis and still sound happily excited. Ah... the joy of bliss.

I, on the other hand, was slightly pissed, partly because I never achieved a state of bliss, but mostly because my morning Philosophication was cut short. I really wanted to explain how the majority of New Yorkers are more tremendously lost than any other humans and how this utterly shitty hand dealt from the deck of destiny indubitably proves that the Big Apple is in fact the Bermuda triangle.

Unfortunately, I had to open one of those financial aid rejection letters from a certain college (here, now, in real life), spill my Diet Pepsi, and get all pissed off at the world. Ah well, boys will be boys, girls will be girls, and Amazing and Somewhat Sarcastic Tads will be Amazing and Somewhat Sarcastic Tads.

Pete was coming closer and I could see from the imaginary sneer in his eye that he was incredibly upset with something he felt to be important, but probably wouldn't care too terribly much about in a hundred years or so.

"Tad! Those two-bit...miserable pieces of.... Why, I ought to kick their rotten...around the block a time or two and then..."

All at once, the feeling of being lost found itself and left. The questions were always hanging around, but Mr. Lost indeed departed. This was considerably uncool because, as soon as I realized where I was, I knew that Pete was in for it.

"...and another thing about that, he is a...if he thinks I...."

"No wait, Pete, stop! You can't curse here. You can't curse here."

"What the hell are you talking about?" he asked.

And rightfully so. I mean let's face it, what are the chances of being in the direct domain of a highly powerful individual who seriously dislikes cursing, racial slurs, and hostility in any form?

Well, under normal circumstances, the odds would be very low. However, given the fact that such a politically proper person made some highly profitable investments, recently retired from whatever the hell powerfully eccentric, highly enlightened, liberalized individuals do, and purchased a comfortable little summer cottage next door, I'd say the chances were increasingly more probable.

"Look, Pete, I don't know how to explain it, but there's this really weird spirit dude who likes to hang out here and he's seriously against language of that nature."

"Oh bullshit. There is no one up here and frankly, I'm getting sick of all these stupid-ass stories. Besides, I don't believe in spirits and even if I did I can curse whenever the hell I want to. Just watch."

"No, Pete, don't!"

The moment was far more tense than you are probably imagining, which is partly my fault I guess. Then again, I'm barely nineteen in real life, so how much talent can you realistically expect? Besides, how can you properly describe an invisible creature that you only saw once in the last four years, out of the corner of your mind's eye?

"I'll...curse if I mother...want to and no stupid ass... is gonna stop me. You hear that you...."

Pete started walking up and down the hill cursing his head off like a God(?) damn idiot. Obviously, this wasn't what he had originally been so excited about. See what I mean, always excited. I couldn't watch. I just lay on the ground, prayed to this ancient forest spirit I read about a few years ago, and hoped my neighbor would be gentle. He was a real asshole.

Suddenly he approached the unsuspecting.... Wait a minute, hold on, now that I think about it, it wasn't suddenly at all. It was slowly, methodically, cautiously, and incredibly suspensefully, and chillingly also. Yes, yes, most chillingly he approached the unsuspecting.... No, no, sorry. That was something entirely different. I was right the first time. It was definitely suddenly. I think. Ah, what the hell. Let's play it safe.

Suddenly, my imaginary neighbor slowly appeared out of nowhere, which was incredibly hard to do (the appearing itself, not the out of nowhere part) because he was indeed, highly invisible. Fortunately for us, he had recently developed an affinity for summer ski suits and, unbeknownst to him, the rayon in the material changed his molecular structure so that he was indeed, highly visible, except for his underarms, which no one wanted to see anyway.

Given the fact that he lives alone, has no friends, no life, and goes around thinking he's invisible when he actually is very much the opposite, I decided to preserve his dignity and let him eventually wander into a bathroom and find this out on his own.

I do this sort of thing with ordinary people as well. I mean, who wants to tell George that while he was giving a keynote presentation on the sorts of things his audience deems to be so vitally important, there was a large, sloppy, green booger hanging out of his nose? I sure as hell don't. It's embarrassing!

I suppose some would say it's just as cruel to set these individuals up for that ever popular, remarkably religious, coming-to-terms-with-your-life-in-general-while-facing-the-bathroom-mirror conversations with the Lord(?). But hey, I kind of like them. They're entertaining. I taped the last one I heard for just this occasion. Here, listen.

"Oh my God, I've got a booger? I wonder how long it's been there. Oh no.... please tell me it wasn't there during my presentation.... Oh pleeeease God, please tell me it wasn't there."

"I can't believe I'm being dragged down to this level," said God, to Himself of course. (I mean, He wouldn't actually want to clear up that ultimate source of human frustration, now would He? You know, like whether our lives have a definite purpose, or if the whole thing was just a horribly stupid, meaningless coincidence as my theory of Accidentalism states. Naw, He's right. Let's keep the little people guessing.) "I've got to deal with famine, disease, incredibly boring prime-time television, and this guy is praying over a nose goblin. No wonder I don't feel like going down there anymore. They've all become so stupid."

"Naw," said George, the above-mentioned bonehead. "That couldn't have been there the whole time I was talking. I mean, someone would have told me."

"Tad wouldn't have told you, you fool, and he was the only guy in the room who actually liked you," said God.

"Yeah, it probably just snuck down there on the way to the bathroom," said George.

"Wrong-o! Get a grip, okay?"

"Yeah, that's it. Don't worry about it, old boy. You knocked 'em dead. Oh yeah, that's right, I was praying. Thanks God. It's good we can still talk."

Then God(?) would grumble to Himself in a seriously irritated manner and postpone the whole enlightenment thing-a-ma-bob until the human race learned to tie its collective mental shoelaces. Perhaps if we spent a little more time learning inter-religious social graces and a little less time in Spanish class, we could appease the supreme one and finally get some answers out of Him. Hey, I can't blame the dude for being pissed; incredibly powerful, ultimate beings must have feelings too.

Anyway, that's enough philosophical rhetoric for the moment. I think it's time we reentered the story.

The above-noticed incredibly non-invisible something was approaching from the exact distance whereby you think whatever the hell you are looking at closely resembles a bucket of Kentucky Fried Chicken. A highly amazing distance if I may say so.

Moments passed as they sometimes do and the formerly fantasized neighbor-like substance projected a more precise image.

He was casually dressed in a long, white robe and exactly nothing else. Well, I shouldn't say that, because he was indeed armed with a Moses-like staff, a Nike headband, and a rather expensive pair of steel-tipped hiking boots. (Please note that the boots were expensive only because he had a size seventeen foot and exactly not because he had a large salary resulting from the formation of a religious system remarkably resembling a corrupt body of ancient European law whereby one can attain passage to a certain wonderful sphere of consciousness by entering little courtroom confessionals, telling stories to a judicial holy man, and then, after some form of monetary and spiritual restitution was presented, this overly dependent individual is given his pardon by a person who has precisely the same amount of knowledge of the afterlife as does a three-legged goat named Bosefus. Ah, as the collection plate passes.)

He was skipping happily through the forest, singing a rather interesting version of a popular Beatles song. He didn't have the greatest voice, but it was strangely pleasing.

I watched. Pete cursed. The interesting something skipped and sang. It was all rather simple. The animals took notice of the happenings and quickly transformed themselves into cartoon images and began to follow the dude (to be named later) in much the same way that women don't follow me. It was quite a spectacle, my social life that is, not the scene in the book.

Be that as it may, the distance between us closed rapidly and the moment took on a suspenseful undertone. You know the kind I mean. Like if the same scene were playing in a *Friday the 13th* movie you would be hearing that, "kill, kill, kill," noise in the background.

Pete stopped cursing when he heard the melody being chanted by the entire forest and turned to investigate. He was awestruck.

"Tad, who the hell is that?"

I didn't answer. It was better that he didn't know. Yes, definitely better. He wouldn't believe me anyway.

"Tad?" asked Pete, with growing concern.

"Imagine there's no countries," sang my neighbor, with the animals picking up the harmony, "it's easy if you try…."

"What the hell is going on here? What do you want?"

"Imagine there's no… "

"Slow down, you psycho! Slow down! Tad, he's coming straight for me!"

"Imagine all the people…."

"Aaaahhhh!" screamed a terrified Pete, as the magical dude landed a solid right hook to his chin."

"….living life in peace. You-whooooooo, well-ell. You may say I'm a dreamer…" sang the mystical maniac, as he continued down the road.

"Wait!" said Pete, as he slowly re-bolted his bearings to the mental structure of reality. "Get back here, you asshole."

"Pete, don't curse! He'll kill you."

"Stay out of this. This is between me and the fairy over there. Yeah, that's right. I called you a fairy. You got a problem with that? You miserable… got to be hitting people when they're not fully paying attention to the happenings of the moment, piece of no good…. I ought to…."

The Pete-assaulting, Disney dude stopped abruptly and came back toward us. Suddenly, my homeboy wasn't too thrilled with the prospect of going another round.

"Oh shit," I thought. (I wasn't about to actually *say* anything.)

"Excuse me, young man," said my neighbor in a gentle off-guard-catching tone. "But do you have any idea who I am?"

"No," said Pete, as the tension lifted itself to a more comfortable atmosphere.

"Well, I'm The Magical, Mystical, and Somewhat Saintly Steve, and I happen to hate violence, foul language, and stand very much for Greenpeace. Now, given this and the fact that this is indeed my land, I'll have to discourage you from performing further outbursts of that nature while in the confines of my compound. You don't curse and I don't beat you firmly over the head with ah... that Amazing and Somewhat Stupid Moron over there."

"You know Tad?" asked Pete.

"We go way back. I used to beat him up in grammar school. Isn't that right ya jag-off?"

"Hey, screw you, Steve. Okay?"

"Watch it, buddy."

"Whatever, jerky. Why don't you make like your mom—and blow this joint?"

"Tad," said a surprised, confused, and concerned Pete. Wasn't that sweet of him?

"Under normal circumstances, I would have to kill you for that," said the Magical One. "However, I recently took a course in how to channel my anger and have learned to relax and express myself in more productive ways. Therefore, instead of pounding your skull into a slimy gray pate, I will simply leave you with an interesting observation of humanity. It is such: *Truth is always the hardest thing to find.*

"Philosophy is rather nifty, isn't it? Good-bye all."

Then he vanished. I don't know how the hell he learned to do that sort of thing, but it really got on my nerves. You see, I'm not the jealous type. I can handle it when somebody is better looking than me, has a nicer car, is more financially secure, or just generally feels satisfied with the ongoings of the universe and his role in it. But when somebody, who by the way comes directly from our particular planet, somehow conjures up the ability to float around, appear, and disappear at will, and basically makes a mockery of every formerly accepted physical law, I tend to become minutely agitated.

"What was that about?" asked Pete.

"You wouldn't understand if I told you."

He seemed to accept that, but the truth was that I wouldn't have understood it if somebody explained it to me.

"Let's get back to the house," I said.

"Sure."

"What time is it anyway?"

"Oh, about nine o'clock.

"Hey, that reminds me. The guys are saying that I lost the bet because of my fart last night."

"Pete, how can quoting me the time remind you of something like that?"

"I don't know, I guess it's just how my brain works. And as long as it continues to work in an acceptable fashion, I really see no reason to question it."

"Fine. Don't get hyper."

"Sorry, dude, but can you believe what they're saying about

the bet?"

"Yeah, it's great."

"It's great!?! What are you talking about? I'm out fifty bucks. Oh…now I see, you're just thrilled that you're finally going to get into Jackie's pants. You really think she's gonna keep her end?"

"Well, that's kinda hard to say."

"No way! You got in there already, didn't you? You did! Last night. You banged her last night! Why, you sneaky little bastard. I can't believe it."

"Yo, yo. I'm not saying anything."

"Ahhh, now I know I'm right. If you didn't, you would have said so. You never lie about that kind of shit."

"You can believe what you want, but don't go saying anything."

"Who, me? Don't worry about it. Man, I can't believe you got in there. Was she good?"

"Shut up."

Don't you just hate how best friends can read you like a comic book? It's really quite disturbing. I mean, what if I were importing drugs from Mexico or made a living via a live-seal-starring *Whac-A-Mole* rip off? Would he know with a glance? I'd rather not think about it.

When we got back to the house, it was a little after nine. The guys were busy doing the sorts of things you'd expect a bunch of morons to be doing in this type of environment. Darien was building a much-unneeded fire, Dawn and Jackie were speaking quietly amongst themselves, and Eric was busy blowing on a blade of grass that tried desperately to pass for a musical instrument. It failed.

"Hey, Tad, did you hear I won the bet?" asked Eric as he

realized, for one thing, that small birds were dropping out of the trees completely dead as a result of the noise he was creating, and for a second, slightly less important thing, that it would be much more fun to gloat to me than to kill those harmlessly useless birds.

"Yeah... ah, congratulations."

I wasn't as excited as he had initially hoped, so he terminated the conversation and went back to killing the birds. The birds took note of this and firmly decided not to like me anymore.

Up to this point I've been in every scene in the book. I didn't plan it that way, but it just sort of happened. I guess it's a first person kind of thing.

In any event, there is one discussion that needs to be shown although I wasn't directly involved with it at the time. In light of this, I must warn you of two things. First, I'm gonna have to switch to the third person for a moment. And secondly, I'm going to have to paraphrase slightly, considering that I wasn't aware the conversation took place until just a few months ago. By the way, if you can follow all this, I'd seriously look into some sort of a counseling program. Here we go.

"Well, what do you think I should do?" asked Jackie.

(Sorry we're a little late, but I did have to explain a few things.)

"I don't know. How long have you felt this way?" asked Dawn.

"Not long at all. I mean, we're friends and I always thought he was kind of cute, right, but I never pictured being with a guy like him."

"Why not?"

"Well, he's funny, but he just didn't seem to be interested in a relationship."

"Is that what you think you have?"

"Not yet, but maybe down the road. Why, is there something I should know?"

"Well, you know...."

"What?"

"Look, I don't know if I should be telling you this or not, but about a month or so ago Tad got depressed about something and decided to go over to Pete's to talk. Well, I had been over there hanging out, and since Pete was too busy working on his car to occupy Tad, I took the task. We started talking and drinking and the next thing I knew we were doing a lot more than talking and drinking."

Jackie started to get misty. (I really wanted to leave this part out.)

"Do you like him?"

"Jack, he's hard not to like."

"I can't believe I fell for him. I really thought...."

"Wait, you're missing the point. I'm not trying to say he's a jerk and you shouldn't go out with him. I'm just giving you the facts. First of all, I was the one who got the ball rolling, so don't go thinking he's a slut."

Jackie giggled.

"Look, all I'm saying is that if you want to be with him you're gonna have to realize the kid's a maniac."

"That I know," said Jackie.

"Well, just don't forget it. These idealistic types are pretty hard to come by."

"So what should I do?"

"Talk to him."

Jackie started to leave, but turned back for a moment. "Hey, what about you and Darien?"

"Oh come on, me and Darien? We'd never make it."

"You're the expert. By the way, do you think there's anything to Tad's philosophy stuff?"

"Who cares? Most guys don't think about anything except cars and sex. At least he's refreshing. A little nuts, but refreshing. Now get over there."

That was pretty damn nice of her, don't you think? Yeah, life may have given me the short end of the stick when it comes to family, money, talent, and penis size, but even I had to admit I had some really cool friends.

Well, nothing tremendously exciting happened that afternoon. I showed them the store where I had bought the sausages. We played a few childish games in the woods. And we made a conscious effort not to concern ourselves with how we were going to get back to civilization.

Anyway, now that things have returned to normal and I, The Amazing One, am back in the familiar, self-loving, first person mode, I think I'll take a break and go order a pizza. However, I will confide this before I leave. Jackie and I had a wonderful day together and, even though I let her do most of the talking, I couldn't help but wonder if that action in itself caused me to disclose the most. If a picture is worth a thousand words, then a woman's glance is worth a thousand pictures. Yes, I guess I was growing up. Perhaps with the right person I could actually learn to, to um, you know, to... somebody. Oh screw it. I can't even say the word.

Ah well, I shouldn't push myself too hard. Even cynical, sarcastic maniacs must learn to walk before they learn to hail a cab.

# CHAPTER 17

Advanced Bee-ben-bobble is a truly remarkable game. Have you ever played? I didn't think so. Allow me to explain.

To play Bee-ben-bobble of the advanced form, you will need to gather the following items: a deck of cards, a Diet Pepsi (optional), an extraordinary understanding of universal cause and effect (completely non-optional), and, of course, a Hypercolor T-shirt. No serious Bee-ben-bobble player would sit at an intergalactic card table without one.

Once you've gathered these items, and are positioned comfortably around a circular table with your favorite bunch of folks, launch a friendly "thank you" in the overly precise direction of the incredibly un-green aliens who, one otherwise-uneventful fourteenth of November, surprisingly landed on my forehead. They, after a brief discussion concerning a few things I couldn't quite understand and yet, strangely reminded me of the spirited, *"I really think frozen yogurt tastes much better than ordinary ice cream,"* debate, introduced me to this highly amazing game.

The aliens' names were Starlapious, Hypergilcemic, and Ralph. Ralph, of course, was the leader and stupendously more intelligent than the other two.

Nevertheless, they told me Bee-ben-bobble was the most confidential, important, and stupendously, mindboggleinglyest difficult game in the universe and that it alone explained the inner workings of infinity.

Besides, if one knew the game's secret, one could easily use it to make a hell of a lot of money in bars. Given the fact that Rhombus 9, which, by the way, is exactly the planet from where the three above-mentioned aliens are directly descended, recently had all its bars removed due to a highly hysterical accident, which would take far too long to explain, they, the three of them, firmly decided that the game should be passed on.

Earth seemed the ideal place to store the secret. First, because its people are so impossibly stupid, and secondly, because the game is so stupidly impossible. Well enough history, here's how it's played.

Bee-ben-bobble of the advanced form is a lot like solitaire, in that you play it alone, and a lot unlike solitaire, in that if you ever completed it you would be ordained The Official Supreme Ruler of Anything Remotely Cool, which, by the way, is a highly sought after position.

The first thing you do is pick a player, hopefully someone amazingly stupid. The game naturally works on smart people as well, but they tend to wager less money. Once you have your sucker, play a hand yourself to prove that it is indeed horrendously improbable. To do this, simply ask the confused-looking gentlemen to your right what his favorite number is. Then, almost immediately after, ask him what his favorite number would be if the originally offered number were kidnapped by Inter-Stupidic Number Stealers and held for a ransom much too expensive to pay given the current economic environment of the galaxy. (This has absolutely nothing to do with the game, but Starlapious, an infamous number stealer in his own right, asked me these questions during our first meeting and I kind of made them a tradition. Perhaps it was a just research project of some sort. Who knows?)

Anyway, after attaining this information, deal the cards face down, into four groups with each group containing six cards. These piles represent the four Winds of the Galaxy. (Please note if people bitch about the number six then, by all means, let them pick another number. The game is still highly impossible.) Next, place a single card face down, in the center of the four stacks. This represents the Orb of the Universe, an incredibly important card. Now turn over the top card for each of the four Winds. Don't try to cheat and look at the Orb.

Now we are ready to play! Just flip through the cards in your hand one at a time and try to get a match. A match is of course two cards of the same suit with a hole in the middle. For example, a seven of diamonds and a nine of diamonds would be a match. The eight represents the hole the two pieces of cosmic matter used to actively form a galaxy-producing atom. Needless to say, the seven could match the five as well, with the hole being the six. See it's all rather simple! One thing to consider is that the king can effectively match the two, with the hole being the ace. This can reasonably occur because the universe is, of course, somewhat circular.

If by chance you get stuck, which you indubitably will, you

can flip over and use the Orb of the Universe. It is rather helpful, but can only be used in times of severe stress. (Note: If the Orb is used for matching purposes, it must be replaced by the currently visible, upper-right-hand corner Wind. If there are no Winds left in that area, you can't use the Orb. Sorry.)

To win the game, some cash, and become an amazingly inventive fellow, all you have to do is end with absolutely no cards in your hand and no cards under the four Winds. For every card that wasn't properly paired with its appropriate counterpart, there is a severely screwed-up galaxy. Also, the Orb of the Universe must be resting comfortably in the middle of the Winds with a partner of its own.

Who is this partner? Well, you will uncover this fact when the time of severe stress arises. When, in this moment of heated anxiety, you flip over the Orb of the Universe and discover, for example, it is a nine of clubs, you must produce another nine (of any suit) to keep the Orb company. Let's face it, even monumentally important symbols of interplanetary congruency get lonely. The catch is knowing what the Orb of the Universe is before you actually play. This way you can effectively plan for its matching. Unfortunately, this, along with any other attempts at creative rule bending, is highly illegal and otherwise frowned upon by the forehead-landing aliens.

It is said that God(?) was quite fond of Bee-ben-bobble (when it was fashionable and still believed to be possible) and effectively won his current position from Frank Sinatra in a small Cleveland-based pub of virtually no importance. However, this belief is generally disregarded, partly because only idiots arrogantly announce such statements, but mostly because none of the galaxy's intelligent life forms actually believe Mr. Sinatra exists.

Oh, by the way, just in case you were wondering, God(?) never completed the game. He did fairly well, but never won it outright. Thus, the three cards/galaxies He(?) neglected to match were destined to an eternity of utter unreasonableness. This is a most profoundly negative way to spend the millennia. But then again, you know this already. Yes, the Earth was located directly on top of the unluckiest spot in the most unwanted of the three forgotten galaxies.

Now billions of hopeful humans wait patiently for the one cool dude who will figure out the bloody game, finish God's(?) handy work, and set things straight with the greater scheme of things. One cool dude in the entire Do Nothing Generation, do you think it's possible?

It was 4:30 a.m. – the third morning of our escapade. A Sunday. The birds were singing, the wind was blowing, and the sun was trying to come to terms with its role in human destiny, now that the majority of people had wised up, realized he was nothing more than a ball of dangerous gas and, therefore, in a rather cold-hearted way, discontinued their Sun God(?) rituals without proper notification. I had just finished my sixty-seventh hand of Bee-ben-bobble. I lost.

Since my camping buddies were all visiting their Inter-Dreamular Fantasy Lands, I decided this would be the perfect time to open my spy kit. Perhaps I was unconsciously distancing myself from a lost relationship, but in that moment Buck seemed a world away.

That's the thing about memories; they are rarely honest. You see, humans have a tendency to invent what's missing. Once the present dissipates, people are free to alter their mental record of prior events into a self-serving generalization more suitable to the story they want to tell. I'm not saying this is wrong. Indeed, it may even be helpful at times. But alas, it is not totally honest. And isn't honesty what we're here to find?

Be that as it may, I abandoned these thoughts and enjoyed the few remaining moments of my relationship with the boss man... ah, former employer. I opened the letter and he spoke.

*Dear Mr. Dreamer,*

*Before I tell you what you have to do, I want to get a couple of things straight. First, whatever happens, don't try to find me. I'm gone. Secondly, don't worry about getting in trouble with the law or anything. Thomas Torri is a captain now and the department would rather have its dick in the dirt than see a decorated man get dragged into a scandal. Everything will be fine.*

*So, here's the plan. As soon as you finish screwing around in the woods, go to the Davenport Beach and Tennis Club and get the box. There's a guy there named Bobby Mancini who runs the place. I phoned him last week and said you would be coming. He doesn't know the deal, and shouldn't ask too many questions. He's a moron.*

*Once you get the box, mail the package inside to me. The doll is worth a fortune and anything that expensive can become a magnet for trouble. The way I see it, you'll have enough of that on your own, so get rid of it fast!*

*Okay, here's the dangerous part. You are going to have to meet Thomas by the old Glen Island Pier. Believe me, I tried to get a more populated spot, but he wouldn't go for it. He swears to God he's important. Anyway, the meeting is set for midnight on Tuesday so, if you are reading this late, you better get your ass in gear.*

*Just give him the money and everything will be all right. I told him you were okay, but he said to make sure you come alone and don't try anything. You know, the typical movie stuff.*

*Oh, by the way, the second part of your payment is included in the fifty grand. Thomas knows about this as well, so don't be a wise-ass and take more than a G. The greedy son-of-a-bitch will probably make you stand around while he counts every last dollar. So just make sure there's forty-nine thousand in that briefcase.*

*Well, it's good to see you have some balls. I knew I could count on you. Thanks a lot, Tad. You're saving my life. I owe you one and I'll make good. Really.*

*Your friend,*
*Buck*

This final promise transformed itself into a friendly stiletto that regrettably, yet fiendishly, severed our lines of communication forever. It was strange that he would end our relationship this way. Yes, ending an era of honesty with a lie, a quick slice at the neck. You know, the kind that doesn't start bleeding for a moment or two, not for a lack of graveness, but rather because the flesh itself cannot believe from whence the injury came. He would never *repay* me. How could he?

# CHAPTER 18

Sunrise was miraculous, yet I all but missed the affair. My head was spinning and my focus blurred about the myriad of details encapsulating the upcoming event. With much to do and so little planned my anal-retentive schemata seemed slightly askew. To ease my cares, I rechecked my pocket for the locker combination and visualized the upcoming transaction for the thousandth time. It all seemed so simple, but then again, so did Bee-ben-bobble and look how hard that turned out to be. So without further Philosophication, I put plan to action.

Yes, it looked as if I would have to finally break down and use Mr. Visa. I wasn't terribly excited about it. After all, I heard tales of how he (Mr. Visa that is) tends to bash you about the brain with a rather unfriendly piece of steel piping when you didn't complete your payments properly.

Given the Zukes, Barley Man, the Transitional Tree, and my overly self-actualized neighbor, I felt I met my quota of strange and somewhat supernatural, imaginary creatures. Unfortunately, some supreme destiny-bending deity had other opinions regarding intergalactic affirmative action. I was trapped. I mean, let's face it. You can't fight Universal Hall. Did I just say that? Somebody slap me.

I returned to the cabin-like shack, satisfied with my morning philosophy session. The guys were awake and huddled around Pete and Eric, the latter of whom had an immense grin plastered in a position slightly north of his overly eccentric jaw.

"Yo, guys, what the...."

My question was answered by Pete's unhappy counting.

"...forty-eight, forty-nine, fifty," grumbled Pete in a hysterically pitiful tone. "I can't believe I lost fifty bucks because of a premature bowel movement."

"Ah, don't worry," said Eric. "If it makes you feel better, I'll by the buy the beer and chips tonight."

"Oooooow," cooed the girls.

Darien was tempted to join in the cooing, but I shot him a halting, *"Come on now, let's at least try to act macho once in a while,"* glance.

"Hey," said the stable one in retaliation for me questioning his manhood, "when are you going to collect *your* winnings?"

Dawn pierced his flesh with an icy stare, but the question grabbed a beer and sat atop a fully reclined Craftmatic II Adjustable Chair. It could not go unanswered.

Eric, who didn't receive one of those, *"If you don't shut up and mind your business, I'm going to smack you harshly on the back of the neck several times and revoke your booty rights for the next five hundred years,"* winks, proceeded to push the issue.

"So, Tad," said the amazingly uncouth idiot, "when are you two going to get it on."

Jackie looked pissed, a bit flustered and embarrassed as well, but extremely more pissed than the other two.

"Look," she said, while trying not to let her voice crack, "whatever Tad and I do is..."

"We might as well tell them," I said, cutting her off.

She looked puzzled, so I continued.

"If you really want to know, guys, we decided to stick to our original fifty dollar bet. So she'll be taking me to dinner when we get back to civilization."

"You got to be kidding," said a sexually repressed Darien, a disappointed Eric, and a soon-to-be-enlightened, *"Wait a minute, Tad. I thought you banged her already... oooooh, I get it. That's really nice of you. God, what a guy,"* Pete, simultaneously.

"That's right," I said. "Sorry."

"Well, I think it's sweet," said Dawn.

"Really? Well, I think the whole affair tremendously sucks. Jeez, what a bunch of fucking pansies," said someone under his breath.

We all knew the guilty party was not among the campers and were desperate to discover the identity of a being callous enough to destroy such a lovely Hallmark moment. Therefore, after a good deal of questioning and the energies from three imaginary, cause-oriented, high-wattage, detective movie light bulbs began to fade, Nobody admitted to making this horrendously antisocial statement. This same Nobody was subsequently tried, convicted, and sentenced to thirty-five years of hard labor in the mostly depressing Something Land, Anything mines. A truly horrible fate.

Satisfied with the Inter-Stupidic Justice System, we decided to spend the remainder of the morning doing absolutely nothing. You know what I mean, the kind of nothing whereby you just sit around, and try not to think about anything more stressful than a bowl of homemade chicken soup. Nobody, not even the Nobodies themselves, can get stressed out by a bowl of chicken soup. It's the third-least-stress-inducing thing in the universe.

As we entered the house, Jackie apprehended my attention with an interesting game of mental freeze tag. She held it long enough to say "thank you" and give me one of those heart-warming looks that could make to reevaluate your whole belief system.

"Yo, Pete," I said, as the rest of the guys went inside. "Got a minute?"

"Yeah, sure."

"What's up?" asked an eavesdropping Darien.

"Nothing really," I lied. "We'll be inside in a minute."

"Sure. No problem."

I thought he was going to be a big pain in the ass and cive into a, *"Oh, come on, man, you guys never let me in on what's really going on,"* bitch sessions. But obviously, he was rather looking forward to the whole "do nothing" affair.

"Where have you been?" asked Pete.

"My morning Philosophication."

"It's almost ten. How long were you out there?"

"A while."

"A long while, I'd say."

"Well, then say it, for it was indeed truly amazing philosophy."

"Yeah, yeah. So what's the deal, Tad?"

"I have to go New Rochelle tomorrow."

"Isn't that your old neighborhood?"

"Yeah."

"Why?"

"I'll tell you about it when I get back."

"What, you going on a drug run or something?"

He was kidding. I was not. He noticed, and that air of secretive seriousness returned to its familiar place by my side.

"Well, if you can't tell me why at least tell me how? What's the plan?"

"The folks down the road are close friends of the family. My grandparents have known them for years."

"So?"

"So, dick-brain, I think I can con them into driving me home. It's only an hour and a half each way."

"Yeah, right. No offense, guy, but you look like shit. Besides, they haven't heard from anyone in your family in years. You honestly think they're going to see you and say, 'Hi, Tad. How's it going? What? You want me to spend three hours in a car for no apparent reason. Okay, that sounds great! Maybe when we get there, I could paint your house, mow your lawn, and let you take a shot at my sixteen-year-old daughter.' You can bullshit. But nobody's that good."

"All right, Pete, I'd definitely say the whole 'knocking the boots with his daughter,' routine is a little out of my league, but they'll at least give me a ride to the Rent-A-Car place."

"Five bucks says you don't get in the door."

"Haven't you lost enough money?"

"Don't worry about it. You game?"

"Yeah, sure."

"Okay, say your plan works. When are you coming back?"

"If things go right, Wednesday."

"Wednesday?"

"Wednesday."

"What the hell are we going to do until then?"

"The same things you would have done if I were here, shit for brains. What's wrong with you? Just tell the others I wanted to visit my grandparents. If they give you a time of it, say that it doesn't make sense for me not to go considering the relative proximity involved. That sounds pretty good, right? I mean, it's only a day or so.

"When I get back we'll still have the rest of the week to hang out. Come Saturday, we'll get another Rent-A-Car and cruise home."

"With what money?"

"Don't worry about it."

"Now I know something's wrong. You never have that kind of cash. Let's have it."

"Have what?"

"The real story."

Jesus(?), this kid is really getting on my nerves. I sincerely hope these years in Florida haven't softened my creatively imaginative truth-bending skills.

"All right," I said. "I'll give it to you straight. You know my boss, right?"

"Sure, Buck Johnson."

"Yeah, well, he's screwed. He has been getting blackmailed for a few years and, well...oh hell, let me start from the beginning. About five years ago..."

And so I told him the whole story. Believe me, I tried to bullshit him a couple of times, but it wouldn't work. Each time I strayed from the path of reasonably accepted insanity he pulled me over, wrote a rather expensive ticket, and subtly threatened my utter existence. Ah, what the hell. I never cared for lying anyway. Enterprisingly inventive philosophy, yes. Lying, no.

"...and that's his basic situation," I said approximately twenty minutes later.

(Oh man I forgot about Darien. I really hope he didn't take me literally when I said I'd only be a second. I'd hate to be the reason for one of his psychological particularities.)

"So, what do you think? Pretty cool, huh?" I said in a positive fashion, hoping to wipe away some of that nasty green, *'Tad is seriously bugging in the highest if he thinks I'm going to let him play cops and robbers with a bunch of Mafioso lunatics,"* pasty goop, currently oozing from Pete's Popeye-like face.

"I'm going with you."

"Don't start that, Pete. You can't go."

"Why? I thought you said it wasn't dangerous."

"It's not, but if you go, then everybody's gonna want to go and I'll have to face the blackmailer feeling like a kindergartener. It's kinda embarrassing, you know? Besides, it's not up to me."

"What?"

"Look, you know I have an interesting relationship with most of the imaginary creatures within the greater scheme of things."

"Yeah... I know. You spent a year explaining it to me one day. Please don't do it again."

"That's the point. There's no time."

Pete's point of "shitafullness" was reached. "I know this will indubitably increase the amount of gastrointestinal acids currently assaulting my soon-to-be ulcer, but I just got to ask. What does all this hyper-galactic crap have to do with us going to New Rochelle?"

"Simple. If we all go I'll have to rent a minivan."

"So."

"So, they're noisy and guzzle gas to the extreme."

"Like you care about pollution."

"No, but with my luck your invisible foe, the Somewhat Saintly Steve, will hear about my 'crying Indian television commercial'-like atrocity and come to the conclusion that he likes to pound on people far more than he likes becoming an overly enlightened, peace-loving liberal. In light of this, he'll sign up for one of those historically improbable maniac conventions and team up with The Incredible Zukes, for an amazingly painful, *Tad's really gonna get it this time,'* inter-imaginary, Battle Royal wrestling match, with a no-holds-bared rule and possible cage involvement. So you see, my man, if you guys go, I'm dead."

At first, Pete just stood there looking flabbergasted. But once his stomach had settled and his eyes had rolled back into a more socially acceptable position, he locked in on my right cheek and fired an incredibly impressive, severely sinister, satanic stare, which made me overwhelmingly thankful there were no idly sitting chain saws in the immediate area.

"I'm going to end this conversation now," said Pete. "Yes, I feel a wholly consuming desire to shave the recently arrived fur from the soles of my feet. I'm not sure how the fur got there, but it better leave."

"Sounds great, Pete."

Boy, I think I stunned him. I really need to be more careful with my comically abusive chatter.

"Oh," said Pete, turning from the door, "I'm still going with you. That whole story sounds a little too perfect."

"Fine, but let's at least keep this between us, okay?"

"All right. Now if you'd excuse me, I have to go reevaluate my standing in the hierarchy of the cosmos. You know, I really hate it when you philosophize at people without giving them the proper warning. That stuff can be pretty painful if you're not expecting it."

At the risk of sounding like a severe wimp, I would like to say that I was lucky to have a friend like him. He's a damn nice guy. Don't you think?

# CHAPTER 19

Monday mornings are generally believed to be a rather shitty time of the week. They've earned this distinction by causing the abrupt conclusion of others creatures' weekends, and wholly reminding them that they've sold their souls to some hysterically useless corporation. Nobody, not even self-actualizing, enlightened, motivated morons, likes them.

They are so intensely disliked that when used as a topic on that historically popular game show, The Intergalactic Freudian Feud, the three most popular neuro-associations linked to the phrase "Monday Mornings" were: First, "They are about as joyful as having every molecule in your body simultaneously go through its mid-life crisis, become severely depressed, and ultimately implode at the speed of light." Secondly, "They are far worse than having your nose hairs individually extracted by the infamous, tuna fish-eating sea lions from Rhombus 7." And the most popular association, the one that earned its submitter a wholly remarkable trip to Shezbot, was, "I like them considerably less than Fridays and I wish they would go away."

I firmly agree with these statements because Mondays indeed suck. However, there is something increasingly more horrible than a regular Monday, and that something is a vactionable Monday morning spent walking seven miles to the nearest Rent-a-Wreck with five highly cranky individuals, and paying one of these altogether irritable humans five bucks for saying things like, "Ah! I told you your neighbor wouldn't give us a ride. What a loser." All this, added to and divided by the fact that I missed my Morning Philosophication, produced a moment in time of considerable un-coolness.

In any event, the morning was spent in verse and stride. We walked. We talked. We laughed. We reached—Otis and Hopson's Rent and Repair. It was an amazingly interesting establishment.

"There's the place," I said, hoping to lift the spirits of the exasperated explorers.

"Finally!" said Eric.

"God, I could use a Coke," said Jackie, wiping her beautiful brow with her sleeve.

"What time is it?" asked Dawn.

"About twelve," said Darien, in a strangely believable tone.

"I sure as hell hope this place is open," said Pete, who was so grossly consumed with the joy of winning that he completely forgot the weekend was through.

We ignored him and entered the shop.

It was oddly normal in a familiarly strange way. What I mean is half of it appeared as you might expect it to appear—dingy and dirty, with posters of naked ladies on the wall and takeout containers scattered haphazardly throughout the area. The other half of the room however, was immaculate. It came complete with some carefully hung, almost-impressive, artwork, a few well-cared-for, exceptionally green, potted plants, and an overly emphasized attention placed in the area of paper clip assortment. What's more, if you listened closely, you could almost hear the faint sounds of imaginary birds crooning to a Springtime Pavarati concert.

The fellas were awestruck. And that's saying a lot, considering most of them wouldn't have known what "awe" was if you struck it with a bat.

"Hello," attempted Eric.

"Why, good afternoon, chaps," said an attendant as he straightened his bow tie "How are you this fine day?"

He was a larky individual with a British nose and incredibly large feet. So large, in fact, I ventured the poor bastard could probably sleep standing up. He also came equipped with greased hair and an obnoxiously long mustache that tried earnestly to twist about in the style of those old-timey barbers. It failed.

"You must be Hopson," said Pete.

"Actually I'm Otis," said the attendant.

"?" looked Pete.

"Surprising, isn't it?

"Hopson!" called Otis. "We have customers.

"We always get that reaction. It has become quite the fancy tickler to say the least."

Hopson entered from the back, looking rather like a chewed-up tennis ball. He was dressed in a loose-fitting, oil-stained garment that could have easily been constructed from the remnants of a ten-year-old painter's tarp.

"So, what the hell can we do ya for?"

"Hopson, I thought Momsey instructed you not to use such language. Honestly, in front of the patrons! You should be ashamed of yourself."

"Her name is not Momsey. It's Ma, you pansy. And if you don't cut all the British shit out I'm gonna ram this tail pipe up your ass."

Otis swallowed hard and proceeded to shut up.

"You got to forgive him, folks. He ain't all there."

"What's wrong with him?" asked Eric, who insisted on denying the existence of social grace.

"Well," said Hopson, "it's a long story, but the truth is he got kicked in the head really, really hard."

"By who?" asked Darien.

"His girlfriend."

I slipped a cautiously curious glance toward Jackie, but she caught it, got pissed, and stepped on my foot.

"Yeah," said Hopson, "ever since, he's been acting like a British fag, calling me Hopson and ha-lew-cin-a-nating this whole opposite brother thing. At first I didn't mind. I mean, shit, the son-of-a-bitch tripled our business. But he's been getting' out of hand lately and it's really startin' to up my dander."

"Ah, what's the big deal, you're making good money, right?" asked Pete.

"Sure, but that ain't the point. He's drivin me batty. The place is so neat I can't think straight. He's got his name first on the business sign. And he keeps calling me Hobson."

"Well, what *is* your name?" inquired Darien. (He really liked the word "inquire" so I imagine he was excited when he finally got a chance to use it.)

"Jethro, as in Jethro and Otis' Rent and Repair—not that

ridiculous Otis and Hopson sign. Get it?"

"Well, look here, Jethro," I said, realizing we were on a schedule, "I feel for your situation and all, but we need to rent a car for a couple of days. What do you got?"

He proceeded to take us out back, where he displayed and discussed various pieces of shit. After about twenty horribly long, mostly miserable minutes, we settled on an ancient, rusty brown, Olds-mo-buick convertible.

"Have that baby back by Wednesday or we'll have to tack on an extra ten percent."

"No problem," I said, while quickly congratulating myself for having negotiated such a remarkable rate.

As we piled in the car I heard a faint siren in the distance. The sound grew louder, as they sometimes do, and a moment later, a long, white ambulance pulled up to the station. At that instant, the formerly silent Otis started to chuckle and sashayed in our general direction.

"There he is, gentlemen," said Otis to the whitely dressed ambulance drivers. "He's in relative proximity to the convertible-seated children."

The drivers caught the good-deal-giving individual, put him in a straight jacket, and promptly cast him into the back of the station wagon. I can only assume that Hopson, or rather Jethro, knew the routine, because he didn't protest, beg for a lawyer, or do anything you would expect an innocent person to do in that situation.

"What's going on, Otis?" asked Jackie and I almost simultaneously.

"Nothing of consequence. Just a little family quarrel. It need not trouble you."

"But, dude," said Pete, "I don't mean any offense by this, but

I thought you were the nut."

"Given the surroundings and the situation, most people do. However, I assure you, young man, I'm perfectly sane."

"Prove it," said Eric, who really shouldn't have, considering that Otis might ask him to return the favor.

"That's simple," said Otis. "I'm sane enough to know the deal my brother gave your friend was seriously unacceptable."

I gritted my teeth. That really didn't do too much for my outlook on society.

"Well," said Dawn, "tell us the story."

"Yeah," said Darien.

"Well, if you must know, my name is in fact Otis and my brother is in fact Hopson. However, what is entirely not a fact is the overly assumed falsity that the above-mentioned Hopson is an uneducated hillbilly."

"Huh?" asked the six of us.

"Allow me to explain. We were born into money, went to Yale, and basically enjoyed a well-rounded childhood. However, sad as it is to say, our father, God rest his soul, was a man of seriously strange humor; thus explaining both my atrocious name and the fact that we are stuck here without our inheritance. Without it, that is, until we can make a go of a business venture on our own. Father quite hated laziness in any form.

"Be that as it may, the point here, gentlemen... and ladies, is that someone was indeed kicked in the head, but I was not the kickee and my lady-friend was certainly not the kicker."

"And..." I said sarcastically, hoping this story would come to a conclusion before someone took *me* away.

"And, ever since my little brother was assaulted by that overly ornery mule, he's been stomping around like a fool, consorting with socially impaired individuals, and generally making a mockery of the family name. I really...."

"How much is the car?" I asked, having had about enough of this shit.

"What did Hopson tell you?"

"Twenty bucks a day."

"Ho ho. You must be joking. I couldn't allow it for less than forty."

"I'll give you thirty."

"Thirty-five."

"All right, you win. But not a penny more than twenty-five."

"Agreed! Ah, what I mean is...."

"Too late, cheddar-brain. See ya in the funny papers."

After I paid him and informed the guys we had a deal, I went over to speak with the ambulance drivers, who had been watching our exchange.

"Hey, guys, how's it going?"

"Good, and yourself?"

"Fine. Look can I ask you something? What's the deal with these two?"

"The truth?"

"It would be nice."

"Well, they're pretty harmless I guess, but crazier than a bug-eyed fuzzle bear."

"What the hell's a bug-eyed fuzzle bear?"

"You wouldn't understand. You see, they take turns calling up the mental hospital and reportin' each other, ya know? Then the two of us come down here, throw one of 'em in a straight jacket, bring 'em back to the hospital, and spend the next few days watchin' the doctors questionin' 'em to death.

"Isn't that right, Joe?"

Joe, the man in the passenger's seat, just grunted.

"The way I see it," said the first ambulance driver, "those two boys are doing the community of Pine Plains more good than anyone else in town. And that includes the Mayor!"

"How do you figure?"

"Simple, for one thing they run a semi-successful business, which is more than I can say for most, and for another, they happen to be the only two lunatics in town. Them being crazy as such, and a possible hazard to the community, led to us bein' awarded the funds for a local mental hospital, which employs two doctors, three nurses, a secretary, a janitor, the two of us, and some guy named Bob. Don't know what the hell Bob does, now do we, Joe?"

Joe grunted again. He must have been a boring fellow.

"So you see, kid, when we ain't chasing these two guys, we don't do squat. As for the rest of the staff, my guess is that they do even less. It's pretty much the way our government works on every level."

"Thanks, man," I said sincerely. "It's been a real pleasure."

"Take care."

"Grunt."

Then they drove off.

"Sorry it took so long, guys," I said when I returned to the car.

"What were you doing with those two?" asked Pete.

"Just discussing the decline of moral fiber in American politics."

Uncertainty reigned as we found the entrance ramp to the Taconic Parkway. Indeed the conversation had been confusing, but even more troubling was the absence truth. It seemed each person lied a little less than the one before, but even that was difficult to confirm. Perhaps if a further party, higher in rank than the others, were introduced into the story line, a new light would be cast on the shadows of the things left untouched and something with which we had endowed our faith would indubitably be proven wrong... again.

Even the most honest of men hide a little something under their beds. Perhaps we should all sleep on the floor.

# CHAPTER 20

New Rochelle was comprised of a kaleidoscope of cultures and built by a slew of multi-generation families, many of which would never have left if Florida weren't invented. Be that as it may, I don't want to tell you too terribly much about my homeland considering the aforementioned nonexistent sequel to this monstrosity takes place there, and I'd hate to spoil the plot. I will note however, that upon our arrival I was surprised to find the city doing a rather convincing imitation of a ball of crud. Time had not been kind to it. But time is a brutal bastard.

Anyway, we decided to stay in a hotel because, to be quite honest, my grandfather wouldn't have been too keen on the idea of having six mentally-defunct teenagers using his home as a spiritual resort and Mafioso planing facility. Besides, there was a Ramada a few blocks from his house and given the whole, *"I *knew the sloppy-looking receptionist since kindergarten and she always had a crush on me,"* factor, we were a shoe-in for a couple of cheap rooms.

The hotel was located in the, *"Gee, I could have been a great city if the governing body presiding over me at the time accepted the onslaught of prospering businesses currently blossoming in White Plains, which by the way, was their second choice of homes,"* city center. This center was created through the convergence of North Avenue and Main Street, the only remaining boulevards in the business district. The overall bassackwardsness of the city sparked a few mild aspersions from my companions.

"You used to live here?" asked Jackie, who seemed completely grossed out by the nonexistence of cul-de-sacs. She happened to love cul-de-sacs.

"Jeez Tad, was it always like this?" asked Darien, looking as if he had bitten into a bad grape.

"What are you guys talking about? So the city needs a facelift. It's a couple hundred years old. Just wait and see what Valrico looks like in a century or so. Now, let's check in."

We got two rooms, something to eat, and a quick tour of the town. Eric had read that Thomas Paine had lived in New Rochelle and wanted to check out his house. Don't get me wrong, the kid wasn't into history or politics, he just enjoyed going into famous dead people's houses and looking in their refrigerators. I tried to explain that he couldn't just walk in and make himself a ham sandwich, but he gallantly argued the opposite.

I would have loved to have seen this historically hilarious pig-out party, but I had to go to the docks to pick up the package. In light of this, I gave them the car, said I was going to visit my grandfather, and thereafter parted company.

As I walked down the street, childhood memories danced through the ballrooms of my mind. Although I never cared for the reality of it, the current experience was strangely comforting. I say "strangely" for I've often wished I could go back through my yesterdays and reclaim the years that time has so unthoughtfully stolen from me. But alas, faced with impossibility, I move on, with my newly awarded faculties in hand and strive to avoid the horror of having to express the same feelings of regret about my todays, in a future moment of recollection.

I assume this is a common feeling and, since I have never been too fond of normalcy, I choose to fugue it out and push on. Perhaps this is cowardice on my part, but at least it's a choice, an action. Too many people never actually do anything.

The theory of Accidentalism states: "Humans are motion dependent. If they are not going forward, they are falling back. Thus, any choice, be it of catastrophic consequence or divine definition, is a thousand times better than a stagnant stance. Death is still and dead men cannot reevaluate." As you can see, Accidentalism is quite an interesting philosophy. I'd explain it fully, but I don't think we have forty-seven weeks to spare.

When I reached the club, I noticed it was busy for a Monday. Well, actually you can't consider that a justifiable comment since I hadn't been there in over two years, couldn't swim for my life, and know less about the beach and tennis business than a pathetically stupid, overly arrogant, three-toed sloth named Steven Nostril. My lack of knowledge however, did nothing to tarnish my mood. I was happy because the client commotion would produce a confusion-causing, *"Don't look at Tad with the secret package,"* interest-intercepting state.

I walked to the front entrance and asked the muscle-bound

moron at the door if Bobby Mancini was in. He looked me up and down a few times, decided that I was about as dangerous as a room-temperature ice cream sundae, and proceeded to pick up the phone.

"Era proprio quello di cui avevo paura. Gli antichi credevano in molti Dei," he said for no apparent reason.

A moment passed, and then a tall, stupid-looking man appeared in the doorway. He walked and dressed like a low-rent pimp, and although I don't like to judge people without giving them at least ten seconds to prove their usefulness to humanity, I must confess, I dubbed him an idiot on sight.

"Yeah, you must be da kid ol' Buck was talkin' about, right? What he send a little guy like you for? You can't be no more than fifteen, am I right?"

Everything's a question with these barbarians. You know, in rare and I suppose harmful moments of extreme prejudice, I've often wished they, the grease balls I mean, had stuck to pizza and construction. I mean, how can one feel fully comfortable at a resort knowing that a man named Tony the Melon is indeed the big cheese? Ah well, I'm half Ginsomanic and I guess I shouldn't snap on the culture. It's just that I hate an overabundance of polyester suits, "skeeve" large women in black dresses who Saran Wrap their couches, and hurl hairy chunks of pre-ingested nutrition at the slightest glance of a B-rated gangster film. Be that as it may, I shrugged the Mancini-induced aspersions off my ill begotten shoulders, and followed him into the locker area.

"There ya go, kid. It's in locker number thirty-seven. You got the combination?"

"Yeah. Thanks."

"Buck rented that locker years ago and has never been back.

Makes you wonder what's in there."

"Yeah, well it's healthy to have a couple of things to wonder about. See ya around, Bobbie," I said, in a voice designed to deliver a possibly undeserved, *"Hey, you're a real asshole, you know that?"* effect.

The guys were still exploring when I returned to the hotel, so I decided to open the box. Things were just as Buck had described. I counted the money and, after coming to the joyful conclusion that case contained fifty thousand and ("and" being the key word) two hundred dollars, I took my share, the two extra c-notes, and hid it under the bed.

The rest of the night went along in a fairly acceptable fashion. When the guys came back, I introduced the culturally deficient, Slurpee-sipping dudes to "real" pizza, showed them a few of the local hang outs, and then, just for the hell of it, we all went buzz bowling. (But don't worry, dads and MADDers of the world. We took a cab both to and from the establishment. I may be negative, cynical, sarcastic, and a bit hard to get along with, but I have no desire to be or cause a humanistic road kill.)

In any event, when we finally got back to the hotel, everyone, including The Amazing, *"At this moment, I can't help but feel tremendously confused, partly because the greater portion of humanity still insists on drinking eggless egg creams, but mostly because I can't understand the reason behind my being highly insominacable unless in a moving mode of transport,"* Me, was dead tired.

Most times this feeling could be rectified by swallowing six rather smug looking gold fish, dancing the dance of the yet-to-evolve Souwantorestuacs, and thereafter falling rather forcefully into one of the most stress-relieving, somewhat sleepy states known to man. Unfortunately, Pete had to go and be a huge pain in the ass and beg me, most pathetically, to describe the events of my package-producing meeting. He was quite insistent so we waited for the others to fall asleep and then headed to the Thru-way Diner for some plain tea with a side order of "not to be used" lemon.

For those of you who don't know (which, now that I think of it, is probably close to everyone) the Thru-way Diner is somewhat of a historic landmark in New Rochelle basically because it has been there so God(?) damn long and is conveniently open every hour of every day except New Year's. Sure it sounds good, but I used to live in the house right behind the damn thing, and personally, I think it sucks. The prices are too high. You could get better service at a do-it-yourself taco stand. And, to be quite honest, the pasta tastes like the chef stirred the sauce with his dick. In light of this, I wouldn't recommend the place. But you must understand my opinions may be biased because the incredibly good-looking hostess never accepted my sexual advances and they, well... they wouldn't give me a job.

"So, what's going on?" asked Pete, once we were seated, settled, and sipping tea.

"Well, I picked up the box and everything checked out, so guess the only thing I have left to do is send Buck the package and give the money to Tom."

"How much did you say it was again?"

"Fifty grand."

"Jesus Christ, I've never seen that much money in one place."

"Me neither."

"So, Tad, do you really think this is on the up and up?"

"Of course. You're making a big deal about nothing. I mean, when has anything exciting ever happened to me?"

"Well, maybe you're due?"

"Doubt it. But I'll tell you this much, I'm not doing anything until this is over. I'm not going to see my grandfather. I'm not going to tell the others. And I'm certainly not going to mail that package until after tomorrow night."

"Why?"

"I don't know, just a feeling."

"Hummmm," said Pete.

"Let's get out of here."

"Fine by me…. I'm going with you. You know that, right?" he asked as we stood. I knew he would. It was only a matter of time.

"Oh shit. You can't."

"Why not?"

"You just can't. Buck said I couldn't bring anyone."

"Why? No witnesses."

"Cute."

"Well, what do you expect? Do you really believe that this Thomas Torri character is going to come alone? Get real. I know I'm from the South and all, but Christ, I'm not that green."

"It'll be too complicated."

"It's a big car. All we have to do is get some blankets, I hide in the back seat and ba-da-bing, instant secret agent. What's so complicated?"

"Ba-da-bing, Pete?"

He smiled at his botched attempt to sound like a grease ball.

"Well, what if he finds you and attacks your balls with a battery-operated power sander?"

"He won't."

"But he could," I said.

"He won't."

"It's too chancy. I don't like it."

"Why, Tad, I never knew you cared."

"Oh screw you."

"What? What did I say?"

"Nothing," I said solemnly.

"You know," he said, "for someone who's supposed to think the world's an accident and tries to fly by the seat of his Monte, you're acting like a real chicken-shit. What gives?"

"What I do with my own life is my business. If my ideas are wrong I suffer. I can accept that, but I don't want to bear the responsibility for dragging you into the whole thing."

"You are so tremendously full of yourself. Aren't you? Do you actually believe you're the only person on the planet who can make decisions?

"Listen, I know you're real smart in a weird sort of way and that must be hard to handle.... Jeez, I can imagine how boring we must seem at times. But let me tell you something, being best friends with a couple of eccentric geniuses like you and Eric really isn't a day at the beach. So before you go off thinking that you rule the universe and everyone else is just a shit-head, remember that some of us shit-heads can be stubborn as hell and have a tendency to try to make sure our friends don't get their balls blown off by Italian psycho maniacs just because they feel like being righteously stupid assholes at the time."

"Would you like to breathe now?" I asked with a smile.

"Yes... yes I would."

We both laughed. Granted, a number of emotions could have relaxed in the catbird's seat at that moment, but we were trying to be men and, given the public setting, I don't think any other response would have been as appropriate.

I wanted to tell him that I was scared for him... and me, but the words wouldn't come. Good. Bad. Whatever happened it would be fine by me, if for only me. After all, I'm a frustrated kid, hopelessly trapped in The Do Nothing Generation. I just want to make sense of it all. I have no religion, strike that of the self-invented philosophy of Accidentalism. I subscribe to no cause other then the triumph of Idealism over Realism. And I don't care what the answers are as long as the topics are properly questioned.

I'm also terribly lost. Lost in much the same way as the children of the sixties, but I'm lost in solitude, while they had each other. But please don't misquote me on this one. I don't mean to say my problems are special, for all my classmates know the fear of inheriting the Earth. After all, it's a big responsibility for someone without a senior driver's license or a legal right to buy beer.

So what next? Will I wander aimlessly for the rest of my Earth life or will the answers that elude me formally introduce themselves during the upcoming exchange? Wow. I have been calling it an exchange, haven't I? How odd of me to do so. It should be called a drop-off, shouldn't it? I am to receive nothing. Or am I? Let's cut the shit and find out.

# CHAPTER 21

Mother Wind is a horribly lovely entity. She has the power to rip through your life, uprooting your existence and the agility to glide effortlessly across your face, roseing your cheeks with her tenderness.

Oddly enough, rather than concealing herself on this bleak occasion, she chose to unleash her fury and arrogantly display her power. She climbed, dropped, and rocketed for the stars. She steadied herself, waited, and then exploded against the hills. She soared, tumbled, and crashed through the trees. All this at stars and hills and trees that bore her no ill will.

The trees most of all, to attack them? What a ghastly thing to do. Hurling herself violently through branches whose leaves had neither the faculty nor experience to comprehend such intensity. What had these leaves done to deserve such misfortune? It was a wicked world. Yes, very wicked indeed.

Disgusted with nothing in particular and everything in general, I fastened a couple of buttons on my windbreaker and skeptically rejoiced in the current climate. Given the highly exaggerated state of Mother Wind's menstrual aggravation, I'm positive she would have much preferred to have been bone-chillingly frigid this day. Alas, it was summer. And given this cooperative time of the year, she could do no more than bury me in blustery atmosphere.

Somehow I sensed this naturalistic confrontation would be the least of my worries in upcoming moments, so I viciously revoked her right to attention acquisition and quickly showed her my psychological front door. She left. I unbuttoned my coat.

It was 11:35, precisely twenty-five minutes before the meeting. I was shitting a serious architectural phenomenon, but the fact that Pete was just a couple of yards and a quick yell away did wonders for my artistically inclined excretion system. Honestly, I was rather glad he had decided to tag along. The fact that he ultimately honored my decision to keep this between us wasn't so bad either.

Being habitually early was a genuine irritant and an official pain in the ass. However, I must admit, the experience was considerably less harmful than puffing away on one of those Eric-endorsed cancer utensils. Besides, the extra time allowed me to discover unique ways of looking at otherwise horribly boring visual stimuli. So, with boredom and several minutes of nothingness in hand, I decided to scan the pier and reflect upon times when my innocence remained.

I gazed outward, toward the Long Island Sound and took pride in the way the lights shimmered off the water. I had nothing to do with the playful dancing, but this was my town, damn it, so I took the pride anyway. The waves noticed my increasingly aroused inspection and being the hopelessly jealous, incredibly dependent fools they are, organized a meeting with the moon's upper management. After considerable memo writing concerning the acquiring and signing of certain official documents, they decided to put on a show of their own.

*They suspended all motion for a second or so,*
*took a deep breath in and then let go.*
*They rushed to the sides, both sides at once,*
*but faced with mortality, appeared the dunce.*
*They joined in the center, to search for a sign,*
*but after a moment or two, gave up on the rhyme....*

Feeling discouraged by their failure at poetry, the waves decided to divide themselves into two sections. A lower portion, which acted as the foundation for reason and reality, and the lighthearted upper area, which glided gracefully along the boundaries of insanity. I must admit, I was rather impressed by the overall effort. However, once I noticed a certain enlargement in a portion of the sea's anatomy closely resembling its cranium, I firmly chose to ignore the hell out of it. This was not due to the scumbag factor mind you. It's just that I hate a show-off.

Nevertheless, a few more moments slid by, and I used these convenient bits of eternity to examine the rocky cliff upon which I was standing. (I realize this may seem odd to note here, but strangely enough, there was absolutely no fence separating the above-mentioned, fishing pier and the highly depressed, play-producing sea below. This strikes a strange note only because Glen Island Park was often inhabited by grossly unintelligent children, who could easily make their way from the not-too-distant swing set to the horribly neglected cliff of doom. These same children could potentially cast themselves over edge in a futile attempt at curiosity stimulation. Perhaps I should bring this up at the next city council meeting.)

I had ten minutes left to feel safe about my existence, but being the horrendously ignorant human I am, I used this fleeing bit of the millennium to question the availability of security.

"Pete!" I yelled in a stage whisper.

"What? What's the matter?"

"Nothing, I just wanted to make sure you could hear me. That's all."

"Christ, you scared the shit out of me."

"Sorry, dude."

After letting out respective sighs and taking in a nice, New Age, cleansing breath, Pete retreated into the bushes. A moment later I heard a slight gagging noise, but I just figured the stupid son-of-a-bitch forgot to exhale again. He was always forgetting the simple things.

In any case, after I had checked his presence for the third time, something interesting happened. I saw a light. A single roving light, cautiously gravitating toward me. It bounced and weaved along the way, surveying the area as it went.

Shit, I thought. I can't believe he came alone. Granted, he's ten minutes late and that really pisses me off, but at least I'm not going to get the crap beat, bashed, and otherwise shot out of me by a group of highly annoyed, psychopathically inclined maniacs.

Yes, yes, Tad, continued the thought, it's much better to be beat, bashed, and otherwise shot by only one highly annoyed, psychopathically inclined maniac. You see, I don't know what you are getting all worried about. You have it easy, my boy.

Somehow the thought neglected to fill the confidence void

currently running amok in the lower-left-hand quadrant of my stomach. Things got worse when Thomas Torri spoke.

"You the kid?"

No, dick-weed, I thought. I'm Fred the ice cream man. I just enjoy disrupting various criminal events by hanging around deserted piers, idly fondling my left testicle, and obnoxiously vocalizing my thoughts on how to ban that stupid-ass ice cream truck music. It can become really annoying if you listen long enough.

"Yeah, that's me," I said, trying to conceal my nervousness.

"You got the stuff?"

"You mean the money?"

"No, wise-ass I mean the beef and broccoli I ordered. Come on, let's have it."

I could see this wasn't going to be as pleasant as I had initially visualized. Well, what could one expect from a pathetic, *"sold out your best friend for a slice of stupidburbia,"* piece-of-shit-loser like him?

Yeah, he was a real schmuck, funny looking too. I mean he wasn't what you'd expect in a criminal. He was thin—well, frail actually—and incredibly pale. Hell, given a can of spinach and a brief moment of self-actualization, I could have probably kicked his ass. Unfortunately, the undeniable presence of a rather healthy looking .38 revolver invited, asked, and eventually ordered me to stop daydreaming, become one with my wimpiness, and basically shut the hell up.

The silence disturbed him. The disturbance sought comfort by cocking the gun. And I, well, I froze, defrosted, and tried to hand him the case.

"No, no, no, just drop it."

I did as he commanded.

"Now open it."

I did that too and he looked pleased. Yes, he looked incredibly pleased for a moment or so. But then, just one state-altering second later, he was much too busy looking dead to concern himself with looking pleased.

"Holy shit!" said Pete. "Jesus Christ! Tad... are you all right?"

"Yeah?" That was all I could manage to say.

"Where did it come from?"

The "it" here, folks, was a single, deadly shot fired from an unknown source. The direction, the motive, and even the sound were masked. Torri was dead. I was stunned. And confusion reigned proudly and politely thanked Andy Warhol for the fifteen minutes.

"So be it." At least that's what some of the more accepting would say. "Torri was evil and this was his destiny. Life goes on, kid. It can hand you roses or thorns, diamonds or coal, life or death. No one really cares which. Just accept it. Random evolution cloaked as some creator's predestination was how this place was designed. Don't question it. That's just the way it is."

Funny the masses would give such a speech at this moment. In a world infested with inconsistencies and irregularities, the one thing that keeps it all flowing along so seemingly smoothly is the presence of the scapegoat, change. This little word bears the brunt of every universal screw-up. "Things change, people change, life is like a party, but the party has to end." What a bunch of horseshit! Blind acceptance is the surest road to insanity. Question it. Challenge it. Confront your problems like a person you wish to be. Rise up. Stand tall. And if they try to steal your child's eyes, bite their heads off, chew twenty times in a dainty-like fashion, and then, if you're still feeling violated, spit the heaping wad down their pathetic necks and laugh like a maniac. Then, as they lie there waiting to die, calmly ask them if shit just happens, or if the world is actually worth an explanation. I bet you get a different answer.

In any event, armed with a certain amount of pissed-off agitation, I turned to meet the murderer. Surprisingly enough, a sole gunman standing approximately fifty yards away had carried out the extermination. Alone, deprived of both witness and conscience, he stole the shadows from the underworld and shrouded himself in darkness, ambiguity and lies. He was cold and, although I couldn't see his face, I knew he was a man accustomed to such atrocities.

"Let's go!" said Pete, who had recently recovered from the shock that had so unthoughtfully accosted his speaking faculties.

A part of me wanted to stay and extract an explanation for such horror, but a second shot, the decreasing distance, and a certain uninvited bowel movement forced me to take refuge. I grabbed the case, ran, tripped, misplaced my darkness, met the eyes of a killer, regained my vertical alignment, forgot I was Caucasian, and sped down the road.

Minutes moved like endless days and breaths came but once per hour. Time was lost, reality reversed itself, and God(?) turned in His deity license for something in a soft shade of blue.

On and on we ran, feet pounding, heads spinning, society mocking our wardrobes. We were going nowhere in particular, but were determined to get there fast. We ended up at College of New Rochelle's fitness center. We sat on the top of the gymnasium steps chest heaving, lungs burning, almost expecting to expire. It hadn't been a tremendous evening, not in the least. When we regained control of our breathing apparatus, we scanned the adjoining street but saw no sign of the killer.

"I think we lost him," I said hopefully.

"Oh shit, man, I don't know. He didn't see you, right? You know, when you fell, he didn't see you, did he?"

I couldn't lie.

"Oh my God. What are we gonna do?"

"Nothing."

"What do you mean, nothing? We have to go to the police."

"And what, Pete, say something like, 'Well, you see, officer, I know Torri is your boss and all. But the truth is that, while I was paying him blackmail money for this pizza guy in Florida, some dude came out of nowhere and shot him in the face with a hand cannon.' Come on now, think about it."

"Well, we can't just do nothing."

"Why? People do it all the time."

"What's wrong with you?"

"What, are you kidding? I've just been shot at, I watched some guy's brains blast out the side of his skull, and to top it all off, I just ran six blocks with a serious load in my shorts."

"You too, huh? I don't know how babies can stand it."

He laughed. It was nice to hear laughter if only for a moment.

"Who would want to kill Torri?" asked Pete.

"Got me. Maybe someone else he was blackmailing."

"But Jesus, the guy's a police captain. Whoever did this has some serious balls."

"Dude, I say we forget about this whole Hardy Boys thing and focus on getting away from the killer."

"But we don't even know who he is."

I hesitated.

"Right?" asked Pete.

"I've seen him before."

"Great! All you have to do is remember and we can..."

Pete's voice was amputated as a half dozen police-cars came

tearing through the neighborhood. Sirens blared, horribly antisocial searchlights destroyed the concept of residential privacy, and chaos replaced fear in the above-mentioned catbird's seat. Interestingly enough, time, being devoid of all tact and good nature, carelessly chose this moment to test its magic wand. Fortunately for us he was out of practice and, an abracadabra later, we were in the hotel sleeping like a couple of children.

# CHAPTER 22

I awoke expecting to find a slaughtered animal lying next to me. To my surprise, however, the only noticeable irregularities were that I was sleeping in a pond of perspiration complete with lush vegetation and a frog named George; and secondly, I had an overwhelming desire to skip my Morning Philosophication.

I showered, changed, and noticed two things: the silence, because it was present, and the time, for it was mid-afternoon. I tried to disregard them, however my curiosity soon stirred, awoke, and kicked me firmly in the ass.

"Excuse me, young man," said the above-mentioned curiosity, "but given last night's events, and your overall position on luck's shit list, I just thought you might want to know where everybody is, and why they are being so quiet."

I hate it when curiosity calls me "young man," but I listened anyway. I stumbled into the adjoining room and found the group huddled around the TV looking terribly concerned.

"What's going on?"

They were frightened to be sure and seemed somehow older. For a moment I thought it was an illusion. Yes, a nightmare of sorts prepared by the Zukes. But this was much more vivid, much more real.

Jackie forgot herself and began to cry. Dawn attempted to steady her, but was swept into the hysteria. Eric went against all his predictable personalities by taking charge of his own emotions and escorting the girls to another room.

"Tad, look at this news report," said Darien, as my attention directed itself to the television. "It's been on every fifteen minutes."

I looked accusingly at Pete, but he issued a glance that ultimately explained his actions. They had to know. It was unavoidable.

"Here it is again!" said Darien. "Watch this."

*"... police are on high alert after the fatal shooting of New York City Police Captain, Thomas Torri.*

*"Torri was allegedly shot and tossed into the Sound around 1:00 a.m. this morning by reputed Mafia boss, Vito Devito at the Glen Island Pier in New Rochelle. Devito was spotted at the scene shortly after police arrived, but managed to evade capture.*

*"Police have not commented as to a potential motive or what Torri may have been doing at the pier. However, Police Commissioner Frank Demarco assured Channel 6 News that a full investigation would begin immediately, as will the search for Devito.*

*"Torri's former partner, retired Police Sergeant Buck Johnson, was head of the Devito investigation six years ago. It's no secret that Johnson and*

*Devito were long-time enemies, but any connection between their relationship and the shooting death of Torri is only speculative at this point.*

*"Thomas Torri was a well-respected leader of the department and there will be a memorial service...."*

"What happened last night?" asked Darien, as he lowered the volume.

"You know God(?) damn well what happened. Somebody killed Torri."

"But why, Tad?" asked Pete. "I don't get it."

"How should I know?"

"But it doesn't make sense," said Darien. "If that Mafia guy wanted Torri dead why didn't he hire some goon to do it? Naw, there's something weird here."

"Yeah, and don't you think this whole thing is a little too coincidental? I mean Devito deciding to go after Torri on the same night you were to meet him. I don't buy it."

"He's right, Tad," said Darien. "This must have been personal. Something only the two of them could have known about."

"What? Vito didn't know about shit. And as far as Torri goes, he couldn't have been expecting anybody to show up. The meeting was...."

"Holy shit, Tad!" said Pete. "Are you thinking what I'm thinking?"

"What are you guys talking about?" asked Darien.

"That son-of-a-bitch. I never would have guessed."

"Guessed what?" asked Darien.

"That Buck would try to have me killed."

"What?"

"It's simple. So God(?) damn simple. Buck set up the meeting for me. He was the only person who knew where Torri was gonna be last night."

"So?"

"So, Darien," said Pete, "he told Vito about the meeting."

"But why?"

"Yeah, Pete, Darien's got a point. What would he say? 'Hey, Vito, it's Buck, you know, the guy that spent half his life trying to put you behind bars. Well, I got a problem. It seems my old partner is blackmailing me and I thought you might want to take care of him. How about it, Vito old boy?' It just doesn't make sense."

"Maybe he lied to him too. I don't know."

"Well look," said Darien, "Buck is definitely involved in this, right?"

"Seems that way, " I mumbled.

"Assuming yes, then all we have to do is figure out what he could have said to get the two of them together. I'm sure whatever it was, it had something to do with you and that box."

"But why would Vito care about fifty grand?" asked Pete. "He's got more money than a Televangelist."

"Well, maybe he thought something else was in the case," said Darien.

"That's it!" I said. "They were both there to retrieve something, but neither expected the other."

"What are you talking about?" asked Darien.

"I think Buck was the mastermind here. Yeah, he was the blackmailer, not the one being blackmailed."

"How do you mean?" asked Pete.

"Well, suppose that during Buck's investigation of Devito he stumbled upon evidence that could hurt him or his crew. But instead of going through with the arrest, he used the info to secure his golden years.

"Yeah, maybe Buck blackmailed Devito, then somehow Torri got wind of the situation. Seeing as how Buck was up for retirement, I bet Torri figured it would be a perfect time to grab a piece of the action, maybe even assume the role himself."

"And?" asked Darien.

"And when things got out of control, Buck decided to let his problems take care of each other. He told Devito that he was sending up some expendable kid with the evidence and that his blackmailing days were over. Then he told Torri that I would be coming up with his share of the take."

"But he couldn't have known what was gonna happen," said Pete.

"Why would he care? It's a win-win. If Vito dies, Torri is left holding his dick. If Thomas bites it, Vito suspects him and me, and gets totally screwed with the law."

"But what if nothing happened?" asked Darien.

"Then everything happens. Torri's got to deal with Devito putting a price on his head, not to mention having to explain the situation to Internal Affairs after Devito leaked word of the meeting. And Vito shits a brick worrying about how many other people know about his little problem. As far as he knows, I could start blackmailing him. You see, no matter what happens, Buck is in the clear."

"So you think his 'poor pitiful me' story is a bunch of bullshit?" asked Darien.

"Yeah. That's exactly what I think. The bastard lied to everybody. Probably grinned himself blind the day he saw a New York reference on my job application."

"Guys, that whole theory is anorexic at best," said Pete.

"But it makes sense, right? Besides, we've got nothing else to believe."

"So what are we gonna do?" asked Darien.

"Well, you're not gonna do anything. I want you, Pete, and Eric to take the girls back to Florida."

"Hell no!" said Pete. "I was there with ya and I can't be sure he didn't see me too. I'm staying."

Since arguing with Pete was as about as productive as a one-legged field goal kicker with a bum knee, I acquiesced. In all honesty, I was glad he pushed the issue. Everybody needs a friend like him.

As for the others, I asked Darien to be a sport and take them home. If we were gonna do anything, it would have to be tonight, and I didn't want them around when the fit hit the shan. Darien dutifully objected a few times, then relented, wished me luck, and drove the group home in my rent-a-shitbox.

I admired him for a moment. It was the first time I ever really did that. You know, maybe his ideals weren't the same as mine, but he really knew how to take care of his own. He was the kind of guy who would always be there for you. Granted, you may not always want him around, but he knew that too, and it didn't really bother him much. He was wise, knowing, and forthright. I pictured him as a father. Yes, a father or a sheepdog. It doesn't really matter which.

Pete and I sat around for a while in silence. But then, our stomachs, who, by the way, were getting increasingly sick of all this running away from crazy killers, decided to protest the hell out of the above-mentioned silence, and grumble like a couple of Inter-Stupidic Grumbleosiphers from the infamous planet of Maniwanaburgernite.

Sensing the overwhelming pangs of malnutrition emanating from the deepest depths of our, *"No really, guys, I don't need any food or anything. That's just my new acordian-banjo-mabob. How do you like it?"* sarcastic storage sack, we ordered an incredibly disgusting, makes-you-want-to-projectile-vomit-through-your-nose, nasty-ass pizza, complete with mushrooms, toejam, and slimy, green refrigerator fungus. The toejam is tolerable, but I considerably hate mushrooms.

Anyway, we spent the remainder of the afternoon scarfing pizza, slurpily sipping some slightly stale Diet Pepsi, and basically devising a most deviously cool plan to facilitate Devito destruction.

# CHAPTER 23

When things are bleak; when you've got a major psycho mobster maniac trying to kill you; when life decides it would be loads of fun to drop kick you rather harshly in the balls, it's a brave man who can sit back with his best friend and lay pizza farts.

Pete and I finished the entire previously described, non-nutritional, sacrilegious substance in a record-shattering five minutes and were currently recovering by violently exporting a kaleidoscope of hazardous pizza-produced contaminants from every available human portal. So there we sat, burping, sneezing, and farting with a considerable amount of smoke pouring out of our ears, while desperately trying to come to terms with our position in life. It didn't look too tremendously good. Our position, or our bodies.

Nevertheless, we had a job to do. So with the sudden realization that we were a couple of amazingly enterprising young men, we came to the conclusions that we needed a plan, I needed a hair cut, and Pete—well, Pete really needed to take a course in social dynamics. Needless to say, only one of those conclusions concerned us at the moment, so with haste in hand, we attacked the problem.

"All right," said Pete, "let's review our position."

"Sure, we're screwed."

"Seriously."

"I am serious. Pete, we've been over this a hundred times. We have fifty grand, a priceless doll, and an unavoidable date with destiny. We're gonna have to meet with Vito."

"That's suicide."

"Look, dude, you don't have to go, but it's something that has to be done."

"Why? We don't even have anything to give him!"

"Doesn't matter."

"What do you mean, it doesn't matter? I bet it'll matter the hell out of Devito. When he finds out he's been tricked by a couple of kids, we're gonna be dead. There's no way we can win. There's just no way."

"Look, I'm not talking about wining or losing. We're way past that. I'm talking about doing the right thing. When people focused on that trust was still alive."

"Oh bullshit, Tad! Things were always screwed up and every day they get worse 'cause people keep selling out. Wasn't that the whole point of this vacation, to notice the path of destruction and to make sure we went the road less traveled?"

"Yeah"

"So, what can we do? Life is a pain in the ass. If you want to change the world, you have to work on yourself. Anything else is a waste of time.

"Look, Tad, I know it might be hard for you to accept, but you can't change things. Vito is going to prison. Torri is dead. And Buck got away with the goods. That's all she wrote, my friend. Going to see him now will get you nothing but dead."

"Remember that bully in freshman year?"

"Jesus Christ," said Pete, sighing into submission. "What does that have to do with anything?"

"Do you remember how he beat on Eric? That was the year he really got quiet, wasn't it? Strange that I never made the connection.

"Of course, I can't be sure. I had just moved to the area. But he sure seemed to change within the first few months of our friendship. Didn't he? Yeah, I guess living in the shadows will do that to a guy."

"You don't know the whole story, Tad."

"Yeah, well maybe Eric will tell me sometime, but until then, there's one thing I do know. Both stories look the same. And I don't like either ending."

"So what are you saying?"

"Simple, if we don't do something about this guy now, then we'll have to deal with him for the rest of our lives. Maybe it won't be physically, but we'll pay the price. Check your eyes if you don't believe me, 'cause faked innocence is worse than none at all."

Pete swallowed and averted my glance. I took note and pushed onward.

"You see, Eric was lucky in that he had friends who could help him fight the bully. We don't have that option. Nobody's on our side this time and nobody's gonna help us. Guys like

Devito don't forget and to be honest, I can't live in doubt."

"What are you talking about?"

"Just that I might want to look someone in the eyes someday and try to convince her that I'm an okay guy. But I'll never be able to do that until I know what I'm all about."

"Come on, man. You know yourself. Heck, you know most people better than they know themselves. You have always had a way of getting inside people's hearts. They trust you enough to disclose themselves without the fear of being betrayed, laughed at, or judged. I've always admired that intuition. These days, it's something the world really needs."

I flipped the pizza box open and closed a few times, considering the compliment.

"Yeah, well, most times it's hard to believe the good things people say. Let's face it, Accidentalism is a cool philosophy for The Do Nothing Generation, but does it really work, or am I just a stubborn kid who refuses to wake up and smell reality?"

"What brought this on? You never doubt your ideas."

"Don't be so sure."

"Well, what is it then?"

"Just something Buck said. Something about a choice I would make that would change everything."

"And you're letting that asshole affect you?"

"Jeez(?), I don't...."

"Shut up, will ya? Everything will turn out all right. And if it doesn't, who cares? It's all accidents."

Pete rose from his place on the sofa and began pacing. He stopped suddenly, as if he had just noticed something that had been staring him in the face for years.

"Look, you were always talking about how you can't trust anybody. Not parents, not teachers, not even a God, right? Well, let me tell you something, dude, no matter what happens tonight, I'm in, okay? You can trust me, if for nothing else, 'cause I have to trust you.

"I never thought I'd say this, Tad, but that theory of yours is true. The only thing worth accomplishing in this world is getting to the finish line with the same exuberance as when you started the race. Nothing means nothing and everything deserves all you can give it. That's the plan, isn't it? That's the wonderfully terrific plan you've somehow managed to imagine. And now you have to balls to question that too! Well don't, just don't.

"Jesus, who would have thought a couple of assholes like us would figure out the meaning of life? Let me explain it to them, Tad, and then you tell me if I missed the plot."

He turned from me, grabbed an imaginary microphone, and faced an audience that wasn't there.

"Listen, book readers of the universe. The secret of keeping your child's eyes, the secret of getting through this horribly wonderful life is to focus the journey. And it doesn't matter which road you take or who you choose as traveling companions. And it sure as hell doesn't matter what kind of car you drive, or what outfits you wear along the way. It's so much more than that could ever be."

He spiked the microphone and began to do a victory dance. I smiled, watching the fool I was privileged to know. But he stopped suddenly and offered a disturbed look.

"I missed something, didn't I?" he asked.

"You figured out what was wrong, Pete, but failed to offer insight as to what is right. That's always the tougher question."

"Well, then what the hell matters?" he asked, obviously disappointed in the premature celebration.

"Nothing," I said. "Absolutely nothing matters. That's the

point. You don't know anything but what other people tell you, and sadly, you can't even be sure of that because you don't know who told them. It's all a game. Don't you see? A big, ridiculous, never-ending game."

"And what, we're supposed to be the players?" he asked.

"No, we're the creators. That's what's so tremendously sad. In our brief moment here we can make anything we dream, but most people don't see it."

"You've lost me again."

"Look, when you're a kid, you want to do and be everything. Nothing is impossible for you because no one told you what impossible means. That's why all babies are beautiful. Greatness is our first impulse. It's natural, built right in!

"But then, at the most malleable moments of our lives, we're beaten down by the failures and influenced by the fears and regrets of others. We're told "No!" a thousand times and soon we associate it to everything. Failure is a cycle, Pete, and we're here to break it."

"But why us?"

"Why the hell not? Life is an amazingly stupid accident and everything that happens is an amazingly stupid result of that accident. So, what I propose is that humanity take the accidental ball back at half-time, line up in a pissed-off formation, and win the thing in the fourth quarter.

"If we can return to the happiness, vibrancy, and unyielding determination of youth by the time we are ready to croak, then perhaps we can change the course of human thinking and leave our kids something decent to follow. We can leave them a path to greatness. That's the road to follow. That's the ultimate journey."

"So what can we do?"

"We've got to play the game out, no matter what."
"Call Vito?"
"Call Vito."
"Shit... all right."

I'm not sure if we discovered the meaning of life, but it seemed to make sense at the time. It was an honest attempt at understanding and I stand by the search. Still, if our spiritual pilgrimage offends your religion and you wish to crucify me for such blasphemy, so be it. Casting stones is a popular pastime.

# CHAPTER 24

I had no idea whether I was doing the right thing or not, but I felt it was important to do something. And seeing how making a phone call to a psycho mobster ranked high in the something category, I figured it couldn't hurt to screw around a little.

It rang. He answered. I was surprised that he answered personally.

"Devito?"

"Yes."

"I want to make a deal."

"Who is this?"

"The kid."

"The kid from last night?"

"Yeah."

"You got some balls callin' me, you know that?"

"Yeah."

"So what's this deal you're talking about?"

"Buck told me the whole story. Well, almost."

"I'm listening."

"He told me how he was making a living from watching you squirm, and how it felt a hundred times better to beat you at your own game than to put you away," I lied, guessed, and hoped at the same time.

"So what is this, a fucking history lesson? I'm a busy man."

"Yeah, I know. Making license plates is time consuming."

"Watch it, kid."

"Shut up, dick-brain," I said. (What the hell, my gamble worked, so why not uncross my fingers and make him feel like a turd in the process? I mean, really now, to quote some slightly famous dude, "You can't fall off the floor.")

He grunted at my bravado, so I continued.

"Personally, I think you're a scumbag, but, lucky for you, I'm more concerned with screwing Buck than making your life miserable. So let's just lay our cards on the table before we go any further, okay?"

He cursed. I laughed. This was becoming quite fun actually.

"First of all, I know how monumentally screwed you are, but it just so happens that you and I have the same goal. You want Buck for blackmailing you, and I want him for getting me involved."

"So what do you want?"

"Another one of those Mafioso meetings."

"When?"

"Tonight. Same place and time. Meet me and I'll give you Buck's address, the evidence, and a big bag of Cheese Doodles."

"No good."

"What do you mean, 'no good'? You don't like Cheese Doodles?"

"You're crazy, kid. The cops got the place taped off."

"It's a big pier. We'll just meet on the Southern end."

"Bullshit. You'd have to be a friggin' maniac to talk with this much balls. Good luck with the trace. Tell the cops I said 'hi'. You're a lousy actor, kid."

"And you're a friggin' chicken shit. Forget it. I'll just testify. Later, asshole."

"No, wait, wait, wait," he said. "I'll meet you there, but this stuff about Buck's address is a crock. The son-of-a-bitch is a million miles away by now. I need something better."

"Picky, picky. All right, dude. I'm feeling charitable. You see, when he sent me up here, I had no idea you were involved. I mean don't get me wrong, Buck was always telling me how much of a loser you were and all, but my mission had nothing to do with you. My job was solely to deliver the money to Torri."

"No shit, Sherlock, I figured that out already."

"Yeah, but what you haven't figured out is that I was supposed to mail Buck one of those stupid-ass dolls he had in the locker."

"So?"

"So, I'm going to sell it and keep the cash, you spaghetti slopper. But I can give you his post office box. You know, the place he's gonna have to go to pick it up. And believe me, that greedy bastard will check every day until it arrives."

"Smart kid. I suppose you want a million for all this, right?"

"Two million actually."

"What?"

"Hey, times are tough, man. A loaf of bread costs two bucks."

"Fine. That's peanuts compared to what the greedy friend of yours was taking me for."

"I'm a simple man, Vito. That's all I'll ever need."

"Good. But this shit better check out, or you'll be one dead asshole."

Click.

Pete and I did a crazy, backwards, jump-up-in-the-air, left-handed high five; cursed at the pathetically appearing individual with the overly redundant name; and laughed in the general direction of fearful ones everywhere. The only thing we had to do now was invent some evidence, kick back, and party.

The day expired quickly, and by the time we were ready to leave for Glen Island, the world seemed a righteous place to be. Mother Wind was behaving herself, all animated creatures seemed momentarily occupied with other things, and the birds, after crapping rather nastily on my jacket, accepted my apology for instigating the Eric-produced, song-like catastrophe, and unanimously decided to start liking me again.

Yes, everything seemed wonderful until we entered the darkness of the pier. The previous night's sin had obliterated all matter and left in its place something, or rather nothing... exactly nothing like I had ever seen.

It was emptiness, complete Nothingness. It left me numb. Even the powerful silence would not show itself in such a place. It was void, distorted, and incomprehensible. And yet, surprisingly, it wasn't cold. This bit of good fortune was not formed out of kindness, I suspect, but rather out of a complete and utter sense of futility, apathy. Cold would be something and Nothings really don't go for that sort of thing.

The tide took note of this strangeness and carefully removed itself from the Sound's chamber, exposing the jagged rocks below. The rocks themselves thought about vacating the premises out of respect for the Nothingness, but quickly realized they were without the ability to formulate thoughts, much less movement. Felling a bit left out, the rocks got incredibly depressed and went to sleep.

Yes, the moment was an abyss where feelings and emotions lay restfully in catatonic stun spells, where time transformed into a frightened puppy, and where thought itself completely lost its mind. I tried desperately to reflect on something beautiful, but only the Nothing came to mind. She owned it and controlled it. This moment I belonged to her.

She stood seductively at a worn-out jukebox, carelessly flipping through the songs of the 70s. I tried to tell her that any selection would do, but in the Nothingness, words are but a useless effort, a memory. She selected one, or so it seemed, but I noticed not the melody. She sashayed across my schemata, casually exposing her private parts to my brain. She was enchanting. She danced, moved, and stole my imagination. I thought only of her. She seduced me, caressed me, and held me in her arms. I was falling for her and I knew it.

"Tad!" said Pete.

The spell was broken and she was gone. Pete's Something scared her away. The lying little bitch, she never even bothered to exist at all. How could she love that way? Impossible. Fraudulent. My friend had saved this fool again.

"Yeah?" I said, lifting my sunken heart.

"Nothing. You did it last night. I just didn't want to break tradition."

"A two-day tradition?"

"Why not? Besides, a little superstition couldn't hurt."

"Then perhaps I should say, 'What? What's the matter? You scared the shit out of me.' Right?"

"Perhaps you should, but not now. It's getting close to that time."

"Right."

"By the way, fellas, how was she?"

"Who?" I asked of a voice yet revealed.

"The Nothingness. She'll screw your brains out, but she won't respect you in the morning."

"Vito?" I asked, wondering if my romantic entanglements with the Nothing had somehow lost their luster. Maybe she was a whore.

"Who were you expecting, Tony Bennett?"

"How long have you been standing there?"

"Ah... long enough to know that I'm gonna have to use two of these bullets. Now, get over here, the both of ya."

Needless to say, the man was huge. He had muscles on his eyebrows, horrible scars in every available location, and an expression that stated, quite matter of factly, that he would rather enjoy us trying something funny.

"I tell ya, it's gonna be a shame killing a kid like you. You got some set of co-ho-nies."

"Hey, Vito, pal, bud, friend-o-mine, there's no need to kill us. We're just a couple of stupid kids who got caught in the middle of something by complete accident. I'm sure a man of your intelligence can understand that...."

"What, you calling me stupid? I'm not stupid. You calling me stupid?"

"No, no, no, Vito, You don't understand what Tad means, basically...."

"So you're saying I'm stupid too? Don't tell me I don't understand what I know I understand. And don't call me stupid."

"No one's calling you stupid, Vito, honestly, you're an amazing moron."

"Bam!" said the end of his gun as it struck me most forcefully on the skull.

It hurt. Pete winced. I fell. Vito laughed.

The experience itself didn't do too much for my modeling career, my overly exaggerated nose, or my outlook on the universe. It did, however, provide me with a unique view of the pier and a remarkable idea. I played dead for a few moments so I could think the whole thing through. To be quite honest, I needed the rest. After all, my nose was killing me.

"Now, shit-head, ah... your name is shit-head, isn't it? Seeing how your friend is... ah, occupied, why don't you be a good boy and give me what I need?"

"Where's the money?" asked Pete.

"Bam!"

A second later Pete was lying alive, but hopelessly unconscious, next to me. This whole affair was becoming quite monotonous in my opinion, so I struggled to my feet.

"Oh, the cocky one is up. How fortunate."

"Did you have a rough childhood?" (What the hell, with death so presumably close, I saw no reason to become a chicken-shit now.)

"Save the wisecracks, tough guy. Where's the evidence?"

"I'm gonna level with ya, Vito. I can't hand it over until I see the money."

"There is no money, you idiot. Do you see a briefcase anywhere, cause I sure as hell don't."

"You mean to tell me that I came all the way out here and you didn't even have the decency to bring the money? That really sucks, you know? I mean it's not like you had to let me keep it or anything. It figures. I finally have a cool experience and some stupid-ass guido has to screw it up. You know, I wouldn't have even minded if you brought fake money. Man, you're really heartless."

"Kid, I think I hurt you with that bash to the brain. Do you have any idea what's going to happen to you tonight?"

"Yeah, sure, you're going to try to kill me."

"What do you mean, *try*?"

"Just toss the gun over the ledge."

"What?"

"You heard me asshole. If you want the evidence you're gonna have to fight me for it."

"Yeah, well maybe I'll just shoot you and get it from your friend."

"Go ahead," I said, pulling an envelope from my back pocket. "This is only a taste of what I got on you. And my friend here doesn't know where it is. Besides, even if he did, it's too late. Looks like you killed him."

He just stood there dumbfounded for a moment or so. Then, to my utter surprise, he looked around as if another option would walk up and introduce itself. When it didn't, he shrugged rather stupidly, and tossed his gun.

"You're nuts, kid. I was gonna kill you quick. Now, it's gonna be painful."

He had experience, four inches, and about eighty pounds on me. But I was youthful, not entirely out of shape, and incredibly pissed off. He charged me, taunting, waving his arms. He was cocky. I hoped that would benefit me. It didn't. He jabbed, lunged, and sidestepped. He was beyond my training. I moved, glided, and used my speed. I danced, ducked, and tried to remember. I punched, missed, slid, and barely recovered. I was buying time. We measured each other for a moment or so, neither hurrying, both savoring the moment.

Bam! The first connection was his. Short, quick, and hard, to the face. He drew blood, and yet I stood. That impressed him. But impressing him was furthest from my mind. He connected again, several times actually. To the stomach, to the face, the stomach again. I lost my mind, my sight, and my wind. The Nothingness returned. Clouded, dizzy, my stability fading. Lost, confused, shrouded in spinning darkness. I stumbled into blow after blow, but counting the wounds became mundane so I struck back, blindly... to the groin.

I wasn't proud of the blow, but it huddled him stopping his attack. My senses were aflame, my faculties were still betraying me, and I had no recollection of the world from which I had come. I forgot the rules. Jesus(?), if it's possible, for a moment, I forgot the game.

I felt strange for a second, not hurt or in shock, just incredibly strange. Then, suddenly, the strangeness transformed itself into a remarkably focused rage. I immediately became aware of what was happening. The single emotion, I was experiencing it, and it was mindboggeling.

I assaulted the killer with blows and kicks foreign in velocity and magnitude. They were punishing, crippling, not my own. They were silencing, menacing, completely unstoppable. I lost control.

The emotion took over my mind and guided my body without acquiring the proper licensing. Things became increasingly difficult to handle. The little people from the Bee-ben-bobble playing planet decided to have a picnic on my left shoulder. The horribly insignificant, Earth-dreaming nerd from Sleepamabob 72 came dangerously close to actually waking up. And yogurt salesmen all over the world came to the conclusion that they could no longer take advantage of the horrendously stupid population by repeatedly convincing them that rotten bacteria was actually worth paying for.

My world was weirding out. Vito was being destroyed. And me? Well, I successfully recovered my senses, saw the effects of the singular emotion, came to terms with the ongoings of this predicament, and then consciously, without reasonable alibi or expected hesitation, kicked the poor bastard off the pier. He died instantly.

I didn't have to turn around to know that Pete had witnessed the whole encounter. With the single emotion upon me, my senses were beyond such trivial actions. I just knew.

"No matter what?" I asked.

"No matter what."

# CHAPTER 25

I found trust that night—trust, honesty, and the simple the truth of things. After all my searching, I finally felt it. Strange, but I never expected the answer to be so close to home.

We went back to the hotel with the intention of washing up and getting out of there, but I was still dizzy from the fight, so we spent the night. Pete rested, recovered, and tried not to think. I tossed, turned, and walked to the door.

The early morning air seemed to cover it all: the feelings, the deed, the memory itself. But it was just an illusion, a careless illusion that mocked the senses and assaulted the imagination with frivolous counterfeits. The deed existed. If not in the real world, then at least in my mind's eye, in all our eyes. That was something I knew for sure.

I looked at Buck's doll. She was beautiful. Funny it took me so long to say so, but she was... beautiful, innocent, a perfectly detailed replication of a child. But her eyes were black, barren, and tainted with the cycle of humanity. The realization crushed me. My hand went limp. She fell, crashed, died a thousand times, and exposed the cancerous note that stole her sight.

*Hey kid,*

*If you're reading this you're better at the spy stuff than I thought. I'm sorry I had to use you, but there was no other way. Ironic, isn't it? You were the only person I could trust enough to lie to. Sure is a funny world.*

*You killed one of them, didn't you? I figured you would find your honesty that way. Lord knows it wasn't going to be through me. I'm sorry for that, really. I would have enjoyed being able to give you that gift. But I was too far gone.*

*Well, I guess you know the story. I used the evidence I found against Vito to make a killing. It really wasn't that complicated until Torri came along. That's when I thought of you. Ah, but what am I telling you for? You know the deal. You always did.*

*Congratulations. Your future has been stolen. You're one of us now. A realist. Remember when I said that someday you'd be faced with a choice, so clear, so obvious, so tremendously tempting, that you would just have to go for it? Well, here it is, buddy boy. There's a million bucks at the pizza shop. You know, where I kept the dolls. It's yours, kid, for a job well done.*

*Now don't worry about old Buck. I've got plenty to last an old fart like me. Nine years of blackmail can produce quite a sum. You see, I told ya, everybody sacrifices their idealism one day. That's just how it is. The dice are loaded, the cards are stacked, and everybody loses in the end. It's unavoidable. Face it, kid, there are no Peter Pans."*

*Good Luck,*
*Buck*

I cried that night. I could have thought, formulated, debated, or argued, but I simply cried instead. I never figured out exactly why.

# EPILOGUE

It was raining and I was thirty. Man, another birthday. I never thought I'd actually make it this far. I went sleepless again, but to tell you the truth, I really didn't mind anymore. They had become quite comforting, these nights filled with questions, visions, and roving thoughts. They provided me with an island, an escape, a place to run to when the world seemed to get out of hand. I loved them for that.

Things have really changed since the Devito days. Pete eventually forgave his father, joined the Army, and married a Korean girl he met overseas. Who would have guessed it? He actually went into the service that Fall. The stupid son-of-a-bitch did six years.

He works at an engineering firm in Detroit. He likes his job, but wrote me a letter the other day saying that his boss is a real jag-off and he wants to quit. Says he's gonna move out to California, raise a family, and start dreaming again. He wants to build something. He doesn't know exactly what yet, but he told me he'd let me know when he figures it out.

The last time I flew there, I asked him if he had any regrets. He just smiled and confessed that he wouldn't change a damn thing if it meant losing his wife. She really makes him happy. I'm glad, 'cause we're still the best of friends.

Jackie and I spent that summer together, but we went to different colleges and time just seemed to fade our relationship away. She lives in D.C., married, with three kids. She says she's doing okay and I tend believe her. She was never one to bullshit.

Darien and Dawn got married about ten months after our vacation. Do you believe that? Their parents pitched in and bought them a small condo about five miles from where they both grew up. They're trying to sell it now so they can buy their first home. I suspect they'll have a time of it, given the market, but they'll manage. Always have.

Neither of them ever went to college, but then again, neither of them ever liked high school all that much, so no one was too surprised. They own and operate a small garage in town. It's nothing fancy, but they like it and it pays the bills.

Currently they're working on their first child and, word is, if it's a boy he's gonna be named Tad. I tried to explain the whole, *"No, guys, please, I really hate my pitiful name,"* concept, but they just thought I was being modest. Ah well, maybe that's just one of those inter-galactic practical jokes I read about.

Now this one's a kick in the head. As it turns out, Eric was fine. He was just acting out his childhood fears in a somewhat eccentric manner. You know, for a while I thought he was gay. Boy, was I wrong. You ever see those slutty 900 numbers on

TV? Yeah, well, he's one of the biggest producers in the industry. He lives in a huge house, has girls hanging all over him, and he's raking in the bucks. Talk about self-actualization. What a maniac.

As for The Amazing and Somewhat Sarcastic Me, well, I'm finally starting to deal with life. It was tough at first, but I managed to find my balance. I came to understand the power and purpose of the not-so-evil Zukes. I all but stopped having regular conversations with irregular spirits. And now, Barley Man only comes out in the bedroom.

I just finished my third novel. It's a philosophical adventure called *Both Sides of Broken*. My agent, that rat bastard, says it's radical. Tops the Larry book even. Ah, but she gets paid to say things like that. So who knows?

Anyway, when I'm not writing, dreaming, or acting weird, I work as a career coach. I make decent money and help people chase their dreams. I dig it and so does my wife. Oh, that's right, I forgot to mention that I actually got married. Her name is AJ, and I love her dearly.

Yeah, I'm full of surprises lately. Just wait until she wakes up and finds out she's a millionaire. She'll be stunned all right, but not nearly as much as the rest of the guys when they go to their mail boxes tomorrow and find their checks.

Oh, come on now, readers of the world, you didn't think I was actually gonna give up the money, did ya? Shit, you must be kidding me. I'm not completely crazy. I told you from the start this was my life, and there was no way that I was gonna let some sell-out bastard steal it.

You see, nobody else knew about the note or the money. All I had to do was deposit it slowly and then wait to see how our lives turned out without the cash. I figured we'd have a good idea as to how things were going when we reached thirty. After all, when you're eighteen you think that's pretty old. And so that little piece of reality sat in a brokerage account for nearly twelve years. Can you believe it? I thought my money man was going to have a coronary. He couldn't understand my lack of interest in the exploding portfolio. Inflation, IPOs, and a landslide of tech stocks made me ridiculously rich and still I let it be. I guess Buck didn't understand me either. He never imagined such a choice. But how could he? His eyes were closed.

Like I always say, you—and only you—control your destiny and nothing, including your past can ever change that fact. Life is most probably a horrendously stupid accident, but as long as we're here, you might as well do something constructive with yourself.

So before you put this thing down and run out to finish doing whatever you were doing before you picked it up, do me a favor and promise me something. Promise me that no matter what road you choose to follow and no matter who you choose to walk it with, you'll try your best to look through the eyes of a child every now and then. If you think about it, living an honest, respectable, inspiring life is really the only decent gift you can give. And believe it or not, people can still be decent to each other. Thank God.............(?).

# About the Author

Tim Toterhi is a blue-jeans kind of guy. He likes rainy nights, top down days, and sipping good wine with cool people. He believes in soul mates, sad songs, and learning through the lifetimes. When not writing he can be found walking the streets of New Rochelle, NY singing, only slightly off key.

# Fiction by Tim Toterhi

## Both Sides of Broken

It's hard to stop a hitman from killing your father. It's even harder when you're dead. Jonathan Holiday and his two brothers are desperate for money. Their comatose father has it, but his hospital meter is ticking away. In an effort to save themselves, the three arrange to have the abusive old man murdered. After hiring the killer, Jonathan has a change of heart. Unfortunately, he also has a suspicious accident.

Now he must battle back from a series of "After-Earths" to convince his self-absorbed, cash-strapped brothers to stop a supernatural hit man from doing his job. Both Sides of Broken is a story about defeating demons – those of this life, those in the next, and most importantly, those within ourselves.

## Two Minutes Too Late

We've all been there – missed the boat, missed the point, missed the chance at that something or someone special now long gone. We ache for a do over knowing full well if the wish were granted it would forever change the person we've become. Two Minutes Two Late is a collection of stories detailing the missteps of a hapless romantic. From career blunders

and criminal exploits to dating debacles to goodbyes unsaid, it reminds us that while follies happen the future is unwritten and ours to explore.

## Lunches With Larry

God and a nuclear fuel broker meet in a sports bar to discuss women, work, and other life mysteries... What sounds like the start of a classic political joke, is actually the beginning of a thought-provoking philosophical adventure. Set against the scandalous decline of the largest, privately-held business empire in the nuclear brokerage industry, Lunches With Larry follows a young, romantically-  challenged, business misfit on his crusade to find true love, lasting friendship, and the answer to the oldest of questions.

If you've ever felt confused, lost or all alone in a world you can't quite figure out; if you've ever thrown up your hands in frustration and shouted, "I just don't understand anything anymore," pull up chair, settle in with a spot of tea, and have a look. You may find something you've never lost and loose something you've never needed.

www.ingramcontent.com/pod-product-compliance
Lightning Source LLC
Chambersburg PA
CBHW070910180626
46817CB00003B/995